# CAMPFIRE CONFESSIONS

### A NOVEL

## KRISTINE OCHU

Cover Design / Typesetting: Stewart A. Williams


Books Fluent

3014 Dauphine Street

New Orleans, LA

70117

*This book is dedicated to Kathy Gram Katterfield, Georgia Glynn, and Cindy Rush Prescott. Three beautiful friends whose laughter I can still hear, smiles I can still see, and love and support I can still feel. Cancer may have taken your lives, but your spirit lives on in all the hearts you touched—including mine.*

## PART ONE

# Is This Really It?

# CHAPTER ONE

ANNIE

# What Happened To My Life?

*Wisconsin*

ANNIE CLASPED HER HANDS TOGETHER, pressing them firmly against her heart. One more deep breath. Finally, the urge to run down the church aisle, shouting *I can't take it anymore* subsided. Her heart ached. No—it actually hurt like hell. She couldn't suppress this growing sadness. It was driving her crazy.

"Goddamn it!" Had she actually uttered those words? So inappropriate for the pastor's wife, especially in the middle of his sermon. Maybe Annie had only thought them? But no, the Petersons, sitting in the pew in front of her, whipped their heads around in horrified astonishment. Alfred fumbled to adjust his oversized hearing aid. Ava, with her short, silver-blue hair, pushed his hand aside, cranking up the volume.

Annie leaned toward her four sons, Matthew, Mark, Luke, and John, sitting beside her. She whispered loudly, "Yes, God demands it, he DEMANDS it!" She nodded at the Petersons, encouraging their agreement while ignoring her boys' puzzled expressions. They didn't look convinced. Better go further. Annie lifted her hand at her husband, Pastor Dan, praising his message when she hadn't been listening, distracted by her wandering thoughts.

The Petersons turned around, satisfied they had misunderstood her words.

A drop of guilty sweat trickled through Annie's thick brown hair. It journeyed down her neck, then underneath her yellow linen dress. It settled on her chest, threatening to leave a spot and betray her. Annie squeezed her eyes shut and silently prayed, *Dear God, please forgive me. I didn't mean to take your name in vain. What's wrong with me? Why does my heart ache?* She paused, hoping for a response. But the only sound was Dan, requesting everyone to join him in the Lord's Prayer.

Annie heard the boys squirming and whispering. John's knee shoved into hers. Exasperated, she rubbed her hands against her forehead and prayed for patience. She opened her eyes and caught Matthew, at the farthest end, elbowing Mark in the gut. Her skin prickled with irritation at Matthew's belligerent behavior. His saving grace was his effort at school and sports. Getting girls to swoon over him was never a problem, with his dreamy eyes and dark, wavy hair.

Another drop of sweat raced down her chest, clearly marking the spot as Mark flapped his elbows like a chicken. He smacked both Matthew and Luke on their sides. It had to be an accident. Mark was her easygoing one, the peacemaker. His only issue was hogging the bathroom. She empathized with him. It wasn't easy being thirteen, trying to hide the pimples on your forehead.

*Oh no, here we go.* Luke might only be ten, but he was a competitor. She held her breath, silently encouraging him to show some restraint. *Come on, Luke, surprise me like you do with your hugs and unexpected kindness to strangers.* But sure enough, Luke wasn't going to take it. He hip-checked Mark, causing his shoulders to knock into John, who slammed into her.

Annie rubbed her forehead vigorously. Shit. She was going to create a permanent indentation like Dan teased her about. Wait—was her happy, sweet, little John, who'd recently turned six, actually shoving Luke back? Causing a reverse chain reaction? Her stomach lurched, watching her sons create a new version of the wave in church.

Annie stretched her arm across them, getting their attention. She shook her head and glared. They immediately bowed their heads. Annie's smile popped out, despite her intention to remain serious. Even though they were all getting older, they were still little kids.

Ava turned around, lips pursed, scrutinizing the boys. Annie's maternal protective instinct kicked in, her blood pumping, ready to fight. She'd love to tell Ava to mind her own business. These were her boys. She loved them intensely. Nobody was going to mess with them. But she couldn't. Reluctantly, she bowed her head and prayed even louder until Ava turned around. Annie raised the knuckle of her middle finger in secret defiance, feeling the sweet taste of gratification.

That small act of defiance felt empowering. Annie's spine straightened. She felt stronger, ready to take on the next bully. How could she hold onto that strength? Was it possible to stop doing everything for everybody? She grimaced, thinking of her high hopes to change things when John started first grade. She was going to rediscover her passions. Dig them out from under piles of laundry, school activities, and endless church projects. What would have happened if she'd finished her music degree? Could she ever get back to that?

Then there was Dan. Thank God, he'd finally finished praying, covering every possible need. Annie rubbed her stiff neck and caught his attention. She kept rubbing it and gave him a smile. Their secret signal to speed things up. Dan cocked his head to one side, ran his fingers through his hair, and grinned at her. In that moment, he looked like he had seventeen years ago—a delicious combination of sexuality and sincerity.

Annie felt her neck tension subside, as her mind drifted back to the day they'd met. Her vivid memory let her step right back into the moment. She'd rolled out of bed to prepare for Dora, her father's physical therapist, not bothering to comb her hair, wearing her ratty robe and old bunny slippers. She knocked on her mother's door, shouting, "Good morning," then traipsed downstairs into the guest room, where her father was recovering from a broken hip.

Annie discovered her dad struggling to pull up his pants, which were twisted around his ankles. His fall had aged him, but he was still striking—silver hair, chiseled facial features, and smiling blue eyes. He usually had a cheerful, upbeat disposition, but that day, his frustration assaulted her like steam from a whistling teapot. Annie decided to use their favorite game to distract him. When she was four and having a meltdown, he'd sung a song, making up silly, nonsensical words to it. They had laughed so hard that she'd peed her pants.

Annie hummed the tune, "When The Saints Go Marching In," while putting on his socks. Then she sang, "Oh when Dad starts walking again, oh how I want to be with him." Her father's face perked up and he hummed along.

The doorbell rang. Annie wondered why Dora was so early. She kept singing, knowing Dora was fun and liked to sing. Annie swung the door open, flung out her arms, and bellowed at the top of her lungs, "Oh when Dad starts walking again!"

And there was Dan—tall, lean, his dark brown hair cut short in a fashionable style. He was dressed in a pressed white shirt and tan pants, looking more scrumptious than a delicious ice cream cone. She wouldn't even mind if he dripped all over her. She knew exactly who he was. His appearance exceeded the most raving descriptions she'd overheard.

Annie envisioned him licking ice cream off her lips. She playfully challenged him, "You're not Dora."

"And you're not Mr. Harrington. You must be the beautiful Annie everyone talks about."

Annie burst into laughter. "Pastor Dan, right? You just told a lie. Isn't that a sin? Now what am I supposed to do? Report you to the congregation? But you're new to the job, so I'm sure Jesus will forgive you."

"Jesus agrees with me. He wants you to invite me inside for a cup of coffee."

Annie frowned, pretending to be perplexed. "Coffee? That's a problem."

Dan leaned against the porch railing, his chest muscles rippling under his shirt. "I'm sorry. Bill, your dad, said to stop by this morning."

"I believe he was trying to get out of his physical therapy again, but this is quite creative," Annie bantered.

Dan backed away from the door. "I'll come back. I didn't mean to impose by asking for coffee."

"I drink ice cream," Annie blurted, not wanting him to leave.

"Ice cream? Is that a new trend?"

"I meant iced tea," Annie laughed, relieved to avoid exposing her ice cream fantasy.

"I love tea." Dan took a casual step forward.

"Are you flirting with me now?" Annie felt a tingle in her

stomach that leapt into her heart.

"Chamomile is my favorite, but it's usually served hot. And yes." Dan cocked his head to one side, ran his hand through his hair, and grinned.

The sound of her dad humming, his walker thumping in unison, prevented her flirtatious response. Her dad winked at her, then sang to Dan, in a smooth, baritone voice that age had graciously allowed him to keep, "So, now you met my Annie!"

Dan shook her dad's hand. "You have quite the singing family."

"Annie has a voice like an angel, doesn't she?"

"Looks and sings like one." Dan gave Annie an intense look, his eyes shooting sparks at her.

Annie's mother appeared in the kitchen, wearing a flowered dress and her favorite pink lipstick. Her blond, shoulder-length hair was curled under in a stylish bob. The only clue that Alzheimer's was taking over were the mismatched tennis shoes, one pink and one blue.

"Pastor Dan, you came like you promised! You have to join us for breakfast. It's oatmeal day!"

Annie's mother was unable to restrain her excitement as she patted Annie's hair. "Annie, you look like a mess. Please excuse her, Pastor Dan. She's been a saint, helping us out, not taking time for herself. She even took a leave from the music conservatory!" Her mother gave Annie an encouraging look, making her wonder if this meeting had been orchestrated. But Annie wasn't annoyed, like the other times; this time, she felt light-hearted.

"Time to run and put my wings on," Annie quipped, marching out of the room while singing the made-up verse. At the top of the stairs, she turned to see Dan looking up at her. Later, he shared that at that moment, his heart left him and high-jumped into hers. And she believed him.

It took three months to fall deeply in love. Dan wanted Annie to finish her degree, but she decided to wait. Her mom's Alzheimer's symptoms had become more obvious. They planned to get help but didn't. Annie never went back to the conservatory or college. She always believed, with her brains and voice, she could have become anything—a singer, doctor, even a scientist. Instead, a year later, she floated down the aisle on her dad's arm. Nobody argued against her marriage to the popular pastor.

To everyone, it appeared Annie had made the right choice. Smiling in church every Sunday, her four sons at her side; teaching Sunday school; helping with the choir. The entire town thought Annie was a saint. But now, she felt like a fake. If they only knew how she was struggling to hold her emotions inside—her frustrations, doubts and, yes, even anger.

Annie snapped back to the present. The memory she cherished had ended in frustration. She rubbed her forehead again as Dan announced the new choir director would lead the congregation into the closing hymn. Her posture slumped. Her throat constricted at her recent sacrifice. That should have been her up there.

Annie opened her hymnal although she knew the words by heart, 'Onward Christian Soldiers.' The song fitted her suffering mood. March on. Be a soldier and carry all the weight. Then John's little fingers wrapped around hers, swinging her hand with his to the beat. John was the one she made up silly songs with, letting go of her serious responsibilities as a pastor's wife. Dan bragged that John was like her, especially his ability to sing and his joyful attitude.

Yet, she hadn't felt that way for some time.

Annie looked down at his small, marching feet. It was these moments that kept her going. Annie took tiny steps to avoid drawing attention and matched his feet to the beat. His happiness was contagious. She could feel the music pulsating inside her.

Annie got lost in the song, holding the last note longer than anyone else. This time, everyone looked at her. She noticed Dan lift his eyebrow almost imperceptibly, questioning her. Luckily, John squeezed her hand, diverting her attention. When Annie looked down at his face, beaming up at her, she didn't care what anyone thought.

# CHAPTER TWO

Annie scooped a misshapen ball of chocolate chip cookie dough and plopped it onto the baking sheet. "Finally! Enough!" A twinge of triumph as she added the spoon to the conglomeration of dirty dishes on the counter. The leftover batter would be a treat for the boys. She glanced at the clock. No! Already late. She hated rushing around in the morning. Her shoulders tightened, hunching up toward her ears.

Annie grabbed the cookie sheet and flung the oven door open. Heat blasted out, threatening to scorch her face. Startled, she stumbled backward, knocking a bag of flour all over the counter. Damn it! Another mess to deal with. Annie shoved the cookies into the oven, assessing the damage. Her heart plummeted: flour smothered the stacks of stunning class reunion cards. All those hours wasted, fastidiously gluing on yellow-and-black hurricanes, for the school team's name—Hayward Hurricanes.

Annie gingerly wiped off the cards. Where was a safe spot? She scanned the room—clutter everywhere except the kitchen table. Annie stacked the cards in the middle as Matthew, Mark, and Luke staggered in.

"What happened, Mom?" Luke asked.

"Remember the cookies you were supposed to make last night? The fuss you made over watching the basketball finals?"

"I didn't know it'd go into overtime. Why didn't you wake me up? I would have helped."

"You needed your sleep. But now you can help by setting the table. Matthew, can you please get the cereal boxes down?"

This counter! She couldn't take the mess anymore. *Just shove the dishes in the dishwasher.* She opened it—plates in hand. Full? Whose turn was it to empty it last night? She could feel the smoke of irritation blowing out of her toes. *Let it go. Try to be positive.*

Matthew grabbed cereal boxes from the pantry, shaking each one. "Mom, these are empty. Didn't you buy more cereal?"

Annie pushed by him and grabbed the last box. "Try this one."

"Yuck, it's one of your weird healthy ones."

Annie set the mixing bowl in the center of the table. "Here. Add cookie batter into the weird cereal and create something magical." She scraped off a hunk and shoved it into her mouth. "Heavenly. Where's John?"

"Here I am." John giggled, hanging onto Dan's back, piggy-back style.

Dan slid John into a chair and sniffed the air. "Smells great. Something special for breakfast?"

"Yes, it's called cereal. The cookies are for Luke's fundraiser. Remember?" Annie pressed her hands against her chest, trying to deflate her anger. Why did she let Dan talk her into letting Luke watch that game?

"They smell heavenly. Can you bring a few to George when you pack up Edith's things today?"

Annie rubbed her forehead with clasped hands. "I forgot about that. Can you stop by and lend a hand?"

"I can't. But be happy. I found ladies to help you organize summer camp today." Dan kissed her on the cheek. Did he really think a kiss would appease her?

Annie felt her good mood pop, like someone had stomped on a balloon. She picked up her legal pad, holding it up to Dan's face. The page was full of action items. "I can't. There's no way I can do anything else."

"You're creative. You always find a way. It's one of the reasons that we all love you." Dan poured a few flakes of cereal into his bowl, then examined the box for more.

Mark picked up an invitation. "Mom, pretty cool hurricanes. You did this by yourself?"

"Yes, nobody else volunteered."

"You could have bought them," Matthew said, his tone challenging.

"Are Jo and Sondra coming this time?" Dan deftly changed the topic.

"They better if they want to remain my best friends. I've reminded them enough. They have no excuses."

"Is Jo the girl who played on the guys' softball team?" Luke asked.

"Yup, she's the one, but Sondra did too," Annie replied, forcing a smile. *Come on, Annie, just get through breakfast and you can take that pill.*

The oven's timer went off. Annie felt her head buzzing along with the timer. "Dan, can you get those out? I can't do everything here."

"You could have bought the cookies too," Matthew said with a smirk.

Annie heard him. *Do not bite back. Rise above.* In fact—a better idea. "Matthew, you need to pick up Mark after practice today."

"I can't. Coach is going over special drills tonight."

Annie turned to Dan, who was squeezing his hands inside her oven mitts. "You'll have to."

"Sorry, I have a visitation. Your meetings will be done by then."

Annie's heart palpitated as Matthew got up and rummaged through her purse. She rushed over and grabbed it away. "What are you doing? You have no right to go through my purse."

"I need gas money," Matthew sputtered defensively.

"Well, you don't go into someone's purse and take their money. It's like stealing. You have no business. Don't you ever do that again."

Dan interrupted her, "Okay, Annie, let's settle down."

Annie glared at Dan. How dare he rebuke her in front of the kids. Wasn't it enough that she was giving up most of her day for the church? Again? Frustration whipped around inside of her like a downed electrical wire. She turned back to Matthew. "There's no gas money and no car for a week unless you pick up Mark."

"What?" Matthew shouted. "That's so unfair. That's your job!"

"My job?" Annie smelled cookies burning. Sure enough, Dan was fumbling to get the cookies out of the oven. The oven mitt slid off his hand, the cookie sheet crashing onto the floor. Her frustration erupted. "All of you—out! Right now! Dan, take them to school. I'll bring the cookies over later."

Dan looked chastened as he herded the boys out of the room. Annie could hear him trying to put his foot down. Matthew was to drive the van, but the blow was softened by a generous amount of gas money. Matthew must be stewing. He hated that minivan, complaining it made him look geeky.

Finally, the car and van left the driveway. Annie's sigh of relief ripped through her like a tornado. Her hands were sweaty as she opened her Kate Spade purse. Her splurge. The hidden zippered compartment had paid off. Thank heavens, Matthew didn't find the pills. She dumped out the bottle's contents. Two tiny yellow pills emerged. *That's it?* Where did she hide the other pills? She'd been in a hurry not to be discovered. *Slow down. Don't panic.* She'd put them out of reach. She looked up. Right—the cupboard above the refrigerator.

Annie shoved aside rarely-used, fancy serving dishes and found the bottle. What the hell? How could it be empty? Despair crept around like an octopus inside her body. *Now what? Think of a plan. Start with a pill and reorganize your to-do list.*

Annie poured a big glass of milk, emptying the container. Careful now. She gingerly placed it on top of the overflowing garbage Matthew was supposed to take out. No way was she going to take care of that too. She took one pill, washing it down with a big gulp of milk. Amazing how something so small could calm her crazy nerves.

Annie grabbed a cereal bowl. Might as well enjoy herself. She sat on the floor and sorted through the cookies, rescuing the ones that weren't too burnt. She poured milk over the warm cookies, then spooned the mixture into her mouth. Chocolate melted on her tongue. Incredibly comforting. The pill kicked in, delivering its blissful calm, until she remembered George. Annie struggled to her feet, hating to leave her peaceful moment. Then a beautiful thing happened. She remembered the extra cookies in the freezer. At age eighty-five, George would never know they weren't fresh. She hated to admit it, but Matthew was right. Next time she was going to buy the premixed dough.

# CHAPTER THREE

ANNIE WAITED AT THE FOUR-WAY stop in her used blue Toyota Camry, appropriate for a pastor's wife. She fidgeted, stuck behind a yellow Mercedes in mint condition. Who was driving that car? As the pastor's wife of the largest church in this town, which had a population of only two thousand, she thought she knew everyone. Plus, everyone shared the same doctors, store clerks, teachers, and coaches. It was impossible to hide your identity for long. Today, everyone was being "Midwestern nice," waving at each other to go first. Dangerous when you were in a hurry.

"Just go, damn it. I have to get to my meeting!" Exasperated, Annie pounded on the steering wheel, accidentally honking the horn. Horror sucked the air out of her body as Mrs. Johnson, the second-grade Sunday school teacher, turned around. Annie immediately smiled and cheerfully waved. Mrs. Johnson waved back, then drove away. *Great. Keep smiling.* She felt like a hypocrite, nice on the outside while seething inside.

It was her turn to go. But where was she going? Too many

things on that list. Oh God, where was she supposed to be now? Annie panicked as that too-familiar ache of heavy sadness rushed into her body. She had to calm down. Use her stand-by. Breathe. In for four counts, hold for six, and out for eight. She repeated it three times, then saw the reunion cards next to her. The post office—only two blocks away.

Annie kept her breathing slow. *Be mindful. Practice what you teach in the church's support group. Look at how green the grass is getting. And those happy, colorful tulips, lining the steps to the post office door.* It was working. Her mood was brightening. As she opened the door, the town's history assaulted her, smelling like stacks of old, mildewed newspaper archives.

Awesome, nobody was in line. Annie almost made it to the counter when the stack of cards began to slide. She wove back and forth like a drunken belly dancer, willing them to stay. They didn't obey and scattered all over the floor.

"Shit." Annie sank to the floor, fighting back her tears.

The sound of footsteps. Annie looked up. Hank. Thank God for her old friend, wearing his postal uniform, looking trustworthy. He was like an oak tree, solid and strong, a stand-out in the forest. She could relate to Hank. They had a blast as teenagers when he dated Sondra. Their real bond formed when they both gave up college to care for their parents. It'd been a while since his mother's funeral. That night, after Dan had left, Annie stayed with Hank, talking for hours. They shared memories, along with a deep conversation about the meaning of life.

Hank grinned, "I didn't think a pastor's wife was allowed to swear."

"Damn, you heard me. We have automatic forgiveness for allowing a bad word to slip, especially when we make a mess like this one."

Hank knelt down to help her. "Don't worry, I won't tell anyone. Remember, I'm good at keeping secrets."

Annie crawled around the floor, retrieving the cards. "How am I supposed to know that?"

"Remember that night in the cornfield? Sondra and I catching you and…"

"Say no more. But that was pre-pastor's wife. I'm surprised you noticed, with you and Sondra being so hot and heavy." Annie flushed, remembering that night. The wind rustling through the cornstalks, covering up the sounds of discovering the pleasure of being touched.

Hank reached out his hand and pulled Annie to her feet. "Will you have a big turnout for your reunion?"

Annie studied his poker face. "You know you can ask."

Hank walked behind the counter and calculated the postage. "Ask what?"

"How Sondra is. I wish that I could tell you. She's lousy at returning my phone calls."

Hank avoided eye contact, fiddling with the credit card machine. "Hopefully it means things are going well."

"Sondra has a big real estate job that keeps her busy. But she promised she'd come and even go camping like we did as kids. Remember how you and the other boys would try to catch us skinny-dipping?"

Annie felt a customer bump her from behind. Really? Did everyone have to eavesdrop? "Oh yes, that's right, my sink still drips. Thanks for your advice. I'll let you know if she comes."

Annie retreated to the car. Had she screwed up again? Saying the wrong things out loud? The sweat again, cold, engulfing her body. She needed a pill and dug in her purse. Where was the bottle? There was too much stuff jammed into it—just like her life.

Annie dumped out the contents in annoyance. She stared into the empty purse. No pill? She wanted to scream. Wait—the zippered compartment. How could she forget so quickly? She popped the pill and waited for the calmness to arrive.

Perfect time to call Sondra. Annie dialed, but no answer. Damn it. She'd have to leave another message with probably no response. "Sondra, It's me. Why don't you ever pick up? I ran into Hank today. Poor guy. He's still in love with you. When you do a number on a guy—that's it. I need you to come to this re-union." Annie choked up and gripped the steering wheel to regain emotional control. "It's not always easy living in this small town. There isn't anyone to tell your secrets to. I need my best friends. Please call Jo and get her to come too. Love you."

Annie hung up. No time to waste. Get that prescription refilled. The risk of going back to the local pharmacy and having Dan find out made her queasy. Annie checked her action list. The next basketball game was in the neighboring town, only thirty minutes away. They had a nice pharmacy. She could try that.

The drive through the picturesque mixture of farmland and forest soothed her soul. Annie felt cautiously optimistic as she parked in a remote spot. She reached under the seat, pulling out a long, black-haired wig, baseball hat, and oversized sunglasses. Instant transformation. She looked a bit odd, but didn't care.

Annie headed inside, encouraged not to see anyone she knew. The pharmacist, a mirror image of Santa except for his slim frame, greeted her. Annie handed him the prescription bottle. "Hi, I need this refilled."

The pharmacist examined the label. "Mrs. Anderson, looks like the last refill. It's a controlled substance, so you'll need a written prescription for the next time." He looked up with a puzzled expression. "Are you related to Dan Anderson, the pastor in Hayward?"

"No, but that's Wisconsin for you, full of Andersons."

He chuckled. "So true. It'll be about ten minutes. I just need your insurance card."

"I don't have prescription coverage. My insurance is so bad. It barely covers seeing a doctor."

"Those darn companies get greedier and greedier. There's a free clinic that opened up on the other side of town. You should check it out. I'll write the address for you."

"That'd be great, thank you." A wave of gratitude rushed through her body. Maybe he really was Santa. An anonymous, free clinic was the perfect gift. She could get more refills and avoid seeing her doctor. Perfect.

Now, how to pull it off? Annie checked her cell phone calendar. The summer school meeting. Easy to skip. She texted the church secretary, lying about a confidential member situation. A mixture of guilt and justification tickled her conscience. Why did she have to feel guilty? They didn't need her. Besides, it wasn't fair for her to have to do everything. Still—she wasn't used to lying.

Annie rubbed her temples. That darn prickly feeling of an oncoming panic attack. What if something went wrong with the refill? Finally, her name was called. Her hunched-up shoulders dropped back into place. Annie paid for her prescription, took the clinic address, and gave the pharmacist a genuine smile.

## CHAPTER FOUR

OH MY GOD, I MADE *it*. Annie looked at her bed like it was a sought-after dream. It was early, but who cared, she deserved it. Just like the logo on her comfy pink nightshirt the boys had given her, she'd been a supermom. Although she ached all over, it had been satisfying to check Item Thirty off her list. She mustered her strength and crawled like an injured spider into bed. It felt amazing. She nestled in the freshly-washed sheets, inhaling the wildflower scent. Yes, this was what she needed.

Annie listened for any noise that signaled her retreat would be short-lived. Good. Heavenly silence. The boys were accounted for in their bedrooms. And Dan was in his office, contemplating what words to share at Daisy's funeral tomorrow. That hellacious leukemia. It was so cruel. Daisy had been a sweet girl, only ten—Luke's age. Daisy's beautiful long hair had been stolen, but not her laugh. The strength of these children was mind-blowing. Annie pressed her hands to her heart to ease the onslaught of sorrow. She had to stop thinking about this. Maybe a book? But that meant moving. She took a deep breath and mustered enough motivation to turn onto her side.

Annie moved the Bible over on her nightstand and reached under the bed. She searched through her personal stash of books. Yes, this one. The cover promised an escape into romance, sex, and intrigue. Soon she was in another world, another woman. Just as she reached the sex scene, an ache of longing rose up from her soul—pounding, demanding attention. What was her soul trying to tell her? She had no clue. *Come on, Annie, lighten up. Enjoy the fantasy.* She read a bit further and her aches were replaced by currents of subliminal bliss.

She heard the door creak and Dan shuffle in. No, not yet. Damnation, couldn't she even finish this scene? She pretended not to hear him and kept reading.

"Can I shut off the lights? I'm beat," Dan said, sounding haggard.

"Give me a few minutes."

"Wait—is that one of your books?" Dan read over her shoulder. "I'm not that beat." Dan whipped off his clothes. He grabbed her around the waist and spun her around, holding himself inches above her body in an impressive plank.

Annie clung to her book, feeling like a startled gazelle being attacked by a lion. He lowered his body onto hers and kissed her. Shit! She jerked away in pain as the book smashed her breasts from a size C to an A.

"It's time you left the party." Dan tossed the book onto the floor. His hands slid over her stomach, like a snake seeking its prey, until they landed upon her breasts. Annie felt a flash of irritation at his lack of imagination. That's how it always started. *Here we go, the same routine.* But damn—he was good, stroking her breasts, causing her back to arch as shivers of delight cascaded down her spine. Still—she wanted more. Sure enough—when she reached down, he was already hard. She didn't want to pretend everything was okay. Her body might be ready, but her mind wasn't. She pushed Dan back and moved away.

Dan whispered with longing, "I love you, Annie. Is something wrong?"

Annie wanted to scream, *Wrong? Yes! There are a million things wrong*. But she didn't, because he smiled at her, clueless as to how she was feeling. Damn that smile. She loved and hated it at the same time. It was genuine. What the hell—she could create her own fantasy—become that character in the book.

Annie slid on top of Dan, so her entire body was touching his. "My turn to be in charge." She kissed him deeply, moving her body in slow circles. His heated response felt like a bonfire, burning through her clothes. When Dan attempted to take her shirt off, she shoved his hand away, feeling powerful.

"Is this what you want?" Annie rolled off him and stood by the side of the bed. She inched her nightshirt off and brought her breasts close to his face. His tongue stroked her sensitive skin, creating waves of ecstasy, spinning her into a whirlpool of exotic pleasure. She buried her face into his hair and breathed in the scent—intoxicated by his excitement.

Annie felt Dan tugging her underwear down, but ignored his request. She walked over to their dresser, slid her underwear off, and leaned over, engulfed in erotic sensuality made bolder by the book. He came up behind her and pressed his naked body against her. She could feel his heart pounding through the skin on her back. The sensation was intense—tantalizing.

"Now," Annie whispered and gasped as he entered her. She moved with him, abandoning herself to the wild rhythm of their bodies pushing against each other, moving him deeper inside of her. Dan's breath quickened like dry kindling ready to explode into flames. No—not yet.

Annie turned around and kissed him hard. The dresser. She lifted herself up to sit on it and turned to face him. The smooth wood felt cold against her hot skin. She flung her head back. The power of being in control fed her desire to be untamed and ferocious. "Make me want you."

Dan didn't hesitate. He became the master of creating pleasure between her legs, touching and rubbing until her entire body convulsed. She grabbed him and toppled onto the floor, pulling him down with her. She landed on top of him. Perfect. She guided him inside, then moved hard and fast. It felt like her body dissolved into his as they climaxed together in a staggering explosion.

Annie collapsed by Dan's side, euphoric, panting.

"You should read that book more often," Dan said, breaking the spell.

"That wasn't in the book."

"Then maybe you should become a writer."

Annie laughed, her anger gone. "I'm a little embarrassed."

Dan gently stroked her hair. "Why?"

"I got a bit carried away."

"Not a problem on my end. In fact, I believe that's how we ended up with four boys." Dan gently kissed her, his lips fuller and softer with all the blood pumping through him.

"That's not entirely true." Annie stroked his chest, treasuring the smooth, silky terrain.

"So, you're giving me some credit?"

"Maybe."

Dan stood, then reached down, pulling her up into his arms. "We better get some sleep. It's midnight."

She clung to him, savoring the moment. It felt so vulnerable, innocent, and real. Their naked bodies touching after all the heated sex. "Right. Reality arrives quickly."

Annie went into the bathroom. She spotted Dan's t-shirt hanging on the door hook. Perfect. One benefit of being married. Nothing like an oversized, comfy t-shirt to slip on. She found her pill bottle hidden underneath the bathroom sink. Did she really need a pill right now? The mirror reflected the fulfillment of her fantasy. Her hair was tousled, and her cheeks were flushed. She had to be able to sleep after all that crazy sex. She put the bottle back, feeling optimistic, and opened the door.

Deafening snores assaulted her ears. Dan. How could she sleep with that noise? It was torture. She turned around and, without a thought, slammed down the pill.

The clock glared 3:00 a.m. as Annie surfaced to consciousness. There must be a thunderstorm. But no, it was Dan, grinding his teeth and making loud, puffing noises. How could he sleep like that? It really ticked her off. He was so oblivious to how it affected her. In fact, things never bothered him the way they did her.

She looked at her wedding ring and remembered when they'd gotten married. Their love had been like a tidal wave, taking down anything in its path. But lately, that love had been replaced by surges of resentment and secrets. Although—tonight had been incredible. She had delivered quite the sex act and maybe was a sinner after all, not Saint Annie, as people called her. Well, if sex made her a sinner, she didn't mind. They hadn't connected like that in months.

It was now 4:00 a.m. *Please God—help me sleep.* The alarm was set for six. Only two hours left. She put on earphones stashed in her nightstand drawer and tuned into a guided meditation. Instead of soothing her, the voice sounded smug, and the words annoyed her. She flung off the sheets in frustration, went into the bathroom, and took one more pill. This time, she didn't look into the mirror.

# CHAPTER FIVE

THE ALARM FELT LIKE A siren blasting through Annie's brain fog. The shower was running. That's right, Dan needed to meet with the Johnsons before Daisy's funeral. It was going to be a tough day. It was a small town and the death of a child affected everyone. Stephanie's suffering must be intolerable. Even with all her training, Annie never felt prepared to ease the grief of parents losing a child. There just weren't any words. It was an area she disagreed with God about.

Annie hit the snooze button. Ten more minutes before she had to face the world. How could she center herself and help others today? She needed to get into the feeling. She looked around the room, searching for an insight. The picture of her laughing with her grandmother. Love heals all—her grandmother's mantra. She never imagined she'd follow in her grandmother's footsteps, taking on the role of a pastor's wife. Annie's hands floated to her heart and rested there.

Those summers had been the best, hanging out with her

grandparents. Her grandmother had been a healer, using her hands to channel energy. She'd believed Annie had the gift, too. Those times practicing how to heal had been magical. But she'd been young, and let her new band and boyfriend lure her away.

*Can I still do it? Why not?* Annie placed her hands over her heart. *Now concentrate on love filling your body.* She placed one hand on her forehead and the other on her lower stomach. A warm glow began to radiate from her forehead to her heart and travel down to her stomach. She moved the stream of energy back and forth, visualizing the loving energy expanding and exploding throughout her body.

The snooze alarm went off, sounding like church bells. It must be a sign. She felt a resurgence of her old self, full of love and joy. Why didn't she do this more often? What about the other things she had learned? *Hold on. Don't start criticizing yourself. Try self-praise for a change.*

Annie grabbed her fuzzy blue robe and headed downstairs to the kitchen. The tantalizing smell of hazelnut coffee greeted her. Good move on programming the machine last night! Coffee was a must for marathon days—like today. Her favorite tea didn't cut it.

Annie reached for her favorite, elephant-shaped coffee cup. It was eleven years old, with chips around the rim. Matthew had made it for Mother's Day when he was still a sweet boy. She filled it up halfway. Now for the milk. Where was it? *Only one container left? There were three yesterday.* She tilted the container. A few drops dribbled into her cup. Unbelievable! The last time she didn't dilute her coffee, she'd had a stomachache all day. How could the boys drink all that milk in one day? And how could she yell at them for drinking milk? She'd like to find out who'd left a few drops behind. But was it worth it? The last thing she wanted was a repeat of yesterday's drama. She couldn't let the sadness in. She had the power to shift her thoughts and create positive feelings.

So now what? What could be fun? She rubbed her hands against her forehead to quiet her mind. Animal-shaped pancakes! The kids loved them and always laughed while deciding which part to eat first, a foot or an ear. She even had a premade mix and chocolate chips left over from yesterday's disaster.

Everything was assembled when John stumbled into the kitchen, sleepy-eyed, wanting his mom. Annie knelt down and cuddled him, cherishing the moment. "What do you think about animal pancakes this morning?"

John's face lit up. "Can I have a rabbit?"

"Great idea." Annie poured the shape of a rabbit into the skillet. "This will make you hop all day."

John hopped up and down. "Like this?"

Annie hopped and flapped her arms. "Yup, and like this."

Matthew walked in and watched them. "You two are corny."

"Okay, grumpy. What animal would you like? Maybe a grouchy lion?" Annie roared, pouring more batter into the skillet. Was she ever going to have her old Matthew back?

"Not funny."

Mark and Luke stumbled into the room.

"Mom, give Mark and Luke turtles for being slow," John said.

"Yeah, they're slow in the head alright," Matthew muttered.

"What did you say? Did I actually hear you right?" Annie gave Matthew a hard stare.

The doorbell rang, saving Matthew.

Annie looked at the clock and flipped the pancakes. "It's six-thirty. I look like a mess."

Luke took John's hand. "I'll get it. But make me a horse so I can gallop. Come on, John, let's go together." Luke galloped as John hopped along.

"This place is a zoo," Matthew said, shaking his head.

That was it! Enough of Matthew's negativity. "If you continue to make derogatory comments, you'll be confined to the house all weekend without a cell phone," Annie threatened.

Mark jumped in, running interference. "Mom, please don't do that. I have to sleep in the same room with him."

Annie took a slow, deep breath in. Mark was right. It wasn't fair to him. What else could she do?

Luke and John were coming back, looking solemn. "What happened?"

"It's Daisy's mom. She's waiting for you in the living room," Luke announced.

"Did she ask for Dad or me?"

"We don't know. She just started to cry," John said, looking bewildered.

"I'll talk to her. Luke, you can flip your horse. Go ahead and add your own chocolate chips. Mark, can you please let your dad know that Mrs. Stephanie is here?"

"Sure." Mark bounded out of the room.

A pill would feel so good right now, but the bottle was upstairs. *Be strong. Reclaim the energy you created this morning. Bring the feeling of love back into your body.* Determined, Annie walked into the living room. Before she said anything, Stephanie, dressed in baggy, gray sweatpants and an oversized hooded sweatshirt, collapsed in her arms, sobbing.

Annie felt a strange calm. *Let your spirit lead this interaction with Stephanie.* Her grandmother's words.

Annie rubbed Stephanie's back in comforting circles until the sobbing stopped. "Let's sit down." She held onto Stephanie's hands, sending her love.

Stephanie pulled back her hood to reveal red eyes circled by smears of mascara. "I'll never see Daisy's smile again or hear her laugh. I can't tell her that I love her or feel her little arms hugging me. It should have been me. Everyone keeps telling me that I'll be okay, but it's not true."

"You're right. It's not going to be okay, not for a very long time. You were her mother. You carried her inside your body. You gave her life and all of your love."

"But it wasn't enough."

"Maybe it wasn't enough to cure Daisy's cancer, but definitely enough for her soul to feel complete. The way Daisy fought and smiled through those treatments—it was inspiring."

Luke surprised them by coming in with a plate full of daisy-shaped pancakes. "Mrs. Johnson, I thought you might be hungry. I sat by Daisy in art class in first grade. We had to draw flowers and I was really bad until Daisy showed me how to make six loops around a circle. She said it was her specialty, since she was named after the flower. I think she'd like you to have one."

"Luke—" Stephanie couldn't finish her sentence.

"Mom made the batter. They're really good. You can even eat one petal at a time. I added some chocolate chips, so you don't need syrup."

Stephanie broke into sobs again. Luke looked terrified that he had done something wrong. Annie gently touched his arm in reassurance, feeling a surge of love and pride.

"I'm sorry if I made you sadder," Luke said.

Stephanie wiped her tears away. "No, Luke, this is quite wonderful. Thank you. It actually makes me happy. I'm going to save the pancakes for later, if that's okay?"

"Sure, I'll put them in a baggie." Luke left, carrying the plate like a prized trophy.

*Finally, Dan.* He brought in the pancakes, covered in plastic wrap. Was that chocolate smudged on his lips?

"Stephanie, Jim called. He's worried. Why don't I drive you home? We can all sit down and talk for a while," Dan suggested.

"That'd be nice."

Annie got up and hugged Stephanie. "I'll be there for the service and afterward to help you through this. Dan, can you stop by the kitchen before you leave?"

Annie was grateful to escape the heavy, grief-filled air. She went to pour pancake mix into the pan, only to find the bowl empty. Her heart plunged—then John handed her a plate with a heart-shaped pancake.

Annie squeezed her eyes. *Don't cry.* But the tears came anyway, with no control switch. Dan came back into the room, held her, and whispered into her ear, "We need you to be strong. Can you do that?" Annie nodded, not wanting to leave his arms.

Dan let her go and turned to the boys silently watching. "Why don't we give your mom a break and clean up this kitchen? Those pancakes were delicious, and she needs time to take a shower."

Annie was surprised by his thoughtfulness and wondered if last night's spectacular sex had anything to do with it.

"You do look pretty bad, Mom," John said.

"Well, thanks a lot," Annie responded, sounding upset. "It would be nice if you boys could make the funeral service. Your sports can wait a day."

"Sorry, Mom, but I have to meet my math teacher after school, something about a tutor," Mark said.

"Yeah, or he'll get kicked off the basketball team," Luke tattled.

"What? Why didn't I know this?" Annie felt like a bomb had been activated in her gut.

"Maybe I forgot to tell you." Mark looked away.

"Did you tell Mom about English?" Luke asked.

"What's going on here?" Annie felt seconds away from a full explosion.

"I've got that covered. I'm doing some extra-credit work."

"Dan—" Annie looked at him, silently pleading for help.

"Annie, why don't you go upstairs? I'll take care of this."

Annie didn't hesitate. She downed her cold coffee for energy and headed upstairs. She overheard John's voice, upset that he'd hurt her feelings and missed his goodbye hug. Thankfully, Dan promised John he'd get extra hugs during a special family meeting tonight. Then Matthew, complaining about another dumb family meeting. Annie wanted to shout down the stairs that he was lucky to have a family. But she was too emotionally drained to fight another battle.

Annie started the shower. Everyone was gone and the house was quiet. The painful, aching sadness reappeared in full force, taking her body over. How to stop it? A pill? Annie placed the pill bottle on the sink counter. Maybe she shouldn't take another one. There were other things she could do. Use a technique from the positive toolbox she'd created at their church retreat. She could meditate, take a walk, play music, even listen to a podcast. But nothing seemed doable or relevant to today. Face it. At this moment, she didn't care or want to try. Impulsively, Annie snapped off the bottle cap and popped the pill in her mouth.

Now for some nice, hot water. Annie cranked the heat up and stepped into the shower. A wave of dizziness crashed into her. She stumbled, trying to keep her balance. What was happening? Damn—she never ate her pancake. Just coffee on an empty stomach. No wonder she felt sick. *Turn off the water. Get some breakfast.* Another ripple of dizziness. She was probably overheated. *Hold onto the shower door and cool down.* There—a little better. Annie gingerly stepped out, wrapping herself in a towel.

A jolting pain shot through her head, startling her. Her legs buckled. She reached for the sink but missed. Her hand knocked over the bottle. Pills scattered everywhere. She was going to fall! Her body shuddered as the countertop rushed toward her eyes. *Please, God—don't let me die.* She threw her weight backward and hit the wall hard with her head. Her world went black.

# CHAPTER SIX

## JO (JOSEPHINE)

# How Do I Get My Act Together?

### *Minnesota*

JOSEPHINE HAD BEEN COMING TO this AA meeting at the local VFW hall for four years. She knew all the regulars, but tonight was different. A lot of new faces. It must be rough out there. Their commonality—the mixture of anguish and hope. The anguish mirrored by old, cracked linoleum tiles, yellowed by countless cigarettes smoked before the clean-air regulations. The hope? Strong coffee—the smell permeated the room, created by the endless cups consumed to stay sober. Jo reflected on how alcoholism was the ultimate equalizer. It had no regard for economic or social status. Everyone here was trying to hold onto their sanity and stay sober for one more day.

"Life sucks! Yeah, yeah, yeah, so I read the first line of Scott Peck's famous book, *The Road Less Traveled*. And I thought, *you don't know shit, buddy*. Life isn't difficult, it sucks! And it really sucks when you're stuck in your job, and paranoid that your boobs are getting flabby. Does anyone want to argue with that?" Jo used her lean, muscled body, topped by long, curly dark hair, to cast a challenging glare around the packed room. She had come straight from the gym, wearing sexy workout clothes that fueled her confidence.

"Okay, I know I sound bitter, but it's how I feel right now. I was told to let my true feelings out."

Jo observed her audience. Many of them just hoped to be better off than the person next to them. Maybe they had been sober longer, had great hair, or a solid job. It didn't matter—just as long as they weren't that person heading toward rock bottom. It gave them a sense of reassurance that their battle was paying off.

Jo's glare lessened as silence pervaded the room, as if someone had wasted a two-hundred-dollar bottle of perfume when only a drop would do. She shifted her weight from foot to foot, trying to rescue herself from her own thoughts, half-hoping someone would reach out and save her.

A soft voice floated across the room, "Do you want to tell us more?"

Darn, it was Phyllis, a regular whose harsh life story was drawn on her face. Pockmarks, deep wrinkles, and a few missing teeth. Phyllis had a gentle heart and acted like the group's mother, after losing her own children in an ugly custody battle. Thinking about it freaked Jo out. If Louie demanded full custody of their sweet daughters, Jessie and Hunter, she would be devastated. Compassion crept in but Jo resisted it, needing to keep up the tough act, perfected from her youth.

Jo's personal trainer had whipped her butt tonight. She was sore all over, but the endorphins felt good. She placed her hands on her hips and jutted them out to the left, knowing that pose made her look strong and confident. "No, that about does it for now."

Chairs scraped against the floor as the regulars shifted positions to avoid Jo's gaze. Yes! Her tactic had worked. Nobody would confront her. They feared her skill at turning a conversation against them, leaving them floundering. She didn't intend to be mean. She felt a pang of guilt slice through her confidence, remembering her commitment to stop using this tactic. Damn that ingrained survival tactic. Someone had told her that she was like a CIA agent who tortured their captives with question after question, until they broke down and confessed everything. In the past she would have bragged about that. Now—it didn't serve her recovery.

"Wait, I have a question." The light Southern drawl wasn't recognizable.

Jo whipped around. Her next words halted in her throat as she zeroed in on the most dripping, mouthwatering specimen of a man.

The vision of an ancient god, maybe Zeus, went on. "I'm just learning the steps but heard that when things aren't great, we're still supposed to act like things are okay. Then give it up to that higher power."

Jo's eyes fluttered, astounded at his boldness. She finally found her voice and was shocked to hear herself saying, "You're right, I'll try that." She sat down, her legs trembling as this Zeus gave her an incredible smile.

Phyllis, God bless her, ended the meeting. People dragged their cheap metal chairs across the linoleum, stacking them in the corner while chatting with each other.

Jo watched Zeus saunter over to her. He stopped to shake hands along the way but managed to keep his eyes on her. He finally arrived and stretched out his hand. "Hi, I'm Zac. I hope you didn't mind me speaking up."

"Not at all, Zeus. I mean Zac." Jo took his hand, enjoying his warm skin rubbing against hers.

"I'm fairly new at this. I'm just hanging on." Zac's upright posture, closely-shaved hair, and bold blue eyes made him look indestructible. But Jo recognized the anguish in his voice.

"Sometimes it's like that...hanging on."

There was an awkward silence as the room cleared and they were alone. Zac shrugged his muscular, hunky shoulders. "I hear people head over to the local diner for coffee and dessert. Are you going?"

"Not tonight. I've got to get home. My ex-husband is dropping my daughters off at the crack of dawn."

"Too bad, I'd love to talk to you." Zac had a pleading look in his eyes. The contrast between his dominant physical presence and his hidden vulnerability captured her attention and drew her closer.

Jo headed toward the door, her hand hesitating over the light switch. "You can come over for coffee at my place if you'd like. I don't live far. You can follow me home. But just so you know—I don't eat dessert."

Zac held the door for her. "That'd be great. I'm more of a main course guy anyway."

Jo flipped off the lights and locked the door. She could hear her own breathing. What would it be like being his main course? *Stop it! Keep your act together!* Jo motioned to her small, white Honda Civic. "That's my ride."

Zac strutted over to his Harley motorcycle. "This is mine."

Jo started her car and looked over at him. A magazine ad for Axe deodorant. *Who is this guy? I'm bringing him home. He could be a rapist, anything. I'm so stupid. What am I doing?* Jo looked in the rearview mirror. Zac was following her. She parked in her townhouse spot as Zac pulled up beside her.

"This is it. Listen, I don't mean to be rude, but I really don't know you. I mean—" Jo felt a rush of anxiety intermingled with anticipation. Her flight-or-fight response kicked in, sending blood racing throughout her body. Her cheeks turned brighter than any blush on the market. She wasn't sure how to continue.

Zac gave her a solemn look as he dug into the pockets of his tight jeans, exposing a glimpse of his six-pack stomach, the sexiness humming from his body. He pulled out his wallet and handed her two cards. "Here's my driver's license and my military number, address, the whole works. I promise you, I'm trained to protect, not to harm. I'm on leave from the Army and I like coffee. That's all."

Jo studied his IDs. "Thanks. I didn't mean to get weird, but I never invite strangers home."

A gasp and a skidding sound drew Jo's attention. Andrea. Her neighbor, in her nursing uniform, probably late for work again, was staring at Zac. Jo lifted her hand to greet her. Andrea winked at Jo, then gave Zac an appreciative look before dashing to her car.

"Do you always have this effect on women?" Jo exclaimed.

"I don't know what you're talking about."

Jo couldn't help but laugh. "I'll let that pass, but let's agree to complete honesty going forward."

# CHAPTER SEVEN

Jo opened her townhome door, which opened up into her living room, decorated in bright yellows and blues. She had wanted to make it cheerful for Jessica and Hunter. And Zac was the first man besides Louie who had been inside it. Jo led him into the kitchen. "Do you like cream or sugar with your coffee?"

"I like both." The words sounded tempting and delicious as Zac took off his leather jacket.

He looked so good. Jo struggled to swallow the ball of nervousness that climbed from her belly into her throat. *Come on, Jo. Focus. Take charge. Start the coffee.* Where was that sugar? Right. Top shelf of the cupboard. Out of sight, out of mind. She tried to reach it but couldn't. Suddenly Zac was there, his body aligned with hers as he grabbed the sugar. They both stopped moving for a moment. His physical energy was magnetic, drawing her closer. Jo turned toward him, and his arms went around her. Their lips found each other, the sensation better than any high she could remember. When they finally pulled apart, Jo's whole body trembled like an earthquake aftershock.

"I don't think we should be doing this. We're addicts and you're new in your recovery. Didn't they warn you about dating, not getting involved, all that stuff for the first year? It's about avoidance."

"I'm sorry, you're right. It just felt so natural and nice without alcohol involved." Zac dropped his eyes so she couldn't read his expression.

"So, when's the last time you—"

"A long time. You?"

"I'm sure, longer than you." Jo winced at her honesty.

"What's so bad about wanting to hold someone? Kiss someone?" Zac looked directly at her, his eyes full of sincerity and desire.

"Right now, I really don't know. Maybe we should skip the coffee?" It had been so long, and she was tired of always being strong, resisting every temptation. She felt a twinge of anger. Why couldn't she let go and be in the moment? She was an adult and almost divorced.

Jo shut off her thoughts, took Zac's hand, and led him toward the stairs to her bedroom. Halfway up the stairs, he kissed her again. He smelled like a mixture of coffee and Dial soap. For some odd reason, it made him more alluring. Jo couldn't wait any longer to look at his incredible chest, covered in a pressed, long-sleeved shirt. What was with these tiny, stubborn buttons! Her fingers felt chunky and awkward trying to undo them. The middle one completely resisted her efforts. Frustrated, she yanked hard. Zac lost his balance and stepped backward into the air. Oh my God—he was going to fall. Horrified, she grabbed his shirt. It ripped apart, buttons sputtering into the air. They caught each other and spun around, performing a comical waltz down the stairs. They finally landed—Jo spread-eagle on top of Zac.

"Hmm…now, this is an interesting position," Zac drawled mischievously.

"I can't believe I ripped your shirt off."

"I'm glad to donate my shirt. Now it's only fair that we make this an equal trade."

"Catch me first." Jo took off, but Zac caught her and scooped her into his arms. He carried her effortlessly up the stairs into the bedroom. Was this actually a dream? He playfully tossed her onto the antique cast-iron bed, the coils squeaking in protest.

Zac spied the hats lining her entire bedroom wall. "You're a hat lady."

Jo's hats. Her pride and joy, besides her daughters. All were different and special. Some inherited and others coming with a special story. Her eyes went to her first hat. Mid-rimmed, black and elegant, discovered at a thrift store with Annie and Sondra. The hat had instantly transformed her from the poor little bar girl to someone beautiful and confident. She was hooked, reinforced by compliments that flowed her way. The hats gave her a special energy. She became selective, choosing hats that matched what she needed at that time.

"That's right. I like changing my identity from time to time."

"A lady wearing a hat is tantalizing and mysterious. Would you wear one for me?" Zac looked at her with such intensity.

Jo shivered at the idea of what might happen next. *Stand up. Play along.* "Just what type of lady would you like me to be, sir?"

"What about this one?" Zac picked a wide-brimmed black hat with small silk flowers cascading down the sides.

Jo put the hat on. "Well, I believe that one calls for this." She slowly inched her shirt and pants off. She sucked in her stomach and hoped her vibrant purple sports bra and matching panties would distract him from noticing her stretch marks. It all felt surreal, like she was an actress in a movie making her antagonist sweat.

"Oh yes, you're quite the lady in that one." Zac pulled Jo to him. His lips were everywhere, creating a free, flying sensation.

*Pain!* Her hair was being pulled from her scalp. She reached up to discover the hat had slid next to her ear, her hair entangled around the small flowers. Jo gasped as Zac tried to unclasp her bra, unknowingly twisting her hair even tighter into an ugly snarl.

"Stop!"

"I thought you wanted—"

Jo bent her head, trying to loosen the pressure. "It's not that. I need help."

Zac's voice took on a calm, authoritative tone. "Hang on. Let me hold the hat in place. Turn around and I'll fix it."

Jo turned. The movement ripped hair out of her scalp. Startled, she jerked back, jamming her elbow right between Zac's legs.

Zac's face turned ghostly white. He slumped back and grabbed his groin. He muttered something Jo couldn't understand.

"Are you okay?"

Zac shook his head and rolled over, his back facing her. *Shit! Don't touch him. Give him some space.*

Jo hurried to the bathroom and freed her hair. No time to brush out the snarls. A ponytail would do. *Ice!* She hurried downstairs, chagrined for smacking the first guy she brought home, right in his balls.

Jo ran back up the stairs and handed Zac the bag of ice. "I'm so sorry. We can just lie here for a while."

Zac kept his back to her as she put her arm around him, hoping to comfort him. His skin was covered with a thin layer of sweat—as if someone had rubbed baby oil on it. It was better than a blanket, as it caressed her skin and lulled her to sleep.

Jo looked at the alarm clock. One a.m. Zac had rolled over in his sleep and had flung an arm around her. Jo sighed. He looked gorgeous in her bed.

Zac opened blue eyes that had regained their spark. "Hello."

Jo touched his chest. "You have beautiful skin."

Zac stroked her bra-covered chest. "And you, my lady, do not have flabby boobs. At least, I don't think so. I haven't gotten to see them yet."

Jo playfully punched him.

"First you elbow me, now you punch me? What am I going to do with you?" Zac touched her face, surprising her with his gentleness.

Jo picked at a loose thread on the quilt, overwhelmed with his sensuality, losing some of her earlier bravado. "Sorry again. I tend to be a fighter when I get nervous."

"I can fix that."

"It's just that I don't know much about you. Are you local? What do you do? You know—the typical questions."

"Mine is a screwed-up story." Zac looked away from her.

"Welcome to the world of alcoholics," Jo said in a straightforward tone. "I don't think you can shock me. In fact, I'll share how I've felt at times. It isn't hard to abstain anymore. What I struggle with is the label—I'm an alcoholic. I get angry when people judge me while they smoke, drink their wine, or take their antidepressants. How do they get to judge? Nobody's life is perfect. What's perfect, anyway? One thing I appreciate about AA is that everyone has experienced destroying parts of their life, sometimes almost their entire life. I did a pretty good job hurting myself and others along the way, but that's where the program helps. So, no judgment here—only admiration for trying. Your turn."

Zac's eyes held a mixture of uncertainty and hope. "I've been in the Army for fifteen years. I was doing okay except for the drinking. I kept getting into trouble. I needed to sober up but couldn't do it there. I left without permission, thinking I could hide out, but knowing I couldn't for long. I've been sober for two months now, finally got the guts to call my parents. Somehow, they still love me and made a few phone calls. Is that screwed-up enough for you?"

"Yes, and I promise to reward you for your honesty." Jo slowly slid her bra straps down, not revealing her breasts yet. Zac reached for her bra straps, but she intercepted his hands. "First you need to finish your story."

"You're tougher than my drill sergeant."

"Maybe this will help." Jo kissed him, still holding his hands.

"You're driving me crazy! I'll confess. I've got to return to base in five days, before it gets too serious. They could throw me in the brig or send me to rehab. But I can't run from this anymore."

"What I've discovered is that tomorrow may be better or worse. The key is to hang in there and never give up. Eventually things will improve, whether it takes months or years. I've been sober for four years. The first two were grueling. In the beginning, not a day went by that I didn't want to get drunk and zone out. Now a lot of days are great, like today."

"It is a great day, and I believe it's time for my reward." Zac walked over to the jar of feathers on her dresser. He picked a crow feather and approached her.

"Perhaps you're ticklish. I know a fun game we can play."

Jo's heart pounded a warning. *Don't share your sacred feathers.* She quickly took it away from him. "I really detest being tickled."

"Not a problem." Zac took a cowboy hat down from a hook. "I bet you'd be a wild and beautiful cowgirl."

"If you're good, I'll let you find out."

"I do promise to be good, hopefully great."

Jo felt fearless again. She reached for the hat and put it on. "In that case, ready for a ride, stranger?"

"Are you going to take that bra off now?"

"Wait, do you like boots?" Jo rummaged in her closet and held up her red cowboy boots.

"Oh yeah—"

Jo put them on and strutted over to the bed. She whipped her bra off and waved it in circles, pretending to lasso him. She straddled him and teased, moving up and down as if she was riding a horse. Out of nowhere, she had a sick feeling in her stomach—like she'd eaten something that had spoiled. Was she making a fool of herself? Was she setting herself up to become fodder for Army jokes? But all doubt vanished as she felt his response pushing up and straining against his jeans. He must be huge. Zac moaned with excitement this time.

"Time to get these jeans off before they rip too."

"That's a mighty fine idea." Zac playfully bucked her around like an unbroken mustang. Jo lost her inhibitions and raised her arm like a rodeo star to keep her balance. It was a crazy, spontaneous moment until Jo's body went up and her leg pulled in the opposite direction. What the heck? No way! The boot's steel heel had separated and was hooked onto the quilt. Zac bucked her again. Jo felt herself become airborne, the quilt acting like a parachute to soften her fall.

An excruciating pain shot through her hamstring. Unbelievable. She gritted her teeth. "I think I pulled a muscle."

Zac thoughtfully draped his torn shirt around her shoulders. "Here, let me see. Maybe it's a charley horse." Zac examined her legs. "No knots. Let's take those boots off before you accidentally kick me. You can use my ice pack. It's still a little cold." He carefully lifted her back onto the bed and slipped her boots off.

"I don't think this rodeo is going to happen tonight." Jo made a pouty face at him.

They simultaneously burst into laughter.

"This is the best sex I've almost had. Wow! It feels great to laugh, much better than drinking."

"And I lost my chance to win the crown and be the rodeo queen. I could have added a new hat to my collection." Jo put the ice pack on her hamstring, drew the shirt closer together, and leaned back on the pillows.

"Should we call it a memory then?" Zac tentatively asked, the tone of his voice hopeful there was still a chance.

Jo moved her leg. Pain exploded in her body. One look at the feathers and all doubt evaporated. "It's a memory. I pray we don't receive any more signs."

"I won't forget you, Jo. I'm going to call you 'Jo, my playful hero.'"

"I like that idea. I'll call you Zeus. Remember that if they throw you in the brig."

Zac leaned back on the pillows beside her. Jo felt a sense of peace as his hand found hers.

# CHAPTER EIGHT

WHAT WAS THAT NOISE? Jo's maternal instinct kicked in, jerking her awake. Zac was talking in his sleep. The time? How did the alarm clock end up on the floor? It had been a crazy night and there was the evidence. Her cell phone was downstairs. Jo shook Zac awake. "What time is it?"

Zac's eyes popped open. His military training was obvious as he jumped out of bed, immediately at attention. "Five a.m."

Jo put on her bra and shirt. "We have to get up. My husband is bringing the kids over early. They'll be here any minute."

"I thought you were divorced?"

"Almost, but that's my problem. Can you act like we're only AA friends? Not two people who spent an incredible night together?"

"You mean tried to spend an incredible night together. The ride was amazing before I bucked you off. Sorry about that."

Jo tossed Zac's shirt to him. "Cover up that gorgeous body of yours before you really get me into trouble."

Zac tossed Jo's pants toward her. "And you better cover up

your beautiful body before I try our rodeo routine again."

Jo ignored the pain as she maneuvered her leg back into her workout pants. She glanced in the mirror. Horror! She looked like a raccoon, with huge smudges of mascara around her eyes. Her ponytail had hair sticking out in all directions. She couldn't let Louie see her like this. She spotted the melted ice pack and wiped away the mascara. Her hair! *Just do your best. Smooth out the ponytail.* Did she smell like sex? Maybe, even if they didn't have it. But Louie would be suspicious. Her jasmine perfume. A quick spray would do.

"Okay, let's go!" Jo looked at Zac in his ripped shirt. She could only imagine what Louie would think if he saw them together. She herded Zac down the stairs and flipped on the television. She spotted her cell phone next to Zac's jacket on the floor. How did that happen? It didn't matter now. Time was more important.

Zac put on his jacket. Thank heavens, it covered his ripped shirt. But it did perpetuate his sexy, bad-boy look. Nothing she could do about that.

"I'm heading to my car. I'm going to act like I'm checking on something. See you out there."

Jo jogged out to her car, her leg screaming to slow down. She opened her car door as Zac straddled his motorcycle.

"Zac, good luck with everything. You're a good man. Stay with the program. Things will work out."

Zac gave her a salute, then sped away. His jacket flew open, exposing his shirt flapping in the wind right as Louie pulled his van beside her.

Jo shrugged her shoulders a few times to relax her body. *Slow down. Release the worry. All is well.* She listened to the birds singing their morning song and was able to capture a sense of balance.

The van door opened and Jessica stepped out, wearing a

black-and-red flannel nightgown, rubbing her sleepy eyes. She had just turned eight and had big, soft brown eyes, like molasses cookies filled with curiosity and intelligence.

Hunter stumbled out of the van behind Jessica. Hunter was six and mirrored her sister in a matching nightgown. Both of them were tall, slim, and muscular. Yet Hunter's eyes were a bright turquoise that darted around, noticing everything.

Jo wrapped her arms around them, loving the feel of their little bodies close to her, happy for the distraction. "I missed you."

"We were gone for one night, Mom," Jessica pointed out.

"I know, but it doesn't mean that I can't miss you. And—your hair?" Jo sniffed both of their heads. Lemongrass with a hint of balsam pine needles. "You smell so good."

"It's one of Grammy's new shampoos. We made a special lotion for you and your best friends," Hunter bragged. "She said you're going to see them at your class reunion."

"If they're your best friends, why don't we know them? And what's a class reunion?" Jessica mirrored Jo's own interrogation skills.

"That's a lot of questions for so early in the morning. Sondra and Annie are my two best friends. They both live far away. Annie lives in Hayward, where Grandma Kate lives. Sondra lives by Hollywood, where movies are made."

Louie got out of the van and joined them. Jo had always believed Louie was the delightful outcome of a magical alchemist, with his mixture of Lac Courte Oreilles Ojibwe and Norwegian blood. He looked like a vision of an ancient warrior forged of steel, with his tall, straight posture exuding strength and courage.

"Who was that guy? I thought we weren't going to—you know what."

Jo felt a twinge of guilt in her gut, a familiar feeling. The truth would hurt Louie, even though it wasn't as bad as it could have been. A little white lie would be okay.

"Girls, why don't you go inside? Cartoons are on. I'll be there in a minute to snuggle with you."

"Okay, Mom." Jessica took Hunter's hand and led her into their townhouse.

Jo turned to Louie. "He's new to AA and needed someone to talk to, that's all."

"The entire night? And talking did that to your hair?"

"What's wrong with my hair?" She touched her ponytail. "I had a big workout at the gym yesterday and forgot to comb it."

"Did your big workout include that guy's ripped shirt?" Louie looked taller than normal. His dark brown eyes dove into hers, prying for the truth.

"I'm not supposed to judge another AA member in need. Maybe he caught it on his bike or something. Besides, you and I are legally separated. I don't need to answer all these questions."

"Yes, but not divorced." Jo could smell woodsmoke as Louie's eyes smoldered with a mixture of longing and frustration. She saw the flicker of light in them, an ember that only needed encouragement to blaze.

*Don't let Louie sense your vulnerability. Too risky. Act tough.* Jo put her hands on her hips and gave him one of her "don't mess with me" looks.

Louie didn't flinch. "That might work on your AA group, but it doesn't work on me, Jo."

"It's just after 5:00 a.m. Time flies when you're sharing your problems. Besides, you've never dropped the girls off so early—it's not cool."

"And it's not cool putting your phone on vibrate. You know our deal in case of an emergency. Your mom texted me five times in the middle of the night trying to get ahold of you."

Jo turned on her phone. A multitude of missed text messages. What happened? Bitter stomach acid floated into her mouth. "Can you wait for a minute so I can call her?"

"I've got five minutes before I need to leave for work."

"I know that you have papers to grade, but you don't teach on the weekend."

"It's not my job. It's Mom's business. It's taking off. I'm working with her. Trying to pay off our debts. Get ahead. The girls deserve a good life."

Jo could hear the frustration in his voice. His words punched at her like hail hitting a car roof, making her feel defensive. "I know. I'm working too."

"True, but now there's rent besides the mortgage, plus all the bills for the house." Louie's voice softened as he opened the van passenger door and handed her three bottles. "These lotions are flying off the shelf. I'm taking a truckload to our southern distributor this morning. They placed our largest order yet. Mom asked if I wanted to quit teaching and become an equal partner."

Jo read the notes taped to each bottle. "To Annie, for Strength and Belief. To Sondra, for Clarity and Wisdom. To Jo, for Love and Forgiveness." The words hit her, making her feel ashamed. She looked up and noticed Louie's hopeful look, like a child making a wish. "She isn't subtle, is she? Are you sure there isn't poison in mine?" The words spewed from her mouth, that stubborn part of her that she hadn't conquered yet. Why couldn't she show more restraint?

Unable to hide his disappointment, Louie's voice fell to a whisper. "My mother is a wise Ojibwe woman, a healer like Thelma, my grandmother. She doesn't carry hatred in her heart. She misses you and doesn't understand why you avoid her."

Regret made her stomach muscles clench. Why couldn't she

erase that memory? "I guess getting drunk, dumping the turkey on the kitchen floor, and making a mess of everything still burns a bit bright."

Louie stepped closer to her, looking directly into her eyes. "That was over four years ago. She doesn't care about that."

Jo knew Louie was right. His mom had saved her job. That day, she'd been so hung over. Maybe even legally drunk. An absolute 'no' for physical therapists. But she'd been in denial, assisting her client out of the wheelchair to practice walking on the parallel bars. Then losing her grip and dropping the client. Shame flooded her body. Jo owed her mother-in-law more than one favor.

"Jo, you're the one saving your life. I just want you to keep me in it. All the way, like it used to be, when things were good." Louie reached out his hand as if to touch her face.

Jo's phone rang sharply like a clap of thunder, startling them both. "Mom, again."

"I'll wait." Louie stepped back, giving her some space.

"Hey, Mom, what's going on? Wait. Hold on." Jo felt her heart plummet and smash onto the ground. She hung up the phone and stumbled as the world started to spin.

Louie caught her from falling. "Jo, what's wrong?"

"It's Annie. She overdosed on pills—maybe—a suicide attempt." Her words felt like chalk, melting and sticking in her mouth.

Jo struggled to clear her throat, which was narrowing, shutting off her words. "She's in the hospital. Mom doesn't have any more information. Louie—"

Jo welcomed Louie's strong, warm, comforting arms wrapping around her. Her heart struggled to understand. Annie. The one who always had her feet on the ground and her heart in the right place.

Jo buried her face in Louie's chest. She wanted to crawl right into his heart and stay there, safe and secure. Louie stroked her hair. She let the sobs escape. Without Louie saying a word, Jo could feel the love cascade like a waterfall from his heart into hers. She finally ran out of breath, pulled her emotions together, and gently released herself from his arms.

No way. Andrea again. Home from her night shift at the hospital. She paused in front of them. "You sure know how to pick them. I want to learn your secret."

Jo jolted at the comment. Oh no, Andrea had seen her with Zac last night.

Andrea nodded in approval. "But I think this one is even better than that guy last night."

Jo wanted to shove Andrea as hurt crossed Louie's face, but those fighting days had ended a long time ago on the playground. She avoided looking into his eyes, not wanting to see the crazy, unconditional love he still had for her. It was too painful.

"I need to call Sondra." Panic now replaced the guilt.

"Will she pick up? You shared she's been out of touch."

Jo's mind kicked in, like a supercomputer scanning the possibilities. "I'll text the secret code."

"I didn't know you still used it."

"Only for extreme emergencies. We need to see Annie."

"Go ahead and make plans. My parents can help take care of the girls. We all love Annie. She'll need you and Sondra. I'm sure the town gossip is going wild."

"I didn't even think about that." Jo shuddered.

"Never easy."

"Thanks, Louie." Jo took a deep breath. She didn't want to cry again. She had to be strong. Tough. Resilient. Be the local bar owner's daughter. People who didn't know her would call her a bitch. Her true friends knew the complete opposite was true. She pulled her shoulders back, took a deep breath and held it, then tightened her chest muscles, holding the tension for fifteen seconds then relaxed her muscles and released her breath. Her technique to acknowledge the pain and release any energy blocks. It helped.

"I better make sure the girls are okay. I'll text you later."

"Call me if you need to talk. Okay?"

Jo nodded and hobbled up her front steps, her leg throbbing. The door opened before she could turn the handle.

Jessica shoved a feather in her face. "Mom, look! This was lying on the top step. What bird is it?"

Jo took it and felt a tingling sensation run up her spine. "A crow. Your Great Grandma Thelma says that a feather is a message from an angel."

"What angel sent it?" Hunter reached up and gently touched the feather.

"I think it's from your Grandpa Colin in heaven. He always liked Annie."

"The one we made the potion—oops! I mean lotion—for?" Hunter covered her mouth, her eyes wide, as she realized she'd shared the secret.

Jo laughed, "It's okay. We should call them 'Grammy's potion lotions.'"

"That's good, Mom. Grammy does add a little magic to each one," Jessica shared.

"Remember, all feathers are special. But my favorite is the crow." Jo stroked the feather with reverence, then leaned down and held the feather to her ear. She gestured for the girls to join her. They were quiet, waiting to hear a message.

"I don't hear anything. What's he saying?" Hunter whispered

with a frown of concentration.

"I know! He's telling Mom to tell us the crow and wolf story," Jessica proclaimed, her eyes sparkling with excitement.

"I'm not sure. I have a lot to do."

"But Mom, you promised the next time we found a crow feather that you would tell us," Jessica insisted, hands on her hips—a mirror of Jo. "You're supposed to keep your promises."

"Who taught you to argue like that?" Jo ruffled Jessica's hair and looked at Hunter's hopeful face. The love she felt for them overcame her hesitation to tell the story that she and Louie had created. It would be good to think of a good memory, elevate her energetic vibration, instead of shuffling around in the sadness. Her whole body contracted. A sign from the universe. She was on the right track.

She closed her eyes and drifted into the feeling of the soulful relationship she'd originally enjoyed with Louie. How they could talk to each other without words, using just a look or expression. When Jessica turned four and Hunter, two, they'd added humor to it, acting the story out. Louie was the wolf and Jo was the crow. At the end of the story, Louie would grab her and the girls. They'd roll around, howling, cawing, and laughing. She knew Jessica missed it, while Hunter was trying to remember.

Jessica tugged on Jo's shirt. "Come on, Mom, let's do our cuddle-bug bed while we listen."

"Will you act it out?" Hunter begged.

"No, silly, she needs Dad to be the wolf." Jessica rolled her eyes, already acting like the older sister.

Jo forced herself not to laugh. "No fighting. It's early and you have to promise me you'll go back to sleep. You can have a special dream and when you wake up, I'll make you pancakes."

"They have to be blueberry," Jessica negotiated.

"Blueberry it is." Jo gathered up blankets and piled them on the couch. She tucked the girls in beside her, so they were all covered up, warm and cozy. Jo sat for a few minutes, letting everyone calm down, hoping the girls would get sleepy. "Ready?"

Both girls nodded. Jo noticed their eyes closing. They snuggled in even closer, giving up their fight to stay awake.

"Once upon a time, there was a wolf and a crow who got lost in the forest after a fire. They couldn't find their families but found each other. They didn't know how to talk to each other, since one howled and the other cawed. After a while, they figured out how to use their eyes to communicate and decided to help each other. After days of journeying and living through harrowing events, they bonded and began to understand each other's words."

Jo paused and looked down at the girls. She couldn't believe it—they were already asleep! Magic. She wrapped up the story for herself.

"In the end, they helped each other find their families and stayed best friends for life. Just like I'm going to be a best friend for Annie."

# CHAPTER NINE

## SONDRA

# What About Sex?

### *California: Four Weeks Earlier*

SONDRA SAVORED THE BUBBLES POPPING and tickling her tongue. Ironic, how the Krug Vintage Brut champagne was more pleasurable than her love life with James. James, never to be called Jim—too casual for him. Actually, it was more sad than ironic. Here she was at the poshest resort in Palm Springs with her husband and their friends. Why did she feel anxious? She needed to change her focus. Otherwise, her energy would sink along with the hope of having sex with James tonight. And that was the problem—it had been months.

*Stop. Be grateful.* Sondra leaned back in her chair and took in her surroundings. The view was stunning. A trellis covered with Japanese white wisteria and jasmine flowers arched over their VIP table. Their deliciously-sweet fragrance created an enchanted atmosphere. Plus, James was enjoying himself, sharing business stories and golf jokes. Maybe it would stimulate his desire to initiate sex tonight. If not tonight, then when? Once they were back home, work and social commitments would consume their lives.

She'd drop everything and make time to have sex. But not James. Frustration leered at her, tempting her to dive in.

What else could she do? Sondra had taken extra care with her organic makeup from France. Every strand of her artistically-highlighted, long, blond hair was in place. Her body was framed in the flaming red Valentino designer dress that commanded attention and demanded action. It was designed for sex, zipping from the bottom up to display her long, sculpted legs.

Did James notice? He looked great tonight. His hair was jet black and naturally streaked with silver that looked sharper than anything a stylist could create. She loved his intellect, the way he could carry any conversation, whether politics, technology, entertainment, or the news. She noticed his hands resting on the table, his fingers perfectly aligned. She yearned for those fingers to rest on her breast and make her feel like a desirable woman. As they had ten years ago.

Yes, Sondra had taken a risk, ignored everyone's concerns. But she'd felt mature at twenty-eight. James had been a young fifty-five, full of life. Now, at sixty-five, he still had enough energy to run multiple businesses, play frequent rounds of golf, and socialize, but not enough to have sex with her. She didn't get it.

It was difficult. They still had fun together. Their vacation with Amelia and David had been enjoyable. David was witty and entertaining. Sondra admired his dedication to keep his large, ex-college-football body in shape. And she got a kick out of Amelia, with her sophisticated Southern charm offset by her unexpected quirkiness and passion to help others. However, nobody could compare to Annie and Jo. They were her true best friends. She didn't miss her childhood, but she missed them. They were the best part. It had been a long time. How old were their children now?

Children. One more thing not to think about. What was with her monkey mind tonight? Sondra hated boarding the high-speed thought train. No use in resisting—might as well flow with it until it slowed down. She could usually quiet it, do a yoga pose or meditate. Not possible here. However, it would be hilarious to see everyone's reaction if she got up and did a downward dog yoga pose. But she could help by tapping. She discreetly raised one hand and gently tapped her sternum. Better. She could feel the cortisol rush slowing down.

Did she really want children? James didn't. She had agreed to no children before they married, but now it felt sad. Still—the lack of a family wasn't the real reason for her discontent. It was the haunting question that woke her up at 4:00 a.m. Should she stay in a sexless marriage? Sondra put her hands under the table and tapped the acupressure points on her hands and wrists. Those morning blues—they sucked. It was when the loneliness hit the hardest—until she started to indulge herself.

That first porn DVD. Her anger and hurt when James brought it home. His explanation that it would help him get aroused. Needing Viagra was one thing, but porn? It was depressing. Wasn't she enough for him? However, it kept their marriage going, even when the porn stopped working for him. Now it was her secret. How she'd get her vibrator when James left for work. Her search for the perfect DVD, letting her imagination soar. Sondra squeezed her hands together, repressing the sick, paranoid feeling in her stomach. James couldn't find out. But why should she feel guilty? She needed something!

Sondra felt uncomfortably warm. Time to escape. The bathroom would work. "Amelia, do you want to join me in freshening up?"

"No, darling, I was there a few minutes ago, remember?"

Right. Sondra smiled to cover her blunder. Her dad used to brag that Sondra's smile could light up the house if there was a power outage. Strange how that memory came up. Guilt jabbed her gut. She hadn't returned his last three phone calls. She'd been a frustrated child after her mom died. And the town—all those people watching her, pretending to care but quick to inform her dad whenever she screwed up. Her dad lost, not knowing how to deal with her antics. Sondra used to call him "Mr. Awkward" behind his back. It had been suffocating. She admired how Annie had embraced staying, loving the small town where everyone knew everyone's business.

"Do you want me to come with you?" Amelia asked.

Startled back into reality, Sondra jumped up and banged her knee against the table. Her forehead broke out in a sweat as everyone grabbed their cocktails to save them from spilling.

Amelia made a funny face and gestured to her. Geez, did she need to rub it in? Sondra was already embarrassed. Now Amelia was moving her eyebrows up and down like she had a tic. *Just ignore her.*

Sondra turned to leave and jerked to a stop. So that's why Amelia was acting strange. Walking toward her was a rakish, debonair hero from a steamy romance novel come to life. He smiled at her, dragging his fingers through a rich crop of perfectly-groomed, shaggy hair, not too short or long, just gorgeous. He oozed confidence, sex, and sophistication, like a template for a young James Bond.

Unfortunately, the image was ruined by the woman who stepped from behind him—the complete opposite of his beautiful self. Whoever she was, she looked like a librarian, with her thick-rimmed, oversized black glasses, pinstriped suit, and high-collared shirt buttoned to the top.

James stood up and enthusiastically greeted this Mr. Gorgeous. "Adam, welcome! We just finished dinner, but please join us for a drink. Ladies, we met Adam on the golf course today. He has a wicked long drive. Put me and David to shame."

"Impossible. You both have great games. I just had a little luck today." Adam began to shake everyone's hands around the table. "Hello, I'm Adam Majors and this is Emily, my assistant."

"Adam is working on a high-end condo project. I promised to show him a few unlisted locations in exchange for his golf tips," James shared. "And his luck is about to get better. This is my wife, Sondra. You won't discover a better agent for finding you a home."

Adam gave Sondra an appreciative look, with enough heat to make ice water boil. "I do believe you're right, James. I'm about to become a very lucky man." Adam extended his hand toward Sondra.

Sondra stepped forward. The left heel of her four-inch Jimmy Choo caught the leg of the chair. This couldn't be happening! She was suspended in air, ready to hit the ground, until her dress zipper caught the arm of her chair. It stopped her momentum until the zipper unlatched and journeyed upward, stopping short of exposing her sheer, red bikini thong. Sondra smacked her face against Adam's chest. Mortified, she pushed herself away, tugging the zipper down.

"That's quite the dress—and the best handshake that I've ever received." The heat in his eyes twinkled with restrained amusement.

Her mind went blank. Where was her usual quick response? *Just act like nothing happened. Be cool and confident. No big deal.* Besides, everyone else was too polite to comment on her mishap.

The waiter appeared with two chairs. Sondra held her breath and willed him to place one next to her. It worked. Adam slid into the chair next to hers like a panther in his perfectly-cut black suit. She felt a firecracker explode in her body when his thigh brushed against hers. Maybe this wasn't a good thing.

"I do like your sense of style."

"I guess being trendy can be treacherous at times." Sondra playfully smiled as she gave the zipper a last tug to ensure it was secure.

"Maybe we can use trendy to our advantage. What if I hire you to find me a house? Would you throw in your design skills? James boasted it was one of your many talents. We could seal the deal right now." Adam turned to James, "Only if that's okay with you?"

Sondra felt a burst of indignation. Permission from James! What century did Adam think she lived in? "Excuse me, shouldn't you be asking me that?"

"My apologies. It's enjoyable to meet an independent woman."

James laughed in amusement. "Sondra is her own woman when it comes to business. It's how we met. I was selling my house after my wife passed away. Sondra was a tiger, fighting off the other realtors to win my business. I couldn't resist that spirit of hers."

"Sounds like I need her in my corner, with or without the decorating bonus. Are you in?"

"Sounds like I'll be showing you some condoms then. Oh my gosh, I meant condos!"

Everyone laughed at Sondra's mistake, thinking she was purposely being witty. Usually she would have laughed along, loving the attention. Instead, she bit the inside of her cheek, quelling her wild imaginings of unzipping her dress and having sex right there with Adam. In a desperate act of self-preservation, she took charge of the conversation.

"Adam, where are you from and how did you get into property development?" Sondra inwardly winced. Her voice sounded so formal and artificial.

Adam slowly looked around the table, making eye contact with everyone there. "I was born on a small horse farm in Kentucky. My grandfather handed it down to my dad. He wasn't good with money or horses and sold the farm when I was ten. I was pretty mad and swore I'd buy it back someday."

"Did you?" Amelia asked, captivated, like everyone else around the table.

"Yes, but by then everything had changed. All the farms around us had sold out. Our old farm was a place where you could lean against a tree and ponder life's big questions." Adam paused and looked up into the sky, as if he was reliving the memory. "I bought a large chunk of land back and built my first affordable condo building. I was more idealistic back then."

Amelia eagerly leaned forward onto the table, ignoring the glasses shaking with the sudden movement. "Adam, that's so lovely. I hope you kept some of that idealism. I'm passionate about my new mentoring program for underprivileged boys. It's mirrored after Sondra's program for runaway teenage girls. You'd be a great mentor."

"I'm still that small-town boy at heart. You can count on me to help."

Amelia was beaming at Adam while David and James nodded in approval. Sondra looked over at Emily. Her eyes were cast downward. Why was Emily so disengaged? Did she feel unworthy? She should draw Emily into the conversation. "Emily, have you worked with Adam for a while?"

Emily shoved her oversized glasses back up on her nose. "A few months." Her tone was curt.

"And she's already organized my chaotic office life. She's a miracle worker." Adam smiled encouragingly at Emily, as if coaxing a shy child to come out of her shell and say hello. Instead, Emily rummaged through her oversized Mary Poppins bag, pulled out a cell phone and began checking messages.

Sondra concluded Emily was either rude or horribly shy. Adam shifted the conversation by flagging their waiter and engaging the men in a spirited conversation about the merits of scotch versus bourbon. By the way the waiter hustled from the table, some expensive drinks were coming.

Adam briefly touched Sondra's hand as he gave her his full attention. Her hand tingled from the contact, as if warm brandy was being injected into her veins. "Besides real estate, what are your other passions?"

If his hand could make her react like that—then what would his bare chest feel like on hers? *Okay, stop it.* That wasn't the passion he was talking about.

"I bet you're passionate about your children," Adam commented, filling the silence.

"My children are a dozen rebellious, Gothic, gutter-language-using teenage girls at the L.A. Have Hope shelter, who hate me 50 percent of the time and love me the other. Well—love isn't the right word. Let's say they occasionally show a glimmer of appreciation and mutter 'thank you' under their breath."

"That's a very different world than this one." Adam stroked the petals of a flower on the trellis next to him then shifted his sensuous eyes towards her. "It sounds fascinating. How did you get involved with the shelter?"

Who was this stranger? Was he an illusion? Sondra looked over at James to center herself and stay grounded. "I could relate to their frustrations. However, I was stuck in a small town. The most trouble you could get into was stealing from your parents' liquor cabinet and partying in the farmers' fields. Not like L.A., with the drugs and crime."

"That sounds pretty tame. You've never experienced anything riskier?"

"We did have a scary experience when a farmer came out with a loaded shotgun."

"Did he actually shoot?"

"No, one of my best friends shouted out her name, figuring he would know her family. Her grandfather was a retired local pastor, so he took pity on us sinners. The worst part was that her grandfather was delighted to dole out our punishment. We baled hay for that farmer for a whole week after school. If you haven't baled hay, you can't relate to the torture."

"I like that." Adam spoke with sincerity, his eyes clear now.

"Like what?"

"That you have a different background than the women in L.A."

"Are you implying that L.A. women are what? Shallow?" Sondra challenged him, enjoying their exchange, liking the powerful and playful taste of the words in her mouth.

"Did I touch another button?" Adam's shoulders leaned closer to hers, offering himself up to her in a physical apology.

Sondra wanted to whisper: *Forget the buttons and just unwrap me like a candy bar and savor me bite by bite.* Instead, she said, "There are a lot of talented women around. You have writers, movie producers, business founders, quite a wide variety to choose from."

"Sounds like you'd fit in perfectly."

Sondra could smell his testosterone, like a blast of ocean air, heavy with salt and minerals, whipping across her face. "Are you working me?"

"What if I was?" Adam questioned as his leg bumped hers under the table.

She looked around the restaurant, noticing everyone engaged in their meals or in conversation. Nobody seemed to notice the electricity flowing between them. Had he touched her leg on purpose?

Why not test him? She stared him straight in the eye and deliberately bumped her leg into his.

"I do like to give pleasure when I can." The heat and smoke in his eyes were back again, so intense that they could trigger a fire alarm.

This wasn't safe. She was a married woman. Her nerves were rumbling like an underground subway. Thank God the waiter arrived.

"Champagne for the ladies and scotch for the men, compliments of Mr. Majors."

James tasted his scotch. "Great choice."

Oh no. The scotch better not interfere with the one she planned to pour James later with the Viagra in it.

A five-piece band took the stage and launched into a slow, soulful jazz number. The sultry notes hung in the air, setting the evening for romance. David and Amelia joined the couples on the dance floor, clinging onto each other. Sondra looked expectantly at James.

"Darling, I'd love to dance with you—you know that." James defiantly lifted his chin. "But I tweaked my ankle playing golf today. I have to play eighteen holes tomorrow before we leave."

*Have* to play with a tweaked ankle? Was this the new excuse? It took willpower not to glare at James. Getting angry rarely worked. It only made him more stubborn.

"If I rest it tonight, it should be fine in the morning. Besides, once we start dancing, you won't want to stop. I'll end up limping."

Sondra seethed inside—what else was going to be limp tonight?

"That doesn't sound good. May I?" Adam asked.

James avoided Sondra's disillusioned eyes. "There you go, honey. Adam can twirl you around the dance floor."

Sondra chafed at James's patronizing tone. But why not dance and have fun? Feel bold and take control. Sondra gracefully glided out onto the dance floor as if she owned it.

Adam slid his hands around her back. "So dancing is a passion?"

"My passion is my secret."

"A woman who stole liquor, sells real estate, and helps with a runaway shelter. What type of secrets does a woman like that have?"

"Let's stick to real estate for now." Sondra implemented her best authoritative tone.

"We have a deal?" Adam's hands slowly crept up her back, just enough to make her wonder if he was taking her seriously.

"Deal? You're playing a very dangerous game with my husband sitting right by us." Sondra glanced over at James, who seemed to be savoring his scotch. Safe...for now.

"A little danger makes everything a little more exciting, don't you think?"

Adam swung her around, then pulled her close for a moment before swinging her away. Her instincts screamed at her to be careful. But her body shouted, *Go for it!*

"As a little girl, I was warned about stranger danger."

"Then I'll have to get rid of the stranger part. Let you get to know me."

Sondra looked over at James again, who caught her glance and pointed to his Cartier watch.

"If you are truly serious about buying a condo, then I can help you. When do you want to start?"

"The sooner the better. I'm back in my office in two days. Emily can contact you."

The song ended on a long note as Adam slid his hands away. They looked at each other, like boxers waiting for the next move.

Sondra caved first. "James just looked at his watch. Guess it's time for me to retire for the night."

"So early? How can you not dance under this magical sky?"

Sondra looked up at the stars as strains of tango music drifted by them.

"The tango, the dance of a thousand different stories. What will ours be? Let's dance and find out."

Adam was right. James could wait. Set the stage to become the woman who conquers the man. Sondra ran her hands down the sides of her dress. She accepted Adam's hand, lifting her chin in a haughty posture. They stood perfectly still, waiting for the starting beat. She felt powerful and alive.

A tap on her shoulder. No! Not now. But sure enough, there was James, along with David and Amelia. Sondra plastered a fake smile on her face to hide her disappointment.

James's hand replaced Adam's on her back. "Sorry to interrupt. But I need to get some rest for golf tomorrow."

Adam released Sondra's hand. "Of course. Your wife is a beautiful dancer. It was a pleasure."

"Stop being such an old man. Think of Sondra. Stay and dance with us," David goaded James.

"Actually, it was Sondra's idea to make it an early night. She wanted some alone time together."

James had remembered. Things were looking up. Hopefully, James could stay up too! Still, it was hard to leave. She had danced from the moment she could walk. Her mother loved to put on music and dance with her, always laughing, until she got too sick to even walk.

"I can understand that. I live with a workaholic husband as

well." Amelia gave Sondra a supportive smile. "I can fill in. I've been known to do an enchanting tango."

Sondra tilted her head toward Adam. "Thanks for the dance. It was fun." She air-kissed Amelia's cheeks, then gave David a hug. "Enjoy your night. See you back in L.A."

James led her away as the music fully kicked in. The throbbing beat matched her heart, full of anticipation of forthcoming pleasure. Sondra glanced back. Amelia was leaping into Adam's arms. She stopped, mesmerized, as Amelia and Adam took over the dance floor in a tantalizing performance. Adam looked masterful, powerful as he twirled Amelia around at full speed. And Amelia—she was crushing her role of the elusive woman. Then the dramatic finish, as Adam dipped Amelia and then pulled her into his arms, chastely kissing her on the cheek. The dining crowd stood up, clapping furiously. That could have been her. Oh well, she was planning on having a climactic ending too.

# CHAPTER TEN

JAMES COLLAPSED ON THE BED that was designed to imitate sleeping on a cloud. Sondra sat beside him, determined to create an atmosphere of playfulness.

"I'm glad we came home early. I do love you." Sondra leaned down and kissed James, tasting the richness of the scotch on his lips.

James pulled her closer and kissed her back, slowly, then more powerfully. His fingers stroked her back in small circles until they reached her neck and rested there. Her chest involuntarily arched forward, her breasts aching to be touched. A tremor of excitement rushed down her spine as his hands slid across her shoulders, brushing the sides of her breasts, to her hips. It was happening.

Sondra leaned in closer but suddenly James pulled away. What had just happened? Had he gotten nervous that he couldn't perform? It had happened before. In an unusual moment of weakness, James had shared his humiliation. It had taken months and Viagra to try again.

"I'm so tired, honey. Maybe if I rest for a bit?"

Better to be patient. Act like she wasn't concerned. "Okay, sure. Why don't I make you a nightcap?"

James groaned as he put a pillow under his ankle. "Great idea."

Sondra poured scotch into the glass with the crushed Viagra already in it. She wasn't taking any risks that James's pride would interfere with taking the pill.

Sondra sat by James and handed him the drink. She smiled at him and stroked his hand.

James took a big sip that seemed to energize him. He lovingly brushed her hair away from her face. "There, I like seeing your beautiful face."

Her patience was paying off. Now let the Viagra do its thing. "Why don't I freshen up while you relax for a minute?"

"Take your time, honey. Can you hand me the TV remote?"

Sondra handed him the remote and hurried into their bathroom. She undressed, then slid the sensuous, deep-blue silk chemise over her head. It whispered against her skin that it wasn't designed for sleeping.

Sondra rushed back into the bedroom. Was James snoring? He had barely touched his drink, but it didn't matter. He couldn't avoid her any longer. She climbed onto the bed and carefully aligned her body against his, so he could feel the silkiness of the chemise and her naked body underneath. Time to wake him up. She wanted to shake him, but wisely chose to tap his arm until he opened his eyes. "There you are." She bent her knees so the chemise rode up her thighs, exposing her slender, long legs, trying to stimulate his libido.

"I'm here. I'm always here for you, Sondra. But my ankle is throbbing."

"Maybe the scotch will help. Why don't you finish it?"

"I've had enough. I don't want to play golf with a hangover. Why don't we cuddle like this? You understand, don't you?" James's face looked innocent, but his guilty eyes betrayed him.

Sondra gritted her teeth. It wasn't fair. He had led her on—now this? Her frustration boiled over. "What's with this ankle? You never said anything about it earlier. And golf is more important than the sex you promised me—your wife?"

"Where's this coming from? We can have sex anytime."

"Anytime? Now that's a joke." The words escaped. It was over.

James got out of bed, looking peevish. "Explain, please. I haven't golfed for months."

Damn. Now he was haughty. James's way of making her feel childish. But her yearning was too strong to keep quiet. "It's been a long time and you promised me a romantic vacation."

"Isn't this romantic? Look around you." James gestured to their lavish surroundings.

"You know that's not what I'm talking about. I want to be together physically. We need that intimacy. Don't make me beg." Sondra felt insecurity weave its cruel threads through her spirit. She wasn't going to win this argument. She hated rejection. Avoiding that feeling had propelled her into the million-dollar sales club within two years. She had learned all the tactics, including how to turn a no into a yes, and make people believe they'd won the lottery. Why didn't it work with James?

"Sondra, I'm sorry. I'll take next Saturday off work. We'll spend it alone and have a romantic afternoon. How does that sound?" James sounded sincere as he caressed her shoulders.

Sondra grabbed his cell phone from the nightstand. "I'll book it."

"Don't be silly. I'll do it myself." James grabbed his cell phone, blocked off the day and showed it to her. "Satisfied?"

"A little." It was hard to hide the hurt in her voice.

"I'm always thinking of you. In fact, I have a present." James opened his nightstand and took out a jewelry box. "Something to remember this vacation by."

Sondra wanted to shout, "Give me great sex! That will help me remember this vacation." Instead, she opened the box—amethyst lilacs woven within delicate silver strands.

"It's stunning. Thank you." Lilacs—her mother's favorite flower. Did James preplan this to placate her? "Thanks, James. It means a lot to me." The salt from her tears slid backward and stung her throat. Hidden, like her feelings.

Sondra closed the box and set it on the nightstand.

"Aren't you going to try it on?"

"Absolutely, I will tomorrow. I'm going to take a shower. You get some rest."

"Okay." James flung his arm across his face and rolled away from her.

Sondra didn't care if he was disappointed. She felt manipulated. His actions confirmed that something would always happen to get in the way of their sex life.

Sondra went into the bathroom, stripped off the chemise, and dumped it in the trash. Hopefully the cleaning staff would realize it was a gift, not something for the landfill. She got into the shower. Grief engulfed her, wanting to swallow her alive. Just like it did after her mother had died. In the past, it had been the fuel of her youthful rebellion. Back then, she had survived by reaching out to Annie, Jo, and her boyfriend, Hank. Now, she had to do it alone and avoid the quicksand.

Sondra lathered the expensive lavender soap all over her. The water caressed her body, like it understood her need to be touched. She could still salvage some of the evening. She stepped out of the shower and left the water running. She grabbed an over-sized thick towel and wrapped it around her dripping body. She reached into her toiletry bag and found the tan travel vibrator. It was her lover tonight.

Sondra dropped her towel, closed her eyes, and visualized James standing behind her, touching her breasts. She made small circles around her breast until she reached her nipple and squeezed it. A jolt of pleasure raced through her body. Every cell came alive, and her body hummed with sensational energy. She visualized James stroking her between her legs and bending her over the counter. She maneuvered the vibrator into the right position and struggled to keep her fantasy going. *Don't give up now.* Her body needed this. She squeezed her eyes tighter, and suddenly James became Adam as he entered her from behind. She moaned as her body responded, shaking. Her legs quivered and she could barely stand. She opened her eyes and looked into the mirror while exploding into an earth-shaking orgasm.

This was awful. The mirror reflected a crazy person. Her face was contorted, and her hair was a mess. Her orgasm face would scare off any sane man. Maybe that's why James kept rejecting her? She stepped back into the shower and released her tears. They blended with the water, carrying the remnants of her crushed hopes and stagnant dreams down into the earth.

## CHAPTER ELEVEN

Sondra couldn't stop smiling as she sped down the highway toward Adam's rental. She loved how her steel-gray Jaguar, the latest present from James, hugged the curves at high speeds. Could she hold this carefree feeling close? Not let it fade away? These last four weeks—so unexpected. Still no sex, but James had surprised her by booking a romantic getaway in Hawaii for two weeks. Plenty of time for James to golf *and* have sex.

Then there was Adam. What an enigma. Sexy, intelligent, interesting, and fun. She'd thought he was just another guy, out to get laid. But she was wrong. He had done a three-sixty when he canceled his meeting with James and decided to help a high-tech start-up company.

Emily—another enigma or a simple story? Sondra had offered to help Emily spruce up her look. But Adam had warned her that Emily would be seriously offended. Whatever the case, it didn't matter anymore. Better to abandon the idea.

Now here she was—on her way for Adam to sign papers for

the condo she'd found him. It had been a feat. A rocky start where nothing had 'spoken to his soul.' Only a few clients had talked like that. She actually loved it. The game changer—yoga. She still felt wisps of disbelief on how it had brought them together. That day driving by her yoga center. Adam asking her to stop. The advanced class. Almost getting kicked out for being disruptive, for trying to outdo each other in holding difficult poses. After that, everything had fallen into place.

Sondra embraced the exhilaration in her gut at discovering the three-million-dollar condo for Adam. Was that why she felt so high? No—the bliss of denial eluded her. It was Adam. Sondra enjoyed Adam's sense of humor. How he could turn a simple situation like ordering sushi into a great story. Then there was his sensitive side. The openness when he shared his inner journey of self-discovery. He was vulnerable, allowing her to be the same. Sondra began to trust him. She even shared how her mother had died of lung cancer and her dad had struggled to raise her alone—not financially, but emotionally.

Sondra pulled into Adam's driveway and her stomach cramped. Was she nervous? Of course. The commission would catapult her into the top sales rank. Not that she had to worry about money, but she had her own business goals. Another stomach twinge, as a thought trickled into her brain. Maybe her feelings for Adam were deeper than business and friendship? After that night in Palm Springs, Sondra had set the boundaries, which he respected. All the sexual innuendos had disappeared.

Did she miss that? It hadn't been easy to stuff her sexual desires even deeper. She even put her vibrator on vacation—it was the only way to cope. She'd been too afraid she'd see Adam's face—not James's. Even her wardrobe was affected. She dressed more modestly, like today. She felt a bit stifled wearing the gray suit and modest slingback pumps. Was it really helping? She didn't know. But she'd been faithful to James and wanted to remain that way.

*Enough thinking!* Sondra grabbed the tray of cheese and crackers, along with her oversized Louis Vuitton purse and computer bag. Were her hands shaking? It must be hunger. She shouldn't have skipped lunch, but the paperwork had to get done. Now, how to ring the doorbell? Her dilemma disappeared as Adam flung the door open. He drew her into a big, unexpected hug. The tray! It tipped and smashed between their bodies. She pulled away, the tray crashing on the ground. Cheese and crackers flew everywhere.

"Five-second rule?" Adam asked.

They both laughed, attempting to scoop up the remnants, but it was a crumbled mess.

"For the squirrels. I hope they're hungry." Sondra picked up the empty tray.

Adam brushed cracker crumbs off his perfectly-white crumpled shirt and tight-fitting jeans. "I'm so sorry. I might have some airline pretzels stashed in my briefcase."

"No problem. I wasn't hungry." Sondra's stomach grumbled at her lie.

"Let me take that tray from you. Hopefully you're thirsty. Come on, let's celebrate!"

Sondra followed him into the great room, its floor-to-ceiling windows framing an incredible view of the ocean. Adam grabbed two full glasses of champagne sitting by two open bottles and handed her a glass. "Time to celebrate." He lifted his glass and touched hers. "To my amazing real estate agent and friend."

Sondra followed Adam in taking a long drink. The champagne was delicious, one of the best she'd tasted. She set her glass down and pulled out the paperwork from her computer bag. "Everything is here, ready for your signature."

"I'm sure it's perfect. But there's something we need to do first." Adam strolled over to his laptop. He hit a key and jogged back to pour more champagne.

What was going on? Adam was acting like a teenage boy who'd gotten the most popular girl to say yes to the prom. His body language was so exuberant that it was contagious. Then the song 'Celebration,' by Kool & the Gang, filled the room.

"Let's toast to dancing!" Adam clinked his glass against hers, encouraging her to drink along. He moved his hips to the music. Why did he have to look so sensuous? She'd prefer to spill the champagne on his chest and lick it off. The thought made her guzzle the champagne.

Adam kicked off his flipflops. "Let's have some fun. Make up for that tango you missed. Kick off those old-lady pumps."

"Old-lady pumps?" No way. Sondra took off her suit coat and kicked off her shoes. Adam's hands encircled hers and spun her around. He tried to lead her into a complex combination of moves. She felt clumsy, stiff, and awkward. This was crazy! She could do better. *Just let go.* She closed her eyes, feeling the music pulsating through her body. Her muscles relaxed into the beat. There, she had it. Her body responded by dancing with joy and freedom. Emotions that she hadn't experienced in a long time.

The song ended. Sondra collapsed on the sofa, laughing and panting. "Enough. Maybe I am an old lady!"

Adam gave her a look that she couldn't decipher as he poured more champagne. "Here, drink up. You must be thirsty. You're definitely not an old lady." He grabbed the second bottle of champagne. "Let's catch the sunset. You'll love it." He walked out onto the balcony overlooking the ocean.

The view was spectacular. The sun splashed colors of orange, yellow, and red onto the water. The waves gently lapped the shoreline, caressing the sand. A pang of melancholy hit her gut. She wanted to be touched like that.

"I have another toast," Adam announced as he topped off Sondra's glass.

Another toast? It was like being at a wedding. It was hard to refuse when Adam was so excited about the deal. Yet, it'd be smart to get the deal done, then celebrate over an early dinner. "How about the papers first?"

"Five more minutes. I really need to say this. It's important. To Sondra, a woman who outshines this sunset." Adam tapped his glass against hers, tossed his head back, and drank the entire glass.

Sondra accidentally took a big gulp. Was she tipsy? She'd drunk only a glass and a half, or was it more? That was the danger when someone topped off your drink. Still, it couldn't be that much. She was just being paranoid.

His voice brought her out of her reverie. "I don't know how you do it."

Sondra watched his lips kiss the rim of his glass as he took a sip. "Do what?"

"Stay with James."

It was the question that haunted her at night. How could she honestly answer that? Best to play it safe. "James is a good man."

"I agree. Here's to James." Adam topped off her glass again. "Let's be reckless and finish this bottle."

Sondra contemplated the situation as she carefully took a small sip. "I think you're baiting me. Are you trying to ask me something?"

"I know it's none of my business, but isn't it hard to be with such an older man?"

"Not at all."

"I apologize. I had the impression that you weren't happily married."

"How would you know? Isn't that a bit rude?" Sondra's nerves pricked. She didn't like hearing her feelings spoken out loud. Besides, it was more complicated than that. Sondra turned and looked out at the ocean.

"I've been there; that's why I know. I see the sadness in your eyes when you're not careful. When you and James are together, I notice that you're the one who reaches out first to touch his hand. Am I wrong?"

Sondra finished her champagne and looked back at Adam. "Been there?"

"I got divorced about a year ago. We had an incredible passion for each other, along with a deep friendship and respect. Then everything fell apart when she couldn't get pregnant. Suddenly, nothing else mattered to her except having a baby. We discovered she had physical issues that were tough to overcome. I was okay with adopting. But she got angry at life, herself, and everyone around her. I tried everything, but she wanted a new start without me. It hurt. I had to let go."

"I'm so sorry."

"I was too—until I met you. It was the first time I've felt such a powerful connection. It's been liberating to know I can feel that way again. This feels inspiring."

Was she hearing Adam correctly? Sondra's ears had a slight ringing in them, and her vision felt blurry. She needed to focus.

Adam stepped closer and placed his finger on her temple. He slid his finger down the side of her face and neck, ever so softly and gently. "I've wanted to touch your face like this ever since I first saw you."

Sondra saw the panther inside of Adam again, remembering how he had gracefully slid into the chair beside her that night over dinner. This time it felt like he was softly and steadily stalking her, hypnotizing her with his eyes and movements.

Adam took her hand. "I care about you, Sondra. Nobody needs to know. Why don't we take a chance? Let's discover what we've both been missing. Maybe we can create something new together?"

"But I do love James. He can't help it that he isn't more..."

"Like us? Some people need to be more physical than others. Haven't you noticed me staring at your lips? I see how full and sensual they are. All I want is to kiss them—like this."

Adam leaned down and took full possession of her mouth. When he let her go, she jerked backward, stunned. Her lips felt seared with his heat. She wiped them, rebuking them for betraying her. Panicked, she looked around to see if anyone was watching.

Adam walked through the door, then turned around. He slowly unbuttoned his shirt and slid it off his shoulders, never taking his eyes off of her. He looked so trusting, waiting there for her. His bare chest rippled with muscles. His perfect hair was tousled from dancing and the ocean breeze. When he smiled at her, it was hotter than sand on a tropical island. She trembled as her defenses cracked, sending fissures into the barriers she'd created.

"Don't do it!" Sondra's mind warned, but her body wasn't listening. The match had been struck and the kindling ignited. Were those her legs moving toward him into the house? She felt like she was watching someone else. If this was a spell, she didn't want to break it.

Once they were inside, Adam lifted her into his arms and carried her into the bedroom. He set her down on a pile of ocean-blue comforters that embraced her body with their softness.

Sondra reached for Adam, discovering that he'd slipped his pants off, letting her touch him. Her head was buzzing. This was a new feeling. But no wonder—she was in the center of a sensual cyclone as he slid her clothes off. He stretched his naked body on top of hers, holding himself slightly up with his arms and moving around so his skin brushed against hers.

Adam touched her breasts as if he was caressing a raindrop off a delicate orchid blossom. Then he trailed his hands up and down her body, making every sensation linger. He twirled his tongue over her arms, breasts, then stomach as if creating a masterpiece of art. He woke up nerves throbbing in her body that had been dormant for years. Sondra tried to touch him, to give him pleasure, but he gently took her hand away. Wait—did she hear a click, like a door shutting? Maybe it was the bedsprings. It must be her imagination, as Adam didn't stop and distracted her with the most sensational, lingering, exotic kiss. She never knew a man could kiss like that.

The unbridled pleasure was so intense—could she be on an astral trip? Sondra couldn't keep her mind and body together as Adam wove his way down between her legs. He devoured her with his tongue, hands caressing her legs, before he finally knelt and entered her. Their bodies were like meteorites racing together, then colliding and showering the sky with a brilliant streak of light. Sondra's body shook from the explosion as she wrapped her legs around him.

# CHAPTER TWELVE

THE NEXT MORNING, SONDRA SAT in her contemporary steel-and-glass real estate office, wishing she could curl up in a blanket. Her mind was spinning faster than a suspended disco ball, thoughts dashing in and out, not knowing how to feel. Her body shivered as she recalled Adam holding her close after their explosion. She loved how their arms and legs had been intertwined, as if they had played Twister in bed. James had never held her like that.

Why were parts of the night blurry? Yes, she'd had three glasses, but to black out? Maybe it was the lack of food and the intensity of being wanted again. Sondra remembered Adam bringing her coffee so she could drive. But there was no way she could go home and pretend nothing had happened. She had forced herself to go to the gym, do a mile on the treadmill, and drink multiple glasses of water before showering. It had been nerve-wracking to see James, but luckily, he'd been on a business call. She blew him a kiss goodnight and went to bed.

*Please, not another anxiety attack!* She felt her body sweat and head pound. What if James found out? Guilt launched through her heart like a rocket. Yet her body tingled when she allowed herself to think about how incredible it had felt. She was so confused.

Was someone knocking on her door? Sondra looked up. Was that Emily? Would Emily be wearing a form-flattering black dress that showed off her curves? What happened? Emily had had her hair professionally styled and had ditched her glasses. Sondra smelled musk, a scent that hunters used to attract their prey, and felt a power shift between them.

"I heard you closed the deal. I thought you might want this." Emily set down Sondra's tray from last night. A large envelope was on top.

"Yes, thank you. It's exciting." Sondra picked up the envelope. It felt heavier than the paperwork she had expected.

"I have to agree. You do look excited in the pictures." Emily fanned her face with her hand as if she was hot.

"Did you take pictures of the new place? Normally, you need the owner's permission."

"Open the envelope. It should provide the clarity you're seeking."

Sondra narrowed her eyes, assessing Emily's body language. She stood up in an attempt to equalize the power shift and casually slit the envelope open with her silver-plated letter opener. She drew out a stack of pictures. There she was, naked with Adam. Adam was kissing her breasts—her back was arched in pleasure. The next—a picture of him between her legs. The blood pounded against her temples, threatening to break through her skin. She tossed the pile on her desk but caught sight of the next picture. Was that her having an orgasm? It was horrifying. She looked so grotesque.

So—it wasn't the vibrator.

Sondra felt a surge of volcanic, white-hot anger. *Act cool. Don't give Emily any clue.* Sondra shoved the pictures back into the envelope. "I'm not stupid. Quite a nice scam. Does Adam know? I'm sure he would be furious. It must be hard to work with someone so handsome and watch him be with someone else."

"That's where you're wrong. He loves being with me. I was thinking no commission for the sale and an extra two million dollars in cash to keep the pictures quiet. That shouldn't be hard to get."

"Are you crazy? Most of my money is tied up with James. Why would I pay you? I can't trust you." Sondra scrutinized Emily, leaning against the door, looking smug.

"I'm not stupid either. I know about your prenuptial. You lose quite a bit of money if you get divorced, especially if you've been unfaithful." Emily picked up the envelope and pulled out the photos. She held up the one of Sondra having her orgasm. "This is my favorite."

Sondra walked around the desk and snatched the photo from Emily. "I can't imagine Adam would go along with this. Why would you hurt him?"

"I found Adam when he was a struggling actor and hungry enough to do a low-budget porn movie. I saved him and taught him how to play in the big leagues. He actually loves me, along with the perks and luxuries that come with the job."

"So, you set him up to screw married women? That doesn't bother you?" Sondra could barely speak the words. Her anger was now spitting ash and blocking her airways. She dug her fingernails into her palms. *Come on, Sondra, keep breathing. Everything is going to be okay. Don't show Emily your devastation.*

"I'm a generous person. I don't mind sharing his body every

now and then, especially with rich women who are sad and lonely. I took pity on you."

"You can screw me over. But you don't want to screw with James."

"James might be physically distant, but he loves you. He wouldn't want those photos all over the Internet and tabloids. How embarrassing for his friends and business partners to see his wife naked with another man."

Sondra's heat turned to ice. It felt like her blood had stopped flowing. "Please don't do this to James. You're asking for the impossible. What's your bottom line?"

"You heard it. That's the deal. If you don't want James to know, I'm sure you can get a loan from your father. I hear you're Daddy's little girl."

Sondra shoved the envelope back to Emily. "Fuck you."

"I think you're the one who will be fucked, but not the way you like." Emily shoved the envelope back. "I have an extra copy. You can keep those for the lonely nights after James leaves you."

Sondra's panic conquered her anger. "Emily, stop. Give me ten days to see what I can do."

"Ten days is a long time."

"You're talking two million dollars. Nobody has two million dollars in cash lying around that's not invested."

"Ten days. Only because I'm feeling generous. But you better reassure me that you're serious by staying in touch. You know how to reach me." Emily blew Sondra a kiss and waved goodbye, as if they were best friends.

"I'm so fucked," Sondra announced to the empty room. "Why couldn't I be happy with what I have?"

Another knock on the open door. Was Emily back? Sondra whirled around to see a delivery boy holding a dozen red roses.

Roses—what the hell? The boy set them down on her desk. "Have a nice day, ma'am."

Sondra's hand shook as she read the card. "Looking forward to our special vacation together. Love, James."

Sondra walked over to the window and leaned her forehead against it. Flowers from James. Unbelievable. What had she done? How could she have been so stupid? Should she pay the blackmail and trust Emily and Adam? Or report them and suffer the consequences? Had she subconsciously let this happen to create a way out of her marriage with James? No—never like this. It was degrading to herself, James, and oh God—what would her dad think? Maybe if she came clean right away, James would forgive her. If he'd been more engaged in their sex life, this wouldn't have happened. Why did she let having sex become such a big part of her life? Why couldn't she be satisfied, just being loved? What was wrong with her?

Sondra realized her whole body was pressed against the window. She shuddered with a terrifying thought of the window cracking, letting her fall and crash onto the pavement below. What an awful thought. Her heart was racing. She needed to breathe before she passed out.

Sondra's despair was interrupted by her phone beeping. Now what? A SOS text from Jo? They had made a pact to only use it when it was a crisis—a promise to be there for each other. How could Jo know what happened? Did Emily and Adam call her? Did they tell her father what was happening? Did he have a heart attack?

Sondra dialed Jo's number, trying to keep the panic level low. "Jo, is everything okay?"

Sondra's heart plummeted further when she heard Jo cry. Jo never cried, only when pushed beyond extreme limits. "Jo, I'm here. I can't understand you. Take a deep breath. Tell me what's going on. Did someone call you about me?"

Sondra sank into her chair. "Wait, did you say that Annie tried to commit suicide?" Her fear turned into inescapable lava, burying her alive with excruciating pain. She finally managed to whisper, "I'm on my way."

PART TWO

# What The Hell Just Happened?

# CHAPTER THIRTEEN

*DON'T WAKE UP. STAY HERE—IT'S so quiet, so peaceful.*

Another flash. Annie's face ready to smash into the counter. Her body suspended in the air. Was that her—naked on the bathroom floor?

Annie's brain kept sending images. *Look at the pills. No—don't look. Go back to sleep. It's just a bad dream.* But wait—was someone calling her name? Did one of the boys need her? She'd better wake up.

Annie fought to open her eyes. Did someone glue them together? What was going on? Wait a minute—there was a light. Was that Jesus shining a light in her eyes? It looked like his pictures—dark brown hair, gentle face, and kind, loving eyes. If that was Jesus, she wanted to talk to him, maybe even give him a piece of her mind.

*Come on—try harder!* Finally, a release of pressure as her eyes popped open. The light moved. "Jesus" was actually a doctor.

"There you are. I told your family that I wasn't going to lose you."

Annie whispered, "Lose me? Fat chance. I can't even take a breath without one of them needing me." The doctor gave her a questioning look. Did she really say that? And why did her throat and stomach hurt? She moved her head and pain shot through her body. Annie looked over at one of the nurses. The nurse looked familiar, maybe a church member? It was hard to tell with that mask. Great, even in the emergency room, there was no place to hide. Time to cover up her misstep. "I didn't mean that. I think there's something wrong with my head."

"You hit your head hard when you fell. Lucky you didn't crack your skull. You must have Norwegian blood in you, like me. We're known for having thick skulls, in a good way."

*Why can't this be a dream?* A shudder coursed through Annie's entire body. "Oh my God, I could have died?"

"A few inches to the left or right—let's say it could have been bad. The antidepressants you were taking might have affected how you fell."

"Antidepressants?" Annie glanced back at the nurse. Shame slithered over her skin. Her secret was out.

"That's why we pumped your stomach. We didn't know how many you took. Your husband said the pills were scattered over the floor. He didn't have time to count. You gave him quite a scare. Do you remember how many you took? It's important to know. With your head injury, we want to be prepared for any withdrawal reactions."

*Pumped her stomach.* That's why her stomach and throat hurt—all those tubes.

"Not many, honestly, and they were prescribed to me. I was overtired. I haven't been sleeping and was stressed over the upcoming funeral. Maybe six or seven—but not all at once and I didn't eat much food." She felt agitated, like a piece of clothing caught in a continuous wash cycle. What else could she say?

Annie's head pounded. *No, don't cry*—but it was too late. Tears erupted like lava from a volcano, streaming down her face.

"I'm going to give you something safe to calm you down. Everything is going to be okay."

Annie closed her eyes. She could feel someone patting her tears away, then a slight pinch on her arm. Exhaustion knocked her back to sleep.

# CHAPTER FOURTEEN

WAS SOMEONE CRYING? WAS SHE still crying? Annie touched her cheeks, but they were dry. Then she saw Dan, his head bowed in prayer. Annie instinctively touched his arm in comfort.

Dan lifted his head. His eyes, red and puffy, lit up as they connected with hers. Guilt rocketed through her body as he put his arms around her. "Annie...I love you." Dan buried his head between her neck and shoulder. His tears ran down her chest and pooled around her heart. Annie held him back. She couldn't speak. Instead, she sank into the depth of his emotions and the supportive feeling of his arms. Something she'd been missing.

Annie could feel Dan's anguish through the tension in his arms. As his tears slowed, his arms became looser until they pulled away. Dan lifted his face toward her.

Annie couldn't ignore his piercing, inquisitive, searching eyes trying to break through her barriers. "It's not what you think."

"You don't know what I think."

Annie cringed. He had found her, half naked, maybe part of

the towel covering her? Maybe not. Pills scattered all over. "I can imagine what you saw. It horrifies me."

"The horrifying thing was not knowing whether you were alive. I could barely hear you breathe."

Was that fear in his voice or was he rebuking her? She had to shake off this heavy blanket of horror. She was burning up. Shit— maybe she was in hell? But no—Dan wouldn't be here. She felt a strange surge of anger. Where had that come from? But once again, words escaped her. "Sounds like I really put on a show. The doctor said you called 9-1-1. By now the whole town must know."

"Nobody knows anything except that you fell and hit your head. Everyone has been praying for you."

"But the pills?"

"Annie, only the medical staff knows about that."

Was there a trace of doubt in Dan's voice? Did he worry about the rumor mill too? What people would think of her? Of him? Dan was practiced at hiding his true feelings in a crisis. "I give it twenty-four hours before the rest of the story gets out."

"Annie, what is the story? What happened? I didn't even know you were taking those pills."

Annie wanted to look him in the eye and pretend everything was okay. It was what she did these days—pretend. But she hadn't meant to scare him, the boys—herself. Couldn't God give her a break? The humiliation of being in the hospital was almost too much to handle. Yet Annie was the granddaughter of a pastor and now the wife of a pastor. She was trained to handle anything. If only her head would stop pounding.

*Find your strength, Annie.* Was that her grandmother's voice she was hearing?

"I was having problems sleeping and was getting anxious over it. The doctor didn't talk about depression. The pills helped me to cope."

The door opened and a refreshing breeze caressed Annie's face. There was the doctor. Wow—he still looked like Jesus. And he'd just performed a small miracle—entering in time to save her from Dan's interrogation.

"I've got good news. We didn't find anything on the brain scan. Annie, you might experience headaches for the next few days. You'll need to rest and take it easy. Because of the overdose, we need to keep you here for the next forty-eight hours. Standard procedure."

Overdose? She'd taken only a few extra pills. Why was everyone overreacting? People took antidepressants all the time. Why did Annie Anderson have to be different? Plus, the boys needed her, and she was already feeling better. Then it hit her—they thought she'd attempted suicide. Annie felt nauseated as another wave of shame invaded her body.

Annie's ears were ringing. She could barely hear what the doctor was saying. Something about a psychiatrist she needed to meet with. Fuck. The word felt good—for some reason it relieved the pressure she was feeling. *Don't say anything. Just nod your head, close your eyes, and wince as if you're in pain.*

Thank God, the doctor stopped talking. God. Exactly where had God been these days? How about a little help here?

Silence.

Annie had nothing to say. She wasn't sure whether to cry or shout to get everyone to leave her alone. Dan looked energized and ready to talk. No way could she handle that.

"Can I sleep for a while?" Annie squinted, acting as if the pain had become too much.

"Good idea. The nurses will keep a close eye on you." The doctor turned toward Dan. "Why don't you come back tomorrow morning? Annie isn't going anywhere."

*Going anywhere?* The words felt rude, but no sense in being offended. Her strategy had worked. Annie closed her eyes and pretended to fall asleep. She could feel Dan gently kiss her forehead.

"I'll come back in the morning. We can talk more." Dan spoke softly into Annie's ear. Damn. He wanted her to explain why she'd taken the pills. It almost sounded like a threat. It made her feel rebellious. Yet, if the roles were reversed? Now that would be something—to watch him deal with everything she did in a day. Yet if she was in his shoes—she would want to understand the secrecy. She had to stop thinking about this, just let it go for now.

Annie lay there. It was quiet compared to the chaos at home. The sounds of the staff doing their rounds were actually comforting. And the nurses had been kind. Did they think the overdose was a mistake? She could only pray—except prayer hadn't helped her recently. She gave up thinking about it and immediately fell asleep.

# CHAPTER FIFTEEN

Morning arrived early. Although, with the constant hourly checks, it was hard to discern when morning had begun. Annie thought of Dan and the boys. How were things going? What had they made for breakfast? She felt a longing for them that surprised her. But there was no way they were going to see her in a hospital bed. She didn't want them to carry that image with them for the rest of their lives.

Annie finished her last bite of oatmeal. Dan was going to be here any minute. What should she say? She should prepare something.

Too late. The door opened and Dan walked through. Could he hear her heart pounding with anxiety?

Dan pulled up a chair and kissed her on the forehead. "Before you say anything... I want you to understand that I know you would never intentionally do anything to hurt yourself, the kids, or me."

Those were the last words she'd expected. Preparation wouldn't have mattered. Sometimes Dan still amazed her.

*Okay, Annie, now it's your turn. Convince Dan to believe you. Give him some irresistible bait and make him swallow the hook. Grovel if you have to. Remember, your goal is to get out and go home. Take a nice, long, deep breath.*

"You're right. I'm embarrassed, humiliated, and ashamed of what happened. You and the kids mean the world to me. Daisy dying really got to me. I kept thinking it could be one of the boys. I couldn't stop my imagination. It kept me up at night and tortured me during the day. I was tired, stressed, and sad. I never thought a little pill could be so powerful. I didn't take that many. It was an accident. I forgot when I took the last one and skipped breakfast. You know the rest."

Dan reached for her hands and leaned in closer. That was a good sign, but did he believe her? Once again, a breeze crossed her face as the door opened. Who was this tall, glamorous woman wearing gorgeous clothes, looking perfect? Maybe this really was one long dream.

The apparition smiled and spoke, exposing the most perfectly crooked teeth. "Hi, I'm Doctor Hensley, the psychiatrist." Annie's mouth quivered with hope. If this was reality, maybe she could deal with it. Her psychiatrist wasn't perfect. Then again— maybe it was a ploy? Maybe those teeth were a trick to distract patients and get them to talk. Geez, was she getting paranoid on top of everything else?

Dan shook Doctor Hensley's hand. "I'm Dan, Annie's husband. I'm the pastor of First Lutheran Church. I'd like to help in any way I can."

"A pastor! Wonderful. You'll understand why I need to be alone with Annie for this visit. Hospital policy."

Now this was intriguing. Dan's smile got thinner, a sign that he didn't like this turn of events. Yet he understood the need for confidentiality.

Dan bent down and kissed her cheek. "I'll check in later." He moved toward the door and halted.

*No, Dan—keep moving. Give him a smile and wave.* It worked. Annie turned back to Dr. Hensley. She couldn't stop staring at her. Maybe those antidepressants were hallucinogens?

"I hope my wearing street clothes and not a doctor's coat doesn't bother you?"

"Oh heavens, it has nothing to do with that. It's your teeth." Annie wanted to crawl under the covers. How could she have blurted that out? It must be her head injury.

Dr. Hensley laughed. "I've been meaning to try that invisible brace. But it slips to the bottom of my to-do list. Maybe you know what that's like?"

"My to-do list would circle the earth a few times."

Dr. Hensley sat by Annie's bed. "Then we have something to talk about. But first I need to make sure you're safe. Do you feel safe at home?"

"With four boys? I daily dodge basketballs and baseballs, but yes, I feel safe."

"Four boys! That's a lot of energy to be dealing with. Just so you know, everything we talk about is confidential. I'm based in Minneapolis and travel to patients. I grew up in a small town and know what it can be like. The last thing you want is to stand by your therapist at the grocery store or at school events."

Hallelujah! Maybe Dr. Hensley could understand. "I'm not some drug addict and I didn't try to commit suicide."

"Did someone tell you that?"

Annie picked at a loose thread on the bed cover. "You said you grew up in a small town."

"That I did."

"Then you know my overdose is the hottest topic since we won the baseball state championships eighteen years ago. Plus, being the pastor's wife makes it even juicier." Annie couldn't stop her fist from curling up, ready to defend herself.

"Being a pastor's wife in a small town can't be easy. All that pressure to devote your time to helping others. Do you feel that way? Do you feel the need to escape? Maybe even feel depressed at times?"

Annie wanted to shout, *yes, yes and yes!* But how could she trust this doctor? "Feel depressed at times?" That would be disclosing way too much. She didn't want to end up in the psych ward for further observation. Maybe give Dr. Hensley a small taste of her life.

Annie clasped her hands together and pressed them against her chest. Her daily routine. It was overwhelming. Might as well dive in. "I don't have time to feel. My day begins with getting breakfast, making lunches, keeping track of sports practices and games, school and community calendars. That's before everyone leaves for school. Then hopefully I can take a quick shower, clean the kitchen and start laundry. Afterward, I head to church to help out with numerous programs. This is followed by attending school and community committees. Basically, anything that people need help with—they call me. I also run errands and go grocery shopping. Later on, it's dinner, going to watch one of the boys' games, homework help, more laundry, and deal with anything else that pops up. That's a typical day, and if someone gets sick or injured—well, that's another story."

"And what about Dan? Does he help out around the house? Or with the boys?"

"The house? Now that's a joke." Shit. Annie heard the angry

tone of her voice. She didn't want to bash Dan to a stranger, even though her frustration was begging for release. No, she needed to focus on his good points. "Dan's incredible with the boys and attends most of their games and school events. But the church demands nearly all of his time. Our membership is growing, along with new outreach programs. He has a lot of responsibility. People rely on him and need him."

"And what about you?"

*Me?* Annie noticed that Dr. Hensley wasn't taking notes. That was a good sign. She liked how Dr. Hensley listened, nodding her head, encouraging Annie to share. She didn't appear to be judging Annie's words. "I'm not sure I understand what you're asking."

"What do you do for yourself? Do you exercise? Have a hobby? Do you have friends that you can grab a cup of coffee with and talk?"

"Nothing and no. I used to do more things. My best friends haven't come back to our hometown in a while. I don't feel comfortable sharing my problems and having them come back in my face. But it's okay. I knew what I was getting into when I became the pastor's wife. Plus, it's rewarding to help others." Annie grimaced at how pathetic her response sounded.

"I agree, helping others is rewarding. I can tell you have a beautiful, big heart. I'm exhausted just listening to your typical day. I'd be on the couch with an ice pack on my head and my feet up on a cushion." Dr. Hensley paused and gave Annie a compassionate smile, flashing those crazy teeth. "Maybe it's time to work on self-love. For women, it's one of the most important things we can do. Yet we find it so difficult, giving ourselves love and care. Would that be okay?"

Okay? It sounded perfect. Annie wanted to break out in song. Music—an unexpected jab of sadness stabbed her heart. Her music—her voice. Where had they gone? Was it where God had been hiding lately? Damn—she sounded so ungrateful. She felt mortified at her thoughts. Was she actually blaming God for everything? Annie longed for one of her pills to quiet her thoughts. But it appeared that wasn't going to happen.

"Annie, if you're not comfortable, we can take a different direction. It's one step on a journey that I'd like to take with you. But I can't force you to talk to me. However, the state does require two follow-up visits. You can request to work with someone else. Trust is important. I want you to feel comfortable."

Words spun around in Annie's head. She wasn't used to compassion being sent her way. It made her feel emotional and teary. She probably needed a minimum of twenty sessions to get her act together. *Shit. Don't have a panic attack right now. Breathe in for a count of four, hold for seven, and out for eight.* All she could manage was, "I'd like to work with you."

A beep sounded from Dr. Hensley's phone. "Our time is up. I'm in the area on Wednesday mornings and have a working office outside of town for privacy. Let's say 10:00 a.m. for the next two weeks. Here's my card with all my information."

"Am I cleared to leave?"

"You need one more night. Think of it as a mini-vacation. Your first practice session on self-love. You can watch television, read a magazine, nap, write a poem, whatever you feel like doing."

A vacation in the hospital—that was a bit of a reach.

"I'd like to start you on a different antidepressant. I'll leave a prescription with the doctor. Think of it as stabilizing the situation. Once you feel better, we can discuss alternative approaches."

"Do you think I'm depressed?"

"Let's figure that out together. There isn't any shame in taking antidepressants. You've endured a lot. There was a reason you were taking the pills. You're likely to feel a mixture of emotions over the next few days. It's normal. Be gentle with yourself, like you would treat a newborn baby." Dr. Hensley placed a pamphlet on her nightstand. "Here's a list of techniques that can be helpful to shift your focus. Meditation and visualization are very powerful. Keep doing your breathing exercises; they're good for your body. I'll see you next week. Call me if something urgent comes up."

Annie watched Dr. Hensley leave the room. So—Dr. Hensley had noticed her breathing. Annie rubbed her forehead. What to do with her free time? Such a foreign question. Watching television during the day sounded decadent but boring. She picked up the pamphlet. Maybe it would guide her. Hmm…a suggestion to think about a favorite memory. Soak in the positive feelings it brought up. She knew how to do that.

Annie pulled the bedcovers over her, placed her hands over her heart, and closed her eyes. She took deep breaths. Her body relaxed and her mind followed, letting go of the battle.

Annie drifted back to a childhood memory when her grandmother had taken her to Thelma's cabin deep in the woods. On the drive, they had sung songs at the top of their lungs. She had felt so happy. She'd clambered out of the car, thinking she'd have to play by herself—until she spotted Jo and Sondra. She had broken out in goosebumps—almost like a premonition.

That afternoon had been magical. They'd spread out on a blanket near a majestic oak tree, looking up at the clouds. They'd taken turns deciding what animal the clouds looked like, making up silly songs about it. It had been one of the best days of her young life.

# CHAPTER SIXTEEN

THREE P.M. WHERE WAS THE doctor? Dan? Annie's vacation time was over. Trying to relax felt like a cruel joke. School was getting out now. How would the boys get to their activities without her help? Annie rubbed her forehead. There—she felt it again, a deep ripple of fear coursing through her body. It was like early childbirth, unexpected pain with no defined pattern. What could she say to the boys? The church members? And why hadn't an angel come in her dreams last night to give her guidance? Did they decide to take a vacation too?

Annie wished she had her cell phone. She wondered if Jo or Sondra had heard anything about what had happened. She could always joke around that she'd taken desperate measures to get their attention. But why put that guilt on them?

Might as well get changed. Annie shrugged off the hospital gown and pulled her clothes out of the worn travel bag Dan had left. What? A striped sweater with checked pants? Was Dan really that fashion-challenged?

No sense in getting frustrated. Besides, by now, everyone probably thought she was crazy. She saw the looks the nurses gave each other and the questions in their eyes. Annie grimaced. She needed to stop this train of thought. It wasn't going to help to be harsh with herself. Better to stay in control of her emotions so the doctor would sign off on her release papers.

Annie went into the bathroom to put on the clothes. Now, where was her makeup? Nothing? Wait—an old tube of lipstick and a small vial of lavender oil. How old were these things? She remembered getting the oil from Thelma, Louie's grandmother. She'd been such an amazing healer. Her special afternoon. Sitting on the famous porch, listening to Thelma's stories, receiving her messages. Thelma had given her this lavender oil for stress, to put a drop on her pillow at night. Here it was—unopened. She felt a surge of remorse. Why hadn't she gone back and sought out Thelma's help? Her grandmother, who was also a healer, had never been too proud to ask for Thelma's help.

Annie took a long look in the mirror. She looked so pale. What was she going to do? She had to rise up. Enough of this self-wallowing behavior. She glided the lipstick on. Bright red. Why not use it on her cheeks? Better than looking ghostly white. She made a big circle on her cheeks and rubbed it in. Why didn't it spread or dissipate? She looked at the label. A forty-eight-hour stain, guaranteed to stay on. She looked like a circus clown. Dread plummeted into her stomach.

Annie grabbed a washcloth and scrubbed her cheeks until they felt raw. A little better, but now her whole face looked red. Damn.

Dan's voice, along with the doctor's, entered her room. Okay—just another day of make-believe and dress-up. One more glance in the mirror and her sense of humor reappeared. *Laugh and roll with it. Go out and be confident!*

Annie added a bit of a jaunt to her saunter back into the room. She noticed the mixture of surprise and concern in Dan's and the doctor's eyes.

"I know. I'm quite the fashion statement. But according to the magazines, mixing stripes and plaids is the new thing."

The doctor grinned. "Very funky for this small town. However, I should check your temperature. You look flushed."

"Ask Dan about that. I don't know who packed my travel bag. But I'm a Northwoods girl and we make do with what we have. My lipstick became my blush. Not exactly what I expected—along with my new fashion trend."

Dan's face turned slightly red. Was he embarrassed? "John and Luke wanted to help. They packed the bag. I should have looked. Sorry, it was a bit hectic getting out the door this morning."

"That explains the flushed face. You're free to go home."

Annie smiled at him. *Keep up the charade. Act confident.* "Thank you, doctor."

The doctor's grin transformed into a furrowed forehead, his concern obvious. "Annie, you're a special person. Be good to yourself, now."

Special? How could he know that?

Dan came over and kissed her on the cheek. "I have a nice night planned for us."

"Then we better get home." Annie smiled at him, hiding the nerves fluttering inside her stomach.

## CHAPTER SEVENTEEN

ANNIE USED HER PERIPHERAL VISION to observe Dan repeatedly running his hand through his hair. So—he was nervous too. *That makes us equal.* Could they make it home without talking? *Turn on the radio and give Dan a loving smile.* It seemed to work. She leaned her head against the headrest, closed her eyes, and hummed along to the song. A trick she had read in that pamphlet to calm the mind and stop obsessive thoughts.

The car stopped. Great—they were home. Now Annie needed to pretend some more. Smile, hug the boys, tell them she had slipped and everything was okay. Annie got out of the car and looked around. Where were they? Why weren't they racing out the door, pushing and shoving and arguing about something?

"The boys left for practice. I thought it was better to keep them on their schedule. Give you time to adjust. Give us time to talk."

"That was thoughtful." Annie kept her tone light, although she felt a pinch of irritation. Dan shouldn't assume he knew what she needed. Yet, if she went with the flow, perhaps she could continue to stall the conversation he wanted to have.

"I'm starving." Annie walked into the kitchen and opened the refrigerator; it was completely full. "Wow, we should change our town's name to Lutheranville, the capital of the casserole."

"I'm glad you've found your sense of humor. I've missed your funny observations of our sometimes-quirky community."

"Right, that's what I was searching for."

"What have you been searching for? Annie, are we going to talk about what's really going on?"

She felt resistance, not wanting to cooperate. She wanted to decide when to share her feelings. Couldn't she ever have some control in this household? "Hold on. I found it! Cherry Jell-O with blueberries, and tater-tot casserole. My favorites."

Annie set them on the counter and started making them each a plate.

"Annie..."

"Dan, I've been serious for three days in the hospital. How about a little break since the boys aren't here? We can talk later."

"Okay. Could you please give me another scoop of that casserole? Thank you."

Annie joined Dan. *Avoid looking into his eyes—that always does you in. Focus on your food.* She took a bite. It was delicious. Her whole body relaxed. There was a reason they called casseroles comfort food. She took a spoonful of the Jell-O and let it melt on her tongue. Jell-O—her mother was a master at making Jell-O molds for church potlucks. She had let Annie decorate them. It had been such fun. Thinking about it helped her anxiety dissipate. She could do this—face Dan, the kids, the community.

Annie looked up at Dan. "Blueberry or apple pie for dessert?" Her voice actually sounded cheerful. She was doing good. What was that saying? Right—fake it until you make it.

"Blueberry, unless you want apple?"

"Blueberry is my favorite. But you knew that." Annie smiled at Dan. "Maybe I should screw up more often. It's been a long time since someone made me dinner. Although I'm so stuffed, it might feel good to have my stomach pumped again." Oops, she'd done it again. Maybe holding back her true feelings was causing her to blurt out her inner thoughts? That was scary to think about.

"That's not funny."

"No, probably not. Why don't we watch a little TV?"

Dan's phone rang and he answered it, walking into the TV room, leaving her with the messy plates. Annoyance clawed at her. *Shove it back. Stay positive and make tonight go smoothly.* The kids should be home soon, and Dan was trying—at least a little. Annie rinsed the dishes and put them in the dishwasher.

Annie walked into the TV room. She squeezed her hands together at the sight of Dan with his feet on the coffee table, flicking through TV channels. "Was that the boys?"

"Yes, they're going out with the coach for some pizza. I told them it was okay."

"Don't they want to see me?"

"Of course, they do. They're dying to see you. I mean…"

"Oh God, don't start being afraid to say words like 'dying.' This is the last time that I'm going to tell you that it was an accident. You either have my back or you don't."

Dan patted the sofa next to him. "Come on, Annie. Settle down. Sit by me."

Settle down? Those were fighting words, as far as she was concerned. But before she could respond, Dan stood up, pulled her toward him, and gently kissed her.

"Maybe I wanted some time alone with you." Dan sat back down, grabbed a pillow, and put it on his lap. Her heart ached with longing. It'd been years since they had taken their favorite couch positions. She'd loved how he would stroke her hair and reach down and kiss her. She swore that was how Mark was conceived, with Matthew sleeping innocently in his crib.

Annie put her head on the pillow. Dan stroked her hair, but thankfully, he didn't kiss her. One step at a time. Now if she could coax back that relaxed feeling. How could it disappear so easily? She was glad when Dan shut the TV off. She realized neither one of them had laughed once during the sitcom.

Silence. Annie watched Dan clasp his hands into a prayer position, a sign he was searching for the right words.

"I thought you were happy with your life."

"I've fulfilled the role of the pastor's wife, haven't I?" Where was her sarcasm coming from? Was she that angry? She never got to be stubborn. It might not be the right thing to do, but she wasn't going to placate Dan. No apologies.

"You do a great job at it."

"That's the problem."

"You're a wonderful mom."

"That's the problem too."

"I'm trying to help here."

"That's the problem too." Annie winced at her unreasonable response. Maybe she needed to lighten up.

"What do you want me to say?"

"I don't know. Did the boys say anything? Someone must have talked about the pills." Annie clenched her teeth, steeling herself for the answer.

"Matthew and Mark did overhear their friends talking about it."

"Great. I'm sure everyone thinks I tried to commit suicide."

"People don't know the truth. They know you took a fall. If someone from the hospital talks, we'll say you had a mix-up in your medicine. That's all they need to know."

"Fine—"

"Annie, we can talk this out. Help me here."

What to say? She was afraid, not trusting herself or what she'd say. Spoken words were hard to take back. This wasn't about not putting the toilet seat down or leaving toothpaste remains in their bathroom sink. She had to at least try. "Okay, knock-knock?"

"Are you serious?"

*Don't respond. Just wait.*

"Alright, who's there?"

"Annie."

"Annie who?"

"I don't know anymore. I have to be more than a mom and the faithful pastor's wife." There—the bottom line without a bunch of accusations, complaints, and ultimatums.

"I didn't realize that was such a bad thing."

"You're not listening to me!"

"So, this is my fault?"

Frustration flooded Annie's body. She grabbed a pillow and squeezed it hard. How could he not get it? Didn't he miss who she used to be? She stood up and threw the pillow at Dan.

Dan caught it, surprised.

"I'm going up to bed."

"But the boys?"

"You can wait up for them. Make sure they go to bed."

"Annie, come on. We've never gone to bed mad at each other."

"There's a first time for everything."

Annie stomped up the stairs. Oh my God—she was acting immature—like Matthew! She couldn't seem to stop herself. She yanked on her pajamas, then went into the bathroom to brush her teeth.

*This is where it happened.* It made her stomach sick. Why was she being so hard on Dan? He wasn't even angry with her. She looked in the mirror. What the hell had happened to her? She looked like a joke with her bright red cheeks. *Please God, come back to me, wherever you are, and let me feel your presence.* Yet instead of comfort, she felt sorrow. The tears came, creating rivulets on her cheeks. Maybe she could start her new prescription, but it was downstairs. Right now, she couldn't bear to have Dan watch her take it, with all his silent questions. Annie splashed cold water on her face and took some deep breaths. *Just get into bed.*

Annie noticed the cell phone on the nightstand. She picked it up. Twenty messages. The tears erupted again. Damn it. She smashed her face into the pillow to muffle her sobs. She had to get it together. Get some sleep or she'd look like a mess tomorrow and scare everyone.

Annie jolted awake. It must be time to get the kids up for school. She glanced at the clock. Four a.m. "Shit, not again."

Dan's arm came around her. "Annie, are you okay?"

"I'm fine. Don't worry. I gave you all the pills that I had. The new ones are downstairs in the kitchen."

Dan pulled her close. "Annie, I didn't mean that. I can go down and get them for you."

Dan's compassion seeped through the cracks in her emotional armor. It struck her. Dan didn't have anyone to talk to. She was his best friend. "I'm sorry, Dan. I failed you...myself...the kids."

"Annie, stop that. You're scaring me. Depression can become quite serious. I've seen too many people stop living because of it. We all need you."

Annie turned to face Dan. "I know. You all need me. But sometimes that's the problem."

Dan reached out and held her hand. "Tell me what to do."

"I need to be me. Remember that person? The one you fell in love with?"

"Yes, she's right here."

Annie pulled her hand away from Dan's and placed it on her heart. "Maybe my shadow is, but I'm talking deeper. I am talking about the level of my soul."

"Annie, nobody can take your soul away."

Annie rolled away in frustration. How could she explain the sacrifices her soul had made for their life? It would come across as a painful accusation. And no matter how frustrated she was, she didn't want to hurt Dan. She had to try again.

"You're right, Dan, but my soul feels sad. It's hungry for a change. It needs to be fed something different. It doesn't mean that I don't love you and the boys. I just need to figure it out, okay?"

"Do you want to pray on it?"

"Not right now. It's something I need to do alone."

Dan was quiet for a long minute. "Okay. If that's what you need."

Annie touched Dan's cheek, a gesture of thanks for not pushing her further. He seemed satisfied as he rolled over onto his side. In minutes he was snoring.

Annie looked up at the ceiling. The truth hit deep inside. *I need to find my soul.* Those were big, deep words. A memory floated into her consciousness. She'd been thirteen, the lead singer in a Christian pop band. She'd written a song about finding one's soul and sung it at local festivals and county fairs. She'd even gotten to sing it at her grandpa's church. She and the song had been popular that summer. She'd felt like a star. Jo and Sondra were her biggest fans. If only she could recapture that uninhibited spirit and joy. She did remember the words. She softly sang the song and let the sweetness of the memory lull her to sleep.

# CHAPTER EIGHTEEN

SONDRA DRAGGED HER OVERSIZED SUITCASE off the luggage belt, almost toppling over in her black, strappy three-inch heels. Besides her sneakers, they were the most practical ones she had in her closet. How did this suitcase get so heavy? It was ridiculous. What did she pack? She couldn't remember. It was a blur. Packing, telling James, covering her schedule, and getting the hell out of there.

Sondra took a few wobbly steps toward the door. Was she tipsy, on only two glasses of wine? She had been wound up and nervous, her mind a seesaw with Annie on one end and Emily's threats on the other. Still—not cool, since Jo was still in AA recovery. Her stomach lurched as she remembered that dizzy feeling after having sex with Adam. No more alcohol for her. Regret tugged at her—she never realized what a painful emotion it could be.

Sondra spied a Starbucks. Jackpot! A mocha caramel coffee would perk her up. She bought an extra-large one for Jo, to assuage her guilt.

Damn. Another dilemma! How was she going to balance
two large cups, her computer bag, an oversized purse, and the
suitcase? She spotted a guy, maybe late twenties, with a guitar
slung over his shoulder, checking her out. A safe Midwesterner
with wire-rimmed glasses, faded blue jeans, and a checked flannel shirt. Sondra knew how to do this. She gestured to her luggage, then put her hands together in prayer and mouthed, "Help?"

The guitar guy hustled over. He gallantly picked up the suitcase and computer bag. "Not often these days that I can rescue a
princess."

"And here I thought real princes had disappeared with the
unicorns."

His smile was playful and non-threatening. "Can I give you a
ride to your castle?"

Sondra silently scolded herself for flirting. This exact behavior had gotten her into the mess she was in. But she did need help.
Sondra flung back her hair and smiled. "Alas, I already have a
ride, just outside at the curb."

He gallantly bowed. "Please lead the way."

"Why, thank you." Sondra walked carefully through the door,
trying not to sway in her shoes.

She was blindsided by strong arms wrapping around her, lifting
her off the ground. Jo. Her bear hugs were notorious. Sondra was
overwhelmed by a wave of gratitude. She blinked back tears, not
wanting to cry. "A present for you. You almost made me spill it!"

Jo took a sip. "Wow. When did you start drinking this?
And…?"

The guitar guy reached out to shake Jo's hand. "And I'm
Sondra's prince."

Sondra handed him her coffee. "Please take this as your reward for helping me. I'm sure there are more princesses to rescue."

"Alas, there won't be any more beautiful than you." He handed her a crumpled business card. "In case you get lost."

Sondra took it. "Dr. Mo, Creator of Literature and Musical Fairy Tales."

Jo blurted out, "She's a married woman."

Mo looked longingly at Sondra. "That's why they're called fairy tales."

A traffic cop blasted his whistle and gestured for them to hurry up.

Sondra climbed into Jo's Camry and stuck her head out the window. "Goodbye, Prince Mo, and thank you."

Jo leaned over Sondra and shouted, "She's too old for you!"

"Never too old to dream about love, especially with a body like that!" Mo lifted his guitar in a toast.

"How in the world do you find these guys?" Jo asked as she drove away.

"I guess my smile still works."

"He mentioned your body."

"Can't be that. I'm being held together by rolls of invisible Scotch tape."

"What? Did some fancy L.A. doctor do plastic surgery on you?" Jo scanned Sondra's body.

"No! It's only a metaphor for how wonderful my life has been."

"If that's what it takes, then give me a whole carton of tape! But I still couldn't match your beauty, brains, and great personality."

"That caffeine and sugar must be going to your head. Where's the crap you always give me?"

"Maybe it's time for a little change."

Sondra noticed how puffy Jo's eyes were, probably from crying. Jo was naturally beautiful, wearing no makeup except burgundy lipstick. Today, she looked like an outdoor sportswear model, wearing skinny jeans, a brightly-patterned flannel shirt, and flashy red sneakers. Sondra gently touched Jo's arm. "Jo, you look great. That young man should have been hitting on you."

"Well—I did have an encounter. Surprised the hell out of me."

"Are we talking sex here? What about Louie? Are you really going through with that ridiculous divorce?"

"Don't hold back your true feelings. Remember, you're my friend first. You're on my side."

"I know, but Louie's one of a kind. He adores you. As your friend, I'm supposed to prevent you from doing dumb things." Sondra flinched at the irony of her words.

Jo gave Sondra a devilish smile. "Let's switch subjects. How's James doing?"

"No, I'll switch the subject. Did you have sex?"

Jo took a few sips of her coffee. "Not telling. Buy more coffee like this and I might let a few details slip. I didn't think you drank this sugary stuff."

"Desperate times call for desperate measures."

"I wonder if that's how Annie felt." The words hung in the air like a moth with no place to rest.

Sondra stared out the window. The sprawling farmland spotted with grazing cows comforted her. However, it didn't soothe the sledgehammer pounding in her head. She excavated aspirin at the bottom of her purse and downed three with Jo's leftover coffee. "It's time we kept our promise to go on our canoe and camping trip. Let's get Annie in the middle of the forest and force her to tell us what's going on."

"Unless the church is burning down, Dan's going to be all over her. I bet he's scared, even with his faith. He won't want her out of his sight. We need a plan." Jo drummed her fingers against the steering wheel.

"Maybe I can dream of a solution. Do you mind if I close my eyes? My head is killing me." Sondra couldn't ignore her body's intense craving for sleep—an escape into nothing.

Jo checked Sondra's forehead for a fever. "Didn't you outgrow those headaches?"

"I haven't been this stressed for a long time."

"I get it. Annie. We both know what it's like to lose someone you love. To watch them disappear—unable to help. But enough for now. Grab my fleece jacket on the back seat. Use it as a pillow. I'll even tell you a story to help you fall asleep."

"I'd love to hear about your precious daughters, Jessie and Hunter."

Sondra eased her head onto the fleece jacket. It felt so good. Jo had always been a fabulous storyteller, thanks to her grandmother-in-law, Thelma. What a powerful woman. Her mother had believed that Thelma healed with stories and teas. Sondra did too. She'd love a dose of Thelma's advice on the blackmail, maybe even on James. But it would be too embarrassing. Time to shut out that world. Sondra closed her eyes. Jo's words softly faded away as slumber conquered her.

## CHAPTER NINETEEN

THE CAMRY RUMBLED OVER THE railroad tracks that ran through the middle of their small hometown. Sondra felt herself swimming back to consciousness.

"Wake up, sleepyhead. We're almost home."

Something funny tickled Sondra's nose, then crawled across her cheek. "Yuck!" Sondra jolted upright and wiped her face. "What was that? Some huge bug?"

She spied the crow feather sticking out of Jo's vest. "Very funny. You're still finding feathers?"

"Not like the old days. Now when they arrive, it's extra special and I pay attention."

Sondra exaggerated her stretch, extending her arm out to touch the feather. Jo's feathers always felt magical. "You still believe Thelma's strange animal and bird totem stuff?"

"Yes. I find it comforting. It's the way nature and the spirit world send me messages."

"Did it tell you to scare me?"

"You know what it means. And don't look at me like I'm weird!" Jo handed Sondra the feather.

"Sorry. I'm still jealous. How terrible is that? You always got feathers from your dad. I never got one from my mom. I always wanted her to send me a message."

"Maybe you did, but you didn't see it. Go ahead and try."

Sondra stroked the feather and gently breathed on it as Jo had taught her when they were eight. She closed her eyes and imagined the feather's energy soaring up to heaven to connect to her mom. She wondered what her mother would say to her now. Would she approve of her? Sondra shuddered with shame, guessing at the answers. Goosebumps covered her arms as she handed the feather back. "No messages."

"You're home," Jo cheerfully announced, pulling up to the impressive mansion constructed of field stone, logs, and massive windows. "If it makes you feel better, I was jealous that you got to live here. How your dad let you hang out with me—a poor kid from the other side of the tracks—was a mystery."

"My dad didn't know who I hung out with."

"He knew. He came to every one of our baseball games."

"Only because he loves baseball."

Jo heaved the suitcase out of the trunk in exasperation. "Are you still a sulky teenager? Your dad isn't getting any younger. Might be time to give him a break."

"Actually, Annie needs the break. Any ideas?"

"With you snoring? I could barely drive. What about you? Any dream messages?"

"No, but I know how to clear our minds. Follow my moves." Sondra swooped her arms up into the air over her head, then brought her hands to her heart in a prayer position. She swung her arms around in front of her body, drawing the infinity symbol in the air. She repeated it, making sure Jo was following her.

"So—you believe these contortions are supposed to clear our minds?

"Yup!"

"Is my mind clear now or is that an illusion?" Jo pointed to Jack, Sondra's dad, driving up in a Honda Odyssey minivan.

"A minivan? My dad?"

"Maybe he wants a second family." Jo waved enthusiastically at Jack, as if directing an oversized bus into a small parking spot.

Sondra watched Jack steady himself with the roof handle to swing his legs around and climb out. Jo was right. Her dad had aged. Jack's dark brown hair had turned shocking white. Yet his outfit spoke otherwise. He wore a neon t-shirt with "Just do it" splashed across the front, running pants, and multicolored Nike sneakers. Who was this man? Her memory was of pressed black pants, collared shirts, and ties.

"Sondra! You're home!" Jack jogged up to Sondra with his arms wide open.

Sondra flinched and took a step back. Was he going to hug her? It'd been years. Their last hug had been incredibly clumsy. She remembered banging her head on his chin, bruising him.

Jo spared them both by giving Jack a high five. "Nice ride, Mr. Wheeler. It's good to see you."

"Thanks, Jo. I got bored with retirement. I'm helping Hank. He's the high school baseball coach now. I drive the kids to their games, that sort of thing."

"So, you got your sons after all." The words popped out of Sondra's mouth, sounding immature even to herself.

"Sondra, it's not like that."

Jo swatted Sondra's back and whispered, "Be nice," then slipped into her car to avoid Sondra's attempt to swat her back.

"I better go. Text me later. I'll be at Kate's Coffee Cup. My mom renovated the old bait and tackle shop. She can concoct us a brew to come up with a plan."

Sondra turned to her dad; suddenly they were alone together. Now what? Should she try to hug him to break the ice?

Thankfully, Jack grabbed her suitcase and computer bag. "What are your plans? I hope you can stay for a while. It's been lonely around here."

*My plans?* Sondra tasted bitter bile from the panic in her stomach. Could she actually ask her dad for money? What could she possibly say that would make any sense? Sondra's tongue felt thick and inflexible, searching for words. She forced a smile and shrugged. That seemed to satisfy him for now.

Sondra followed Jack into the foyer, with its sixteen-foot ceiling and massive crystal chandelier. This was where her mother had taught her to dance, all dressed up, pretending they were princesses at a ball. Now the chandelier just hung there, its magic gone.

"I forgot how big and empty this house felt." Sondra saw her dad's smile disappear. Shit—was she a sulky teenager, as Jo said? Her old, critical behavior seemed stale and out of place. "Sorry, Dad, bad habit."

"It's okay. You're right. The house does feel empty. I've been thinking about selling it. What does an old man like me need with all this space? I guess I always hoped you'd come back, but I get it. Looking back, I wasn't the best dad. I was always confused, never knowing when to talk or leave you alone. I was bogged down in mud, not knowing what direction to take. I can't expect you to understand."

"But I do. I'm buried in mud at the moment." The words were out. Sondra's heart pounded. She wanted to take them back. Her dad's unexpected openness had caught her by surprise.

"What do you mean? Is everything okay with Jim?"

"James is fine."

"James...so stiff and formal."

Sondra wanted to shout, *look who's talking, Mr. Stiff-as-a-Board*. One of her many nicknames she'd had for him growing up. But he was trying. Besides, hadn't she caused enough hurt? Maybe more to come? Time to change the topic. "It's about Annie. I wasn't there when she needed me. She could have died and left those kids alone, like Mom left me."

"I don't know what to say." Jack lifted his arms again, as if he was going to hug her.

Sondra froze. Unexpected compassion was more than she could handle right now. She didn't want to cry in front of her dad. Still—she managed to take a step toward him.

Jack's phone alarm beeped. "Time for team practice."

Sondra blinked rapidly. *No tears! Avoid eye contact. Dig around in your purse. There—the phone. Any text messages?* She tapped on her sternum while she checked, ignoring her dad. Better. The rush of cortisol slowed down. The flood of disappointment had caught her off guard. She was finally here, and he was leaving already. She wanted him to stay and reassure her that everything was going to be okay. But they'd never had that type of relationship. She unconsciously kept tapping while she put her phone back. *Just act casual. It's no big deal.* She looked back up at him, dropping her hand from her sternum.

"Where's my head today? I'll tell them I can't come. They can get by without me."

That's right, he knew about her tapping to relieve anxiety. Sondra surprised herself by responding, "Don't worry about it. Why don't I come with you? It'll be fun."

"Really?"

"I've never ridden in a minivan before. It's about time, since I won't have any kids to need one."

"I know Jim—I mean James—is too old, but you're not."

"Dad..."

Jack was right. But after years of searching for love through sex, Sondra had been ready for James. James had created a place to come home to. Now, everything was about to change. Even her anger at James's manipulation of their sex life didn't excuse what had happened with Adam.

Sondra didn't realize how long she'd stood there, thinking, until her dad apologized.

"I promise not to say anything negative about James." Jack held out the van keys. "Want to drive?"

# CHAPTER TWENTY

SONDRA TOOK ONE MORE DEEP breath. The fifth time had to be a charm when it came to parking this van in the narrow spot. *Concentrate.* She squinted and steered it between two oversized pick-up trucks. Finally, she did it. The Midwest had morphed into the land of minivans and trucks. She clambered out, grateful that she hadn't caused any damage.

There it was—the old baseball field. Fresh paint on the dugout and new sponsor banners were the only changes she detected. Good things had happened here.

"You still okay with hanging out for an hour?"

"Not a problem. Aren't Annie's boys on the team?"

"Yes, but I'm not sure if they're coming today. I better hustle out there. Get the boys warmed up."

Was her dad always this nice, and she hadn't seen it? It had been only an hour, but coming home was already offering Sondra comfort. Might as well head over to the bleachers and watch the practice. Treat herself to an escape. Ignore the emails in her inbox.

She didn't want to see anything from Emily or Adam.

Sondra reached the bleachers and spotted a familiar figure. Hank. A tsunami ripped through her body, uprooting memories and tossing away her excuses for not coming back home. She'd been a junior and Hank, a senior—the team star. Hank hit home runs and pitched like a hurricane, but was always humble. Everyone loved him, including herself.

Sondra remembered that day, years ago. Early spring. Alone, waiting for her perpetually-late dad. Hank had walked over. He had a new pitch and asked if she'd catch for him. She'd hid her wobbly knees, faked confidence, and struck a bargain. That's how she'd learned to pitch a wicked curveball. They'd begun to meet after practice to work on it. Then, when Jo had gotten injured, Sondra had convinced the coach to let her pitch. She'd shocked the crowd by striking out player after player, giving up only one run, winning the game. It had been a really big deal for her.

"Hey, stranger," Hank called out. Damn if her knees didn't wobble as he strode up to her. His tattered baseball cap and yellow jersey, tucked into form-fitting baseball pants, were sexier than a tuxedo.

Sondra tamed her impulse to jump into Hank's arms and have him swing her around like he used to. It had been pure joy. Would she ever experience that feeling again? Hank was closer. Should she hug him? If she couldn't hug her dad, how could she hug Hank? Maybe it wasn't right. Sondra wasn't sure. She took a casual step toward him.

Sondra felt a loss of balance. What was happening? She glanced down at her high-heeled shoes sinking into the ground. Her body lurched forward into Hank, bowling him over. She landed on top of him—their faces inches apart.

Sondra looked into Hank's sparkling blue eyes. Did she still have the power to turn them smoky blue? She inhaled the smell of Irish Spring soap emanating from his skin. The years disappeared. Dreamlike, she moved her head toward him, desiring the long, exploring teenage kisses they'd shared.

"Now, that's quite the hello." Hank laughed, moments before her lips could touch his. "Did you just try to kiss me?"

"Of course not!" Sondra sputtered, trying to disentangle herself.

Hank sat up with Sondra straddled across his lap. "Come on, admit it. You did."

"No, I was going to do this." Sondra shoved him backward, then somersaulted over and onto her feet. "How about that self-defense move?"

"Impressive." Hank retrieved her shoes and inspected them. "These are some serious weapons."

"I was in a hurry when I packed. Forgot my sneakers."

"I'll check the lost-and-found for you."

Sondra dug her feet into the warm, trampled grass. "Don't bother, this feels good." She gestured toward the boys, who were doing the sloppiest jumping jacks she'd ever seen. "Those boys are going to hurt their necks watching us. Haven't they seen you with a woman before?"

"Nobody like you." Hank returned her shoes. Their fingers accidentally intertwined. His hand was warm and strong, as if it carried the weight of the world but did not suffer from it.

"I'll take that as a compliment," Sondra said, trying to keep things light.

"You should." Hank slowly peeled his fingers off the shoe.

"Get going before I tackle you to the ground again." Sondra playfully waved her shoes at him.

"Is that what you did?"

Sondra couldn't continue to flirt with him. Hank wasn't like

Mo, the airport musician. Hank was real. Sondra could see his integrity, the love he'd once had for her—the love they'd once had for each other. Better to switch the topic to Annie.

"Yup, I'm preparing to wrestle Dan to let Annie escape for two days. Take her canoeing and camping like we used to. Jo and I could use your help."

"Oh boy, I smell trouble."

"Hey, we're here to rescue her. Let her relax, then get her to talk. She needs to know that we're here for her."

"I'm sure Annie could use the break. It can't be easy taking care of four boys and helping with the church. When that little girl died of cancer—it was too much. Annie has a heart of gold, so when someone—anyone—hurts, she hurts."

Sondra's stomach sank at the word *cancer.* "How do you know so much?"

"Kate's coffee shop. It's where everyone gets the 4-1-1." Hank's voice was light, but the way he rubbed his neck betrayed his concern.

"The 4-1-1. Quite hip." Sondra scrutinized Hank, trying to figure out what had changed. She liked his quick wit and how his confidence exuded a tender maturity.

"Look at who I'm hanging around with." Hank gestured toward the boys missing and dropping balls. "Looks like I'm needed. It's good to see you. By the way, your dad and Annie aren't the only ones who've missed you. Nothing like an old friend." Hank tipped his baseball cap to her and jogged onto the field.

Sondra felt dizzy and out of balance. Seeing Hank rattled her at a deep level. It was why she'd stopped coming home—all those memories slapping her in the face. The ones she wanted to forget were the ones that battled hardest for her attention. She needed to ground herself. She tapped her cheekbones. Better. Where could she escape? She spotted her favorite seat at the top of the bleachers.

As Sondra climbed the steps, she thought of Hank. Theirs had been a sweet love. She shivered, thinking about their first time, a few weeks before she had gone to college. How the candles in her room had illuminated Hank lying in the middle of her frilly pink bed. And that *Cosmopolitan* magazine she had read, about how to turn your man on. She had acted brave, undoing her bra in front of him, but sweating with nerves. How he'd put his arms around her and kissed her until they swam in the luxury of their naked bodies finally touching. It had been awkward but beautiful, both being virgins. She didn't have an orgasm that first time, but did later, and it had been mind-blowing. Suddenly, it was all she wanted.

Sondra felt her nerves pulsating. She reached the top bleacher and sat. She didn't like thinking about how college had changed her. But the memories kept coming. Her roommates were appalled that she'd been in a committed relationship in her freshman year. Finally, in her sophomore year, she broke up with Hank so she could 'discover herself.' What she discovered was partying and her sexual power over men. She was mortified, thinking of the sex she had with her college professor. She had used her body to get an A, and he used her naïveté to lead her down a road of self-regret. One that cost her thousands of dollars in therapy to learn to forgive herself. Through it all, Hank had always been a gentleman.

Sondra looked around. The town didn't feel so small or stifling. It actually felt good. Familiar. So many hours spent here, dreaming about creating a life with Hank. He would play professional baseball and she would write books. But life had thrown them too many curveballs, like Hank quitting college and giving up his baseball dreams to take care of his parents. Now Hank was back in the town he loved, while here she was, still running away from her mistakes.

Sondra grimaced. Her mindset seemed determined to sink her into sadness. Maybe she should take a walk.

Sondra spotted an old, beat-up minivan pulling into the parking lot. Four boys spilled out and headed toward the baseball field. Sondra glanced at her watch. Whoever they were, they were definitely late for practice—only fifteen minutes left. Wait—the tallest one looked like Dan. They must be Annie's sons. This was her chance. Sondra scrambled down the bleachers. Matthew and Mark ran past her. *Don't let the other two escape.* She hurtled over the last two steps, banged her knee, and almost tumbled into Luke and John. Sondra stopped short, her arms windmilling. She couldn't look any stranger. The boys' puzzled expressions confirmed her thoughts.

Sondra pulled herself into an upright position. "Luke and John, remember me?"

"How do you know our names?" John asked.

"I'm one of your mom's best friends."

"Are you Jo, the baseball player?" Luke asked.

"No, I'm Sondra, but I played baseball too."

"If you're one of Mom's best friends, why don't we know you?" John asked.

"Because I live far away across the United States, in L.A."

Luke gave her a suspicious look. "There are planes."

These boys were tough! No surprise. Annie had raised them. "You're right. I should have come more. I goofed up. Now I want to make it up to your mom. I'm trying to think of a plan to help her escape."

"Why does she need to escape?" Luke asked.

John stomped his feet, his eyes filling with tears. "I don't want her to do that."

Shit. What had she just done? Sondra wanted to kick herself for upsetting them. The hole she kept digging for her life was growing into a gigantic pit! Time to back up a bit and not scare them.

"I'm so sorry! I didn't mean escape. I meant to go camping. Jo, your mom's other best friend, is here too. The three of us made a promise to go on an overnight canoe trip. It was your mom's idea. To be silly, laugh, and have fun. I promise from the bottom of my heart that we'll take special care of her."

John put his hands on his hips. "Mom needs to have fun. She's been sad a lot lately."

Luke nodded. "She's big on keeping promises."

"The problem is, your dad may not want her to go. He might be feeling overprotective. People do that when something has scared them. Do you understand that?"

Luke turned to John. "It's like when I fell off the jungle gym and broke my arm. Mom didn't let me go to the playground for weeks. Remember?"

"Yeah, like when I fell off my bike and Mom made me wear a helmet and knee pads."

"Exactly!" Sondra gazed from boy to boy. "So will you help me and Jo?"

Sondra studied their serious faces as they thought about it. They were so precious. A surge of protective feelings engulfed her. She wanted to gather them in her arms and hug them—but that would scare them. Annie had sacrificed her music dreams for them. What other dreams had she let slide away? What had caused her to possibly give up on her life?

Their silence was broken by the team whooping it up as they

ended practice. Luke waved at his brothers. "Matthew might have an idea. He's the oldest and in charge."

Sondra watched Hank run toward her, passing Matthew and Mark, challenging them to a race. So there still was a little boy inside of Hank. While her dad trailed far behind. Poor Jack. He looked tired after managing that motley crew of teenage hormones.

Luke and John dragged their feet in the dirt, creating a makeshift finish line. Hank barreled across the finish line first, the boys a foot behind.

Sondra high-fived Hank. "Sorry, guys. Close race, but your coach won by his big nose."

"What? Are you dissing my nose?"

John giggled. Good. Sondra wanted to break the ice.

Hank patted Matthew and Mark on the back. "Nice try. Boys, this is Sondra, one of your mom's best friends. Sondra, this is Matthew and Mark."

Sondra shook their hands, treating them like grown men. "I remember when you were toddlers. I can see that was a long time ago. How's your mom doing?"

Mark shrugged his shoulders. "Don't know, but she should be home by now. Dad made us leave and come to practice."

"Maybe she needed to rest."

Sondra hesitated, watching Matthew kick the dirt. Better use a direct approach—avoid another faux pas. "Matthew, I heard that you're in charge. We need your help to take your mom on a camping trip."

"Who's we?"

"Jo and myself."

"The baseball player?"

Really. Jo again? Go figure that Jo would become a local

baseball legend. Sondra sighed, "Yes, that one. We want to get your mom out of the house and on the river tomorrow morning. All without your dad knowing."

"No way. I'm already in enough trouble."

"Dad says it's not your fault," Luke said.

Matthew shot Luke an angry look.

This wasn't going well. Oh good, her dad was walking toward them. The boys seemed to like Jack; maybe he could help. Jack made a show out of tossing Hank a baseball.

Why was Hank touching his nose, his ear, and straightening his cap? Right. His pitching signals.

Shit! The ball was coming right at her, but Hank had tossed it at a gentle pace. Sondra instinctively caught it. What was going on here?

Hank winked at her. "I've got an idea. If Sondra can strike Matthew out, then all of you have to help. A deal?"

"Sounds good to me," Matthew said.

John frowned. "Isn't that betting? Dad says it's a sin."

"No, this is just a game," Mark explained. "They're joking around because Jo was the star of the team."

Sondra pulled Hank to the side. "What are you thinking?"

"Listen, you were the better pitcher. Jo just had more of a killer instinct. You know how to throw that curveball. I'm betting on you."

"So, you're going to commit a sin?"

Hank smiled at her. "Not the first time. You can even borrow my good-luck cap."

Sondra took the cap and adjusted it on her head. "All right. I need some cleats."

Jack held up a pair. "I already thought of that."

"How did you—?" Sondra caught the look passing between

Jack and Hank. "I should have known. Let's do this. Mark, will you catch for me? Dad, you can be our umpire."

"Sure." Mark put on his mitt and jogged to home plate.

The rest of the team must have sensed something was happening. They gathered behind the fence to watch.

Sondra sauntered onto the pitcher's mound. Time to get into the zone. Do her old routine. She shook her arms and legs. One good spit on the ball. Now polish it up. Sondra rubbed the ball against her jeans and glanced at her dad. He was beaming! She felt a pang in her heart. When was the last time she saw him look so happy? *Stop thinking about the past—it's getting beyond irritating. Just focus on the now.*

Matthew was ready.

Sondra let the first one fly. It went wild to the left.

"Ball."

No problem. *Visualize how you used to strike Hank out.* She wound up again and let it fly—straight across the plate.

"Strike one."

*That's more like it. Now take your time. Look around.* Sondra observed how Matthew looked more serious, digging his feet in. The boys on the sidelines were quiet and respectful, with Hank standing by them.

Sondra stepped off the mound and stomped the dirt off her cleats. Her old trick to keep the batter guessing. She hustled back on and immediately threw another pitch, catching Matthew off balance.

"Strike two."

The boys, now hanging over the fence, cheered her on, clapping. Now all she had to do was to stay relaxed and let the ball fly. She threw again.

"Ball two."

Still room for error. Let Matthew think she was nervous. Sondra took off Hank's cap, studied it, then put it back on. *Now wind up and throw!* The ball soared out of her hand. She blinked in disbelief. That was the fastest curveball she'd ever pitched.

"Strike three!"

Matthew looked at his bat in disbelief, as if it had betrayed him. He dropped the bat on the ground, as if it was poison.

Sondra's nerves prickled, watching Hank talk to Matthew. *Please don't let Matthew be mad.* Had she just made things worse? Matthew could be embarrassed for losing in front of his friends. Her tight muscles melted in relief when Matthew looked over, giving her a thumbs-up.

Sondra tipped the baseball cap to Matthew in return. She watched Matthew's teammates gather around him, as if he was actually the hero. Interesting. She wondered what Hank had told them.

Mark ran up to her. "That was awesome. It's about time some-one put him in his place."

"Mark, it wasn't about that."

"Yeah, but sometimes he can be hard to live with."

"Is that right? I never had a brother or a sister. You'll have to share with me what that's like."

"I will. Why don't you come back with us for a cup of tea?"

Cup of tea? What teenage boy talked like that? Right—Annie's would.

Sondra's phone beeped with a text. She grabbed it out of her back pocket. Jo. Perfect. She read: "Ready to meet up. Pizza? Any plans yet?"

Sondra looked at Mark. "Would you be okay with a raincheck on the tea? How does pizza and meeting Jo sound? We can put our heads together and make a plan."

"Awesome." Mark looked her straight in the eye and shook her hand. "I'm glad you came. My mom needs a friend."

Sondra bit the inside of her cheek. Tears from her would really freak the boys out. She cleared her throat. "Me too."

# CHAPTER TWENTY-ONE

THERE IT WAS, KATE'S COFFEE Cup, the most popular place in town. A pleasant surge of happiness flowed through Jo's body. Her mom, the iconic Kate, reached a lot of people with her unconditional love. It used to bug her, competing for her mom's attention. Now—only gratitude.

Jo had tested that love, just like her dad, both of them alcoholics. Remorse trickled in. Was Jo ever there for her mom? She'd been a coward, never coming back home after her father's funeral. What had she been so afraid of? She hadn't even made the extra effort to attend the shop's grand opening. Then canceling Christmas—the snowstorm providing the perfect excuse. Hours later, the knock on her door. Her mom, beaming with joy after braving the elements in her ancient blue Ford truck filled with gifts.

There it was again, the ugly jab of guilt. Did she avoid people who loved her? How many people had she pushed away? Too heavy to think about right now. Time to go in.

Jo swung the café door open and was swallowed by strong arms. The famous hug. Her mom claimed it was a gift, handed down through her maternal ancestors. On her father's side, affection was shown differently, through tall tales, song, and rambunctious behavior. After a few drinks, her father would swing her around in the air, scaring her mom. But Jo loved it; even with the whiskey on his breath, her dad never dropped her.

Her mom turned to the customers scattered around at tables. "It's a celebration—Jo's home! Free muffins in the baskets!"

Jo bowed to her café audience, accepting their cheers.

"Mom, you're making me feel like the prodigal daughter."

"Take it any way you like. I'm happy you came home. It's been—"

"Two years since Dad's funeral." The words stopped Jo. Two years. Her body felt stonelike, immobilized at the enormity of her selfishness. She had never come to check on her mom and make sure everything was okay. Another one on her AA list to make amends to. Damn. She was going to be one hundred years old before she finished her list. "Sorry, Mom. I've been a coward, afraid of facing the ghosts of my past."

"You? A coward? Never. You're my brave daughter, here to help your friend when she needs you the most. Think about that." Kate handed her a muffin.

Jo noticed the bright red wooden hearts hanging around the room, intermixed with large photos of colorful flowers. "This is beautiful, Mom. I love it."

"I do too. It was a blessing to sell the bar and buy my dream."

Jo sniffed the air. "I can't smell rotting fish anymore, just delicious coffee. It must have taken a ton of work. Why didn't you just renovate the bar?"

"I couldn't get rid of the smell of stale beer and cigarettes. I swear it permeated the wood and sank into the floor, along with all the sad stories."

"I thought you and Dad had fun running the old place."

"We did—for years. People came in to celebrate special occasions, tell jokes, and hang out with friends. But over time, things changed. The world seemed harder to live in. It was depressing to watch people coming in to drink their troubles away."

"Like Dad?"

"Luckily, he was a happy drunk. But forty years together, hearing the same jokes and stories—it became more annoying than funny."

"Now, I'm getting depressed!"

"No! Be happy! I've discovered that coffee and tea have a nice way of bringing people together. In fact, try my new concoction." Kate poured Jo a mug of tea from a thermos and handed it to her.

Jo inhaled the scent. "I knew it."

"Knew what?"

"Sondra and I want to take Annie on a camping trip. I told Sondra you'd concoct a brew to help us be creative and come up with a plan."

"Actually, Thelma and I invented this together. Our own alchemy."

"Thelma. How is she?"

Kate pulled an envelope from under the counter and handed it to Jo. "This is for you. Thelma said you'd understand."

A letter? Was it about her divorcing Louie? It'd been hard enough to avoid the conversation with Louie's mom. Now his grandmother, too? Might as well open it. A necklace fell out— Thelma's. The one with the crow and wolf etched on it. Her heart somersaulted, making her feel disoriented. Jo took a deep gulp of tea, letting the feeling pass.

"Are you okay?"

"This is Thelma's favorite. Remember when she would babysit me? If I was having a rough day, she'd let me hold it and make a wish. I hated that word, babysit."

"Oh, I remember quite well. Your independence began the minute you started to walk. In fact, our customers swore they never saw a toddler walk with such an attitude."

"Hey, you gave me that attitude."

Kate smiled. To Jo, the smile was like a powerful sunbeam drying up the rain. Had she ever given her mother a compliment? Her list of things to consider was becoming a scroll. "You know, I was eight at the time and very mature."

"I remember you clinging to me, begging me not to leave, that Thelma was scary."

"That's because a customer said Thelma could shapeshift and become an animal or a bird. When we got there, Thelma was sitting on the porch with two ravens next to her. Then all those crows flew at me when we got out of the truck."

"I don't remember that."

"I'll never forget. Thelma walked over, looked at the crows, and thanked them for their message. I asked if she talked to crows. She answered that all living creatures share messages in different ways. The crows had told her they wanted to get to know me. I was so confused. Why would a bird want to know me?"

"Now I remember! You squeezed my hand so hard it was sore for days. I felt bad leaving you with her that time, but money was tight. We had to try something. Your dad convinced me to hold our first and last wet t-shirt contest. I didn't want you anywhere near that. Thelma offered to babysit you in exchange for fixing her roof."

"And here I thought that plastic swimming pool in the parking lot was for me."

"That's what we wanted you to believe. It didn't take long before you begged to go back and see her."

"It was a magical playground. Plus, Thelma was even better at storytelling than Dad. My favorite one was about the crow and the wolf."

"Then Thelma giving you this must be meaningful. Let's put it on." Kate clasped it around Jo's neck.

Jo knew she was supposed to inherit this necklace after Thelma journeyed to the other side. Was Thelma sick? "Mom, is there anything you're not telling me about Thelma?"

"Jo, she's ninety years old. That's all I need to say. Do you want to borrow my truck? The road going back to her place is worse than ever. With all the rain we've had, there's deep mud and potholes everywhere. I don't know why she never let anyone fix that road."

"Thelma believes it keeps out people with bad intentions. The key?"

"In the same spot. Now, be careful. You must be tired after that long drive. Promise to text me later with your plans. I want to help, too."

"I promise. Love you, Mom."

"Love you more."

Tears pricked at the edges of Jo's eyes. All this love—it made her feel vulnerable.

Jo hurried outside. Sure enough, there was the pickup truck. The door was unlocked and the key under the mat.

The truck started like a dream. Now this was fun, sitting up high. Jo sighed, the tension oozing out of her body. Much better. She could barely keep her eyes on the road. Spring in full bloom. The wildflowers were so beautiful. What a delicious time to come home.

Jo cranked her window down. No automatic button here. The air blowing in her face was invigorating. The pureness of the oxygen and the smell of pine trees infiltrated her senses. She loved spotting the fallen trees, covered with moss, creating a mysterious land where fairies created their magic. They had occupied her imagination for hours as a child.

Was that her feather floating toward the window? Jo caught it and checked her pocket. Sure enough, it had worked its way out, eager to see Thelma too. Memories streamed through her head like a movie. Sitting by Thelma on a blanket under the oak tree, watching the crows in the branches. Within minutes, a crow feather had drifted right into her hands. It had sounded like it was humming a song as she examined it. It became her first lesson from Thelma—the magic of birds and animals.

Spirit birds. Thelma had drawn her into a story about birds sharing their special powers and skills with humans. Jo had asked if the crows could help her hit a home run. Thelma hadn't given her a direct answer. She never did. Instead, Thelma had explained that crows were magical, creative, and very intelligent. She'd instructed Jo to hold the feather up to her ears and listen for a message. Jo had been hooked.

That feather. It comforted her at night. She'd used to fall asleep thinking of magical stories. She'd kept it for years. Perhaps the crows could send her a message on how to help Annie. And if she was really honest—how to help herself.

# CHAPTER TWENTY-TWO

*OUCH!* **JO'S CHEST SLAMMED AGAINST** the steering wheel. The driveway was horrible, no way to avoid hitting potholes. It was like being in a blender on the chop cycle. The last time she'd driven out here, her dad had been alive. Why did she have to think about that now? That burning flash of anger at him—for drinking and dying.

Ugh! One last pothole before the cabin appeared. There was Thelma. She looked peaceful in her rocking chair, as if she'd been waiting for Jo.

Jo clambered out of the truck. Where was her hello? Louie had mentioned that Thelma was going blind. How was her hearing? Jo let out a big "caw," like Thelma had taught her. Sure enough, Thelma "cawed" back.

The crows in the nearby tree joined in, chattering up a storm. Jo's soul ignited and her body raced toward Thelma. *Slow down. Easy.* Jo gently hugged her, feeling the fragility of Thelma's bones. Her heart thudded. She couldn't lose Thelma.

"Come, sit with me. I already made you a cup of tea."

"But how—"

"The crows told me you were coming."

"Thelma?"

Thelma cracked a grin as she pulled her cell phone from her pocket.

Jo sat on the rocking chair next to Thelma. "Finally—I get to graduate from the kids' blanket to the adult porch. When I think back, I see my mom, Sondra's mom, Annie's grandmother, and you, all rocking in rhythm together. It was quite the eclectic group. A bar owner, a Bible-stomping pastor's wife, the town's philanthropist, and a healer, all whispering and laughing together. Whatever did you find in common?"

"Different on the outside, but not on the inside."

"We were convinced that you were all creating recipes for secret potions. Do you have something Sondra and I could use to help Annie?"

"Help. What a wonderful word. Annie has a soul ache. She feels empty inside."

"Did she tell you that?"

"My dreams did. But I did see the three of you, sitting around a campfire, singing and laughing."

Jo sipped the tea and sighed, "Always the best."

"I made a special package to bring on your canoeing trip."

"Okay, don't tell me the cell phone told you about that?"

Thelma let out a soft wolf's howl.

"Louie."

Thelma squinted, her hand fumbling as she patted Jo's shoulder, then felt for the necklace. When had the lenses on Thelma's glasses gotten so thick?

"I'm glad you're wearing it. Josephine the Crow and Louie the

Wolf."

"I always thought this necklace was magical."

"Thought or believed?"

"I believed back then."

"Why not believe it'll bring you magic to save Annie and Sondra?"

"Sondra needs saving?"

The crows started chattering again.

"Maybe. It's up to her. Now, how about you? Are you happy? Are you following your dreams?"

"I've been thinking of doing something new. It's difficult to change paths when you need a paycheck."

"That damn paycheck! I bet the universe is already using your intentions and collaborating to open up opportunities. What else is holding you back?"

"Fear? Confidence? I don't really know."

"When the time is right—you'll be ready."

"I hope so."

"Hope. Another beautiful word. I've missed you and my beautiful granddaughters. I haven't seen them since your dad's funeral. That was such a beautiful day. He was finally released."

Damn. Thelma had done it again, planting a seed. Her words weren't random. That seed would grow and then bam—the answer right in front of you. "The girls are growing up. I'm sorry I haven't brought them to visit. But I promise that will change."

The camp forms on her kitchen table back home. Why not bring the girls here for part of the summer? Give them a chance to be with their grandma and discover their amazing great-grandmother. Jo knew Louie would agree with her.

The sun was fading. Time to tell Thelma. "Before I go, I need to give this back to you." Jo took off the necklace and handed it to

Thelma. "Louie and I are getting a divorce."

"A divorce? Those wolves aren't perfect, but their sense of family is always strong and loyal. Has Louie changed?"

The same question—it kept slugging her on the shoulder. Jo wanted to shout, *yes,* but it wasn't the truth, and this was Thelma. "No, it's me."

"I shouldn't be so nosy."

"It's fine. You have a right to ask."

"Jo, you don't have to be alone to find the answers. There are helpers all around you. And remember, you are my fearless granddaughter-in-law, the mother to my great-granddaughters, not just by marriage but also by spirit. I know you'll figure it out." Thelma took Jo's hands and placed the necklace in them, folding them over the talisman. Then she hugged her.

Thelma's aged arms still held strength. Jo's body quivered.

"Now come inside and get the tea for your adventure."

Jo followed Thelma inside the cabin. It still looked like an advertisement for the Discovery Channel. Books, maps, rocks, crystals, and all kinds of unique items lay everywhere. Jo loved those rainy days when she was little, discovering treasures hidden in a bookcase or a nook.

Thelma slid two large Ziploc bags toward Jo. "Your mom and I had fun creating these concoctions. There should be a tea for any occasion. Did she tell you about the herb garden we started? It's a co-op open to the whole town. Besides that, she still brings me fish on Friday nights. Not just for me, but for others that can't drive anymore."

"No, we haven't had time to catch up." Another sensation of being slugged on the shoulder. What was going on? Whoever was trying to share a message didn't have to be so rough. Okay—what else didn't she know?

Thelma began beating on two small drums.

What was this? Were they supposed to drum to help Annie?

"For Jessica and Hunter. They can reach me any time. Beat their drum or use their cell phone."

"Looks like they'll be taking drum lessons. I haven't given in to cell phones yet." Jo took the drums from Thelma. "Thank you for the childhood happiness that has seeped back into my heart. I'll stop by before I leave."

As Jo walked to the car, the crows flew by her, lifting themselves into the air, circling high above her. They looked so free. When had she felt like that? It was dangerous thinking, the type that could lead to having a drink.

She had a lot to be grateful for.

# CHAPTER TWENTY-THREE

Jo GOT INTO THE TRUCK. One more stop to make before she lost her willpower. Thelma had called her fearless and her mother, brave. What did that feel like? She was going to find out.

The cemetery. Jo parked in front of her dad's grave. It was so peaceful and welcoming. She traced her finger around the eagle engraved on the tombstone. Her mom had spent more than she could afford, but Jo understood. Her dad had loved eagles. That day fishing on Lake Windokini by the sacred island. The fledging eagles learning how to fly. Her dad didn't drink that day. Instead, he shared stories of young warriors who journeyed to the island for their vision quest. The place was sacred.

There was also levity. Her dad catching a big walleye, battling it to the boat. The eagle soaring down, snapping it off the line. She had screamed so loudly that he swore his left eardrum exploded. It became his excuse—that he couldn't hear to get out of doing a chore. But he always gave her a special wink. He had been fun, and she had loved him.

A memory floated to the surface. That tourist claiming that Lake Windokini was named for a powerful, mysterious, and frightening spirit. Thelma refusing to answer her questions. Her terrifying dreams, recurring for months when she was a teenager. Young warriors battling a ferocious creature to fulfill their vision quest. Then her birthday present from Louie, to spend the night on the island together.

Sondra had covered for her. Their huge fire to keep the formidable spirits away. How Louie held her in his arms all night. Every time she woke up and shared a nightmare, he would hold her closer. He had been so calm, navigating to shift her attention to an owl hooting or a loon calling for its mate. The night had become more magical, then terrifying.

It all came rushing back at her. The sunrise, swimming in the lake, washing away the residue of the campfire smoke and the last threads of her dreams. How the nightmares stopped. She'd always wondered what happened while she was sleeping. Louie never shared. Yet he seemed to become stronger—protecting her and comforting her at the same time. It made her fall more deeply in love with him.

Jo pulled out the crow feather. Those days were gone. A wind whistled around her, snatched the feather out of her fingers, and whisked it out of her reach.

Why weren't the leaves in the trees fluttering?

"Okay, Dad. You want me to talk, is that it? Am I mad? You bet I am. You left me and Mom too early. You didn't get to see your granddaughters grow up. They didn't get to see the fun side of you. The one that made me feel I could jump high enough to touch the sun. Instead, they saw you in a hospital bed with your liver disease—from drinking."

Jo sank to her knees and pounded the ground. *Damn it. I'm*

*not going to cry.* She lifted her head and watched the feather disappear out of sight.

"Don't leave yet. I need you. I'm a mess. This divorce with Louie. Should I go through with it? I'm so mixed up. Why did you teach me that drinking was fun? It destroyed your life and almost mine. It really sucks. How do I get rid of this anger?"

Jo looked around for a sign, but nothing. It was so quiet, as if all the spirits were holding their breaths. It had been two years. What was she waiting for? It was time to speak the words. "Okay, Dad—I forgive you."

There. She finally did it. The words buried with her dad had now been spoken out loud. A shift inside her body. The sensation of a stone sliding down her throat, freeing up space, giving more room to breathe.

The last light of the sun intermingled with the light and energy of the moon as they changed places. The solitude was broken by a single crow calling from the forest.

Her phone beeped. A text from Sondra. Pizza with the boys. Their plan was coming together. Better text her mom.

Jo touched the eagle on the tombstone one last time.

She felt lighter, more determined, and confident. It came from a place deep inside.

It felt good.

## PART THREE

# The Adventure Begins

# CHAPTER TWENTY-FOUR

SONDRA LOOKED AT THE CLOCK. Six a.m. She had this. Just tie the apron a little tighter around her waist. There. That should distract any grumpy customers. Her waitressing talents were untested. Sondra glanced over at Jo, Hank, and Jack, her practice customers. Five minutes left before they initiated their plan to rescue Annie. No doubt that Kate, with her mothering skills, could convince Dan to leave Annie and the boys in her capable hands.

Sondra still didn't agree that Jo should go along and not her. She had scoffed at Jo's argument that Dan would be suspicious that an escapade was brewing if Sondra showed up. Those days were over—even though some of the townspeople still remembered her bad behavior. She would show them all how much she'd changed. And at least Kate appeared supportive of her efforts this morning.

Hank. Her next victim. Maybe use a sexy, Southern drawl? "Well, sir, do y'all want sugar or cream in your coffee? And might I suggest a homemade blueberry muffin to keep those muscles lookin' so good?"

Jo spit out her coffee. "You're not supposed to act like a prostitute! Just give them some breakfast."

"Hey, I was having fun. You don't mind, do you, Hank?"

"I was ready to buy five muffins to keep listening to that pitch."

Jack appeared to gasp for air, then cleared his throat. Had he swallowed wrong? "You might give my friends a heart attack if you walk up to them like that."

"Don't pick on Sondra. She's great!" Kate exclaimed. "The whole town will be buzzing in minutes. My revenue should skyrocket. But they'll be bummed later today when you're gone."

"You can spread the word that I'll give an encore performance before I return to L.A. Heck, you can say that I'm auditioning for a part as a waitress in a movie. That'll really get the gossipers going! Take their minds and mouths off of Annie."

"Excellent idea. But time to hurry up. The mail waits for nobody. However, I do need to finish this muffin. Kate, that was one of your best. You put magic in everything you bake and brew." Hank took a big bite and washed it down with coffee.

"Actually, Jo did the baking this morning."

Sondra checked out the muffins. Carbs? Why not? It might be a seven-hour workout canoeing on the river. Cranberry. Healthy and a way to support the local farmers. It was delicious. A compliment? Jo wouldn't be expecting it. "Jo, great job. Let's pack a few extras."

"Really? What's up? That's your second compliment in two days."

"Maybe you better get used to it." Sondra relished the startled look on Jo's face.

Jo clapped her hands. "Focus. Let's execute our plan. Mom, let's go make breakfast and get Dan out of the house. Hank, you'll help Jack load the canoes and our backpacks into your truck."

"Not a problem."

"Once we get Annie, I'll text everyone. Hank, got it?"

"Hank, don't take it wrong, Jo's always this bossy." Sondra finished her muffin, showing all the crumbs in her teeth as she grinned at Jo.

"And some people never grow up, therefore causing people like me to be bossy."

"Do they always act this way toward each other?" Jack asked Kate.

"You haven't seen anything yet. We usually end up holding our stomachs from laughing so hard."

"And these days, we need to cross our legs so we don't pee our pants," Jo added.

Hank wiped his forehead with a napkin. "Ladies, that's TMI for me and Jack. Have a little mercy."

"There Hank goes again, showing off how hip he is," Sondra joked.

"Exactly when did Hank show you how hip he was?" Jo asked.

Sondra shook her head. Just ignore Jo and get them out of here. Hank did look sexy today, even in his postal shirt. Sondra flipped the window sign to 'OPEN.' She pushed on the door and directed them out, using her Southern belle routine. "Y'all scoot. Get going now. I have work to do."

"She always gets the last word. Doesn't it drive you crazy?" Jo asked Jack.

"I heard that!" Sondra shouted, then quickly lowered her voice. Her first customer was approaching. This was going to be fun. She held the door open, with her best smile and sugary accent. "Good morning, looks like you rose with the sunshine today. Get settled right in and let me make you the best coffee you've ever had."

## CHAPTER TWENTY-FIVE

Jo PULLED THE TRUCK INTO Annie's driveway. "Okay, Mom. Time for the call."

Kate dialed her cell phone. "Dan, I'm so glad I caught you. Are the boys up yet?" Kate nodded to Jo.

Step one. Accomplished. The element of surprise. Jo climbed out of the truck. Wow—the flowers planted in the front yard were stunning. When did Annie have time to plant and tend to flowers? Jo could barely keep the few potted plants by her door alive.

Jo rang the doorbell while her mom continued to chat with Dan. The door opened. Dan. His eyes were bewildered as he hung up the phone.

"We brought breakfast!" Kate whipped past Dan, like a bike speeding downhill with no brakes.

"Surprise!" Jo's stomach quivered as a mixture of anxiety, gratitude, and relief spun together like a tornado. Jo hugged Dan harder than she meant to. It had been too long. Dan had always been her friend. For a pastor, he never seemed to judge anyone. Quite amazing.

"Your famous hug. You've got some muscles. I'd hate to see an angel try to arm-wrestle you."

"I'd let the angel win. I don't want to mess around with getting into heaven. I've already used up my free passes. These muscles were sculpted from lifting clients during physical therapy. Much easier than lifting people's souls, like you do."

"I haven't been doing a good job with that lately."

"Blarney. Nothing that Kate's famous farmhouse breakfast can't fix."

Dan sniffed the air. "The smell of bacon. It's like a call for hungry wolves. The boys will be charging down any minute."

"So how are you and Annie holding up? If any silly, small-town gossipmongers mess with you, let me know." Jo flexed her bicep.

"I'm fine. Annie hasn't been out yet. I think people bought the story that she mixed up her medication, got dizzy, fell, and hit her head. They expect a pastor to tell the truth."

"Isn't it the truth? Has she said anything?"

"She's talking in riddles. I'm starting to understand that she's frustrated. But why did she need the pills? And why hide them? I'm afraid to leave her alone. She seems so fragile. I've never seen her like this before. Maybe I should take a few days off work?"

"It's going to be okay. Kate and I can hang out with her today. Maybe she'll talk to me. I've been down a rough road. I may be able to relate."

"I'm her husband. I know her better than anyone."

Was Dan the problem? *Be smart. Keep your mouth shut. Make Dan feel that it's safe to go to work.* "Of course, you do. Annie loves you. You've been married for seventeen years. Women need to talk and process, even if our words don't make sense. It's why

AA works for me. Being anonymous allows me to dump it all out without hurting anyone's feelings. Nobody reminds me of what I said and there's no pressure to be correct. It's hard to explain something when you don't understand it yourself."

"I get it. I'm sorry if I sounded defensive." Dan squeezed his eyes shut and rubbed his hands over his face.

Jo recognized the motion, a sign of fatigue and confusion. "Don't worry, Dan. Annie is my best friend. I want to help however I can."

"What's the news on Sondra?"

"Wait! What's that noise? Sounds like a stampede." The boys—perfect timing.

"Jo, where are you? I could use some help!" Kate shouted over the boys' laughter.

"Dan, I left a bag of muffins in the truck. Could you grab them? I promised to be the chef's assistant."

"Sure, be right back."

Jo raced into the kitchen. "Our plan's working! But we can't let your dad dawdle. We need to get him out of the house ASAP. Ready?"

The boys nodded.

Dan walked into the kitchen and handed Jo the bag of muffins.

"Thanks, go ahead and sit down. Mom already fixed you a plate."

Kate set a plate full of eggs and bacon in front of Dan. "Here you go. Just what you'll need for a busy day of work."

Jo placed the muffins on a plate and held it out in front of Dan. "How about a delicious muffin to go with your breakfast?"

Dan looked them over. "They look fantastic. Boys, Mrs. Kate is the best baker in town."

"Actually, Jo made these," Kate said.

"Safe to eat?"

Jo snapped Dan with a dish towel. "Okay, buddy. No wise-cracks. They're so good that you might declare it a miracle."

Dan laughed. "You got me. I do want one. Maybe I should wake up Annie and bring her down?"

"No, you can't do that." Matthew raised his voice.

Dan frowned and gave Matthew a stern, reproachful look.

Jo's eyes twitched. Dan looked formidable. Was he going to launch into a sermon? Was there something going on with Matthew and Annie?

Mark jumped in, "Matthew thought it'd be nice to surprise Mom with breakfast in bed."

"We want to have special alone time with her," Luke chimed in, right on cue.

"Yeah, Dad. You got to see her last night," Mark mumbled, his mouth full of a muffin.

John hopped up and down. "I'm going to wake Mom up by singing her favorite song."

Dan's frown vanished, replaced by a look of astonishment, his eyes opened wide. "I'm really proud of you boys. I just thought it'd be nice to talk as a family before school."

Kate sat down by Dan. "My mother, God rest her soul, taught me that mornings were a time to rejoice. Be happy for the day. And dinner was a good time to reflect and have serious discussions. I mean—it's none of my business, of course."

Jo could see Dan wavering. Better jump in. "I'll make sure the boys get off to school. I'm sure everyone is worried about Annie and will be calling the church. You're the best person to reassure them that she's doing great."

"Don't worry, Dad, I'll even drive the stupid van to school," Matthew offered.

Jo could see Dan's shoulders relax and the worried look leave his eyes. "Alright. I see that your mom is in excellent hands. She's going to love your surprise."

Dan's phone beeped and beeped again. Great, Jack and Hank had remembered to text Dan, asking for updates on Annie. "I guess the questions have already started. I'll head into work, but let me know how breakfast goes. Text me a picture. I'll see you all later. Kate and Jo—thank you."

Dan headed toward the door.

Finally! Jo expelled a sigh of relief. Wait. What? Dan had stopped and turned around. "Jo, got a minute?"

"Sure." Jo hurried to the front door and stepped outside. "What's up?"

"I'm glad you came. It was a better morning than I could have imagined. I'm going to think about what you said. Maybe we can talk later."

Was Dan asking for her advice? A sensation, like a spiral of energy, erupted from the ground and raced up her spine. Mother Earth was surely giving her signs that she was on the right path. "Absolutely. Now stop worrying."

Jo watched Dan drive out of sight. Mission accomplished. It was Annie time.

# CHAPTER TWENTY-SIX

ANNIE ROLLED OVER. WHERE WAS Dan? She glanced at the clock. Could it really be that late? It was so quiet. Had Dan taken the boys to school before she'd gotten to see them? How could he? She felt a surge of anxiety. She needed to see the boys. They must need reassurance that she loved them and, just as important, that she was okay. And to be honest—she needed their love. Better hurry and check it out.

Giggling. The doorknob jiggled, then the door banged open. John charged in, carrying a huge bouquet of flowers, dirt dangling from the roots. Her garden—how much damage was done? *Oh well, who cares.* Now Luke, with a plate of scrambled eggs; Mark, with toast and bacon. Incredible. Was this an out-of-body experience? Kate with a teacup! Annie sniffed the air—maybe cinnamon?

They surrounded her bed, singing, "Good morning, good morning to you, good morning, good morning, and how do you do."

It was their send-off song, the one she'd sung every day of their kindergarten year. When they began first grade, they didn't want it anymore, except John. It had felt good, dosing them with motherly love, part of her process of letting go.

Where was Matthew? Annie rubbed her forehead. He was probably embarrassed by her—or angry. Understandable. She was disappointed in herself too.

It had to be an illusion. Annie pressed her hands against her heart as she spied Jo with Matthew, arms hooked together. Was Jo dragging him? Matthew's lips were moving, so he was either singing or mumbling.

There was a pause. Then the boys belted out, "Good morning, good morning, and how we love you."

Her spirits soared. Maybe everything would be okay?

Annie moved over as John and Luke crawled into bed next to her. Mark arranged everything on the breakfast tray and placed it in front of her. Annie reached out and patted his hand. Her signal that she loved him. Mark had been the first to pick up on the silent message. She remembered when he responded that he loved her too. A good memory.

Now Matthew, clearly uncomfortable. He stood at the foot of the bed, avoiding eye contact. Better to let it pass for now.

"I can't believe this! Thank you everyone. Jo, when did you get here? Kate, this must be your doing."

Jo rolled her eyes. "Why does my mom keep getting the credit? I got up early and slaved in the kitchen to help make the food. So, eat up while it's hot. We have something to share."

"I see you're still bossy."

Jo put her hands on her hips. "And what's with everyone calling me bossy? Is it the word of the day? And I told you to start eating."

Kate threw her hands up. "That's my Jo! She was born bossy. When I was pregnant with her, all she wanted was cheeseburgers with extra pickles for breakfast, lunch, and dinner. Anything else made me sick."

"See—it's genetic. I can't help it. But I'll try harder to lighten up. Let's start with the plan." Jo turned to Matthew. "Sondra said you were in charge, since you lost the bet."

"What bet? Is Sondra here?" Annie asked.

"You'll see her soon. She's running the coffee shop for Kate. Probably mixing up orders and still getting excellent tips."

"That's our Sondra." Annie laughed. "So, Matthew, what's this plan?"

"We agreed to distract Dad so you can go camping and canoeing with Jo and Sondra. Sondra swears Dad won't get mad, maybe just worry. Coach Hank, Mr. Jack, and Mrs. Kate are bringing over dinner tonight and will hang out. Just to make sure."

"And the bet?" Annie asked.

"How was I supposed to know that Coach Hank taught Sondra his famous curveball?"

"She even had high heels on," Luke shared. "But she fell, and Coach Hank caught her. She went barefoot until she borrowed some cleats."

"Sounds very interesting. Camping sounds like fun, but you're more important. It might be better for me to stay at home, just in case you need me for something. I'm sorry you all had to worry about me. I'm sure you have questions."

"Mom, are you okay?" Mark asked.

"I'm fine. The doctor gave me medicine for insomnia and headaches. I got the pills mixed up. It made me dizzy and I fell, that's all."

"What's insomnia?" John asked.

"It's when you can't go to sleep even when you're really tired."

"Why didn't you sing yourself to sleep, like you do for us?" Luke asked.

Mark interrupted, "Stop bugging her. Mom, you should go. We'll be fine. Have fun. All that fresh air and paddling will help you sleep. Right, guys?"

"Yeah, Mom, you should go. Sondra and Jo are really funny. You'll laugh a lot," Luke added.

"Matthew?"

"A bet is a bet. Plus, Jo can train me in giving orders before you go." Matthew cracked a small smile.

There. A glimpse of the old Matthew. The one with the sense of humor. If only Annie could see more of that.

"Not a problem. Just follow my lead," Jo declared. "All of you, bring this stuff downstairs. STAT. Mom, call the schools and let them know the boys will be late, but make up a good excuse, like a flat tire or something, so they don't get a tardy mark. Boys, go and pack what we agreed on. Then we'll head out for the canoe landing. Oops—please."

The boys took off with lightning speed.

Jo stepped toward Annie. "Now, get up and get dressed."

Oh no. Annie tried to duck under the covers, but too late. Jo pulled her out of bed and gave her a huge hug.

"You can release me now so I can breathe."

Jo dropped her arms. "Sorry. Seems I've been a bit exuberant in my hugs these past few days. I'm just excited about our trip."

"Jo, you know that I can't go. Dan will have a fit."

Jo pressed her lips tight and covered her ears with her hands. "I can't hear you." Her shoulders drooped. Her eyes were disillusioned. Jo was good at pretending, but not with Annie.

Annie touched Jo's arm. "Come on, give me a break here."

Shit—could she actually go? A reprieve with her two best friends. After what had happened? She didn't deserve it.

Jo dropped her hands. "That's exactly what I'm doing. Giving you a break. One night. You'll be back early Saturday evening. All refreshed. On Sunday, you can walk into church, your head held high. Sure, Dan might get a little nervous, but he'll survive. Plus, he knows how to pray."

"Is this an intervention?"

"I'd call this a retreat. My intervention was hell, but I was an addict. Not like you."

Was Jo right? Maybe she had become addicted to the pills. They did relieve the stress of struggling through the days lately. But like Dr. Hensley said, "No judgment." A glimmer of anticipation buzzed inside her mind, like a firefly, flickering in and out. Why not? The boys were supportive. Dan—at this point, what difference would it make? A whole day and a half on the river with her two best friends. God must not be too mad at her.

# CHAPTER TWENTY-SEVEN

ANOTHER SURREAL MOMENT. ANNIE WAS shoved against the window of Hank's truck, with Sondra beside her. If she could link these moments together, it'd be a hell of a dream. They pulled up to the canoe landing with Jack's van parking beside them. Jack, Jo, and all the boys spilled out of the van. To think they'd conspired to get her here. Amazing.

Why this dread, this negativity creeping in? Residue from the past few days? Annie patted her pocket, feeling for her pills. Nothing. Damnit. She'd changed her pants at the last minute. If she didn't constantly overanalyze everything, this wouldn't have happened. Now what? Shit. She couldn't make everyone turn around. Annie squeezed her hands together. *Count backward from one hundred by two, like that pamphlet suggested. Ninety-eight, ninety-six, ninety-four... Better. Stay in the present moment.* She was going camping. *Just step out of the truck.* Not like she had a choice, with Sondra hip-checking her to move.

Everyone began unloading the canoes and camping gear.

Except for Luke and John. They raced over and clung to her legs as if they'd had a nightmare. They were afraid. She knelt down and pulled them close.

"I'll be gone for one night. Like a sleepover."

John's cheek pressed against hers. "The nights you were in the hospital felt like forever."

"Don't worry, John, you can bunk with me tonight. I'll tell you funny stories," Luke promised.

Annie stroked the top of Luke's head. He was so precious. "Thank you. You're a great big brother and an excellent storyteller."

Luke beamed. She kissed the tops of their heads, cherishing the scent of their hair. *Keep it together. Don't get emotional.* She looked up and spotted Jo heading their way. *Perfect timing. Break the intensity of the moment.*

Jo growled and grabbed both boys. "Hey! How about me and my bear hugs?" Luke and John squirmed and escaped.

Jo took a sharp detour, caught Mark off guard, and gave him a fast squeeze. Sparing him with brevity. Perhaps she had noticed Mark's face, morphing into dark red like an overripe strawberry. He was still so innocent.

Matthew. How was he going to handle this? Really—hide behind Jack? It was quite the dance: Jo and Matthew sidestepping, with Jack in the middle.

"Don't even think you're going to hide behind me. A bear hug is a gift. Take it like a man," Jack ordered.

*Way to go, Jack. Interesting.* Matthew stopped and stretched out his hand. Jo grabbed it and yanked him into a huge hug. "I changed your diapers! There's no escaping me, buddy."

Matthew took it well. Embarrassed, he shoved his hands in his pockets and kicked a rock out of the way.

Annie felt a twinge of jealousy. Why couldn't she have that

relationship with Matthew, instead of walking on eggshells, conscious of every word she spoke?

Jo did have a way about her. Now she was standing on a tree stump and waving her arms. "Everyone, pay attention. Before we launch, here's the story of our fearsome threesome. The day I met Sondra and Annie."

Fearsome threesome. Their nickname. How long since she'd heard it? Too many years. They had earned that title. All that fun and a little trouble. A tingle in her throat grew stronger until it became a hum. The tune they'd sung that day. So how would Jo spin the tale this time?

Jo looked like an evangelist on the tree stump with everyone gathered around her. "When I was Luke's age, I spent my summers with Thelma, an Ojibwe woman who was known for her wise and healing ways. Later, I married her grandson, so she become my grandmother-in-law. She taught me about the forest, what plants were safe to eat, and how to listen to the sounds. What do you hear?"

Annie observed her sons' serious faces, tilting their heads, listening. She took a mental snapshot. They were exhausting, drove her crazy, and the demands were never-ending. Then there were times like this.

Luke spoke first. "I hear water running, birds calling, and squirrels running on branches."

"Perfect! On that day, those sounds were interrupted by a car and two voices blaring out the song, 'Onward Christian Soldiers.' Thelma exclaimed, 'Virginia!'"

"Our great-grandmother," Mark said.

"Yup. A tall, striking lady with white hair. She was skipping and singing at the top of her lungs, along with a girl wearing a pink dress, pink tights, and white cowboy boots."

"Our mom?" Luke guessed.

"You got it! Thelma was so excited. I actually got jealous. Your mom begged me to lead her on a spooky walk through the forest. At first, I wanted to scare her. But your mom was so happy, chattering up a windstorm. She made up silly stories about the animals and acted them out. I couldn't stop giggling."

John sprang to attention. "Mom still gets silly and acts like an animal."

"That's right. And I am the master giggle monster!" Annie tickled John, who squealed with laughter. "We also learned how to canoe. Your great-grandfather had a summer cabin about fifteen miles down this very river."

"Why haven't we been there?" Mark asked.

"It's not there anymore. Bets were that your great-grandmother would burn it down. She loved to bake cookies but would forget them in the oven. She had Alzheimer's. It was my job to keep an eye on her. But actually, a lightning strike burned it down."

"Is that how you learned to burn cookies?" Matthew asked.

Annie frowned. "Hey, there isn't anything wrong with a burnt cookie now and then."

Matthew shrugged. "Guess not. Better than that gross cereal."

Annie cocked her head. Decision time. Get irritated with Matthew or let it roll? At least he was engaged. Better than avoidance. Keep going.

"Anyway, Jo and I were making up songs about the clouds when the fanciest car in town pulled up. Sondra bounced out of the car, along with her mom, the most elegant, beautiful woman I've ever seen. Sondra's bubbly personality was irresistible. She plopped down in the middle of us, no fear, and sang along. She had no clue how off-tune she was."

Jo placed her hands over her ears and squinted. "It was painful.

Sondra made your mom sound like a Broadway star and me like a backup singer."

"I wasn't that bad," Sondra protested.

"Boys, it's like your dad says: God gives us different gifts, and our quirks make us special." Annie looked at Jo. They burst out laughing. "Anyways! We let Sondra sing, and within minutes we became best friends. Therefore, nobody needs to worry. We'll take care of one another. I promise."

# CHAPTER TWENTY-EIGHT

SONDRA THOUGHT ABOUT THE DAY she'd met Annie and Jo. She'd been fascinated, watching her mother put on her makeup. How the dark shadows under her mom's eyes disappeared. Her pale lips turning bright red with her signature lipstick. Then, of course, the dab of perfume. Lilacs. She had dabbed it on Sondra's wrists. Her mom was so ill but still beautiful—except for the cough. The row of pills on the bathroom vanity couldn't stop it. Her dad had been out of town, her mother declaring it was time for an adventure. They were going to meet the wise woman in the forest. Thelma—a healer. If only the tea had worked miracles. Who knows—perhaps it did give her mom more time.

Sondra glanced at her dad. He appeared so alone. Had she ever seen him hang out with friends? Not that she could remember. Perhaps an occasional golf game. What else didn't she know about him? Maybe take the first step. It could be small. She straightened her shoulders and tapped her chest. She was strong. Nothing bad could happen.

Sondra walked over to Jack. "Dad, thanks for helping us. Since I don't have any kids to practice a bear hug on, you'll have to do."

*Close your eyes. Relax. This is your dad. He's trying.* One quick squeeze. There, she did it. Not too bad. She felt a slight squeeze back.

"Go have fun. Be a kid. Your mom would like that."

His words mattered. Her mom. A dragonfly flew by, grazing her nose. Now, that was strange. A fluttering in her stomach. Then an image of herself and Adam in bed slapped her in the face. How was she going to tell her dad? Anxiety rushed in. *Not the time for this. Push it away. Focus on Annie.*

"You're right. Mom loved Annie and Jo. Time to go."

Hank had shoved the canoes into the water and was holding onto the ropes, waiting for them. Was he always waiting? Had he ever found someone? She'd been too self-centered to even ask. He must be late for work by now. Yet there was his smile. He was watching her. The sound of a baseball cracking off a bat. The cheers for a home run reverberated through her body. They had history. When she got close to him, somehow her body felt lighter, the air was easier to breathe.

Sondra tossed her backpack and their tent into the first canoe. "Thanks, Hank." She stretched her legs over the bow and climbed in without getting her feet wet. Her yoga was paying off.

"All set?"

Sondra nodded and caught the rope.

"You already got your curveball back. What about your canoe moves?"

"They do deserve payback for their singing comments." Sondra backpaddled into the river. She knew all the strokes, thanks to two weeks of summer camp. She grimaced, remembering her antics. Her poor dad. She pushed him to the limits that summer. Even Annie and Jo were grounded. But she had perfected her paddling skills. It had given her something to focus on and burn off her angry energy.

Yes! A circle, a fast spin, a few cuts left and right, zigzagging—perfect. She knew it bugged Annie and Jo.

"I may not be able to sing, but I can out-paddle the two of you. Hurry up! Stop being such slowpokes." Sondra twirled the canoe in circles.

"Are you showing off for the boys or Hank?" Jo asked. "We've already suffered for years watching you. Besides, your spin was quite slow." Jo nudged Hank's arm and whispered, "Darn—she's still good. What do you think?"

"She looks great. I mean, she's really good at working that paddle."

Jack clapped his approval. "That's my girl!"

"Don't tell her that." Jo grabbed the remaining backpacks, slinging one on each shoulder. She stepped into the water. "This water is freezing!" She tried to hop into the canoe but instead banged her knee. "Shoot—that hurt."

Annie waded in behind Jo. "'Better cold than the fires of hell,' my grandpa used to say."

Jo swung one leg inside the canoe. Shit. A muscle spasm—that pulled muscle. Jo jerked around, feeling like a disjointed puppet. The canoe rocked dangerously, threatening to capsize. She grabbed the crossbar and pulled her body in. Something caught. Her face kissed the bottom of the canoe, her butt in the air. She wasn't going to live this one down. She tried to sit up but was trapped. What? She reached around. The backpack strap had wrapped around the paddle.

Annie set the cooler in the middle of the canoe. "Jo, what are you trying to do?"

"I'm trying to get my backpack off."

"Need a lesson over there?" Sondra paddled over for a closer look.

Annie unhooked Jo. "I'm supposed to be getting away from taking care of kids." She rolled her eyes, pretending exasperation. Damn—the water was cold. No dawdling here. She had to admit to herself, though, it was enjoyable to see Jo's face contort, searching for a witty comeback.

Annie hustled to the bank to retrieve the rope. Hank offered his hand, and she took it. Acting like a queen ascending her throne, she gracefully stepped into the canoe.

Hank gave the canoe a slight shove into the river.

Matthew waved his arms. "Wait! Stop! We promised Dad a picture."

Jo grabbed the side of Sondra's canoe and pulled it closer. "Okay, big smiles!"

No problem with that. Annie felt a huge grin stretch across her face. This was actually happening!

Matthew snapped the picture with his cell phone. He showed it to Mark.

"Dad's going to love that," Mark said.

"Let's hope so, or I'm in big trouble," Matthew muttered. "I'm going to wait a few hours before I send it to him."

"Come on, Jo. Let's get ahead of Ms. Showoff, who can't carry a tune," Annie said.

Jo shoved Sondra's canoe away, causing it to turn backward. "Quick! Paddle hard!"

The game was on.

Sondra expertly turned her canoe around. Within moments, she passed them by. *Now,* she thought, *fling my hair back and kick my feet onto the gear. Act as if that was easy and I don't have a care in the world.*

If only that was true.

## CHAPTER TWENTY-NINE

THE RIVER. THE FOREST. THE sky. Jo connected to it all, absorbed the energy—filling herself up. She inhaled the air. It was better than any drink she'd ever had. The sky was a magnificent blue, dotted with linen-white, puffy clouds. She could even hear the butterflies and dragonflies flutter around, dancing on the flowering bushes that lined the river. There were no words.

This time, a tap on her shoulder. Better than that slug. She knew the question. What was she doing with her life? Staying away from the forest, her mother, Thelma, her friends—and Louie. A clunk. Her stomach. Fear again. Releasing her anger and forgiving her dad had allowed the next big question to surface. Couldn't her spirit guides just give her the answer? No. A harder tap.

Okay, Jo got the message. Go into the basement of her mind and dig out the suitcase. Dust it off, open it, and deal with memories she'd prefer to forget. AA's steps had taught her how to face her mistakes and make amends. She was grateful for the program's guidance and support. It reminded her of what Thelma used to teach. Release and bless any negative energy; give it love, then send it back to the earth.

Where did Annie get her support? Dan? The church? Was it what she needed? Hopefully, Annie would open up and share what had happened. How could Jo help her? Maybe look for a sign.

There on the bank—an intricate, colorful formation of rocks. What had caused it? Jo squinted to get a better look. A natural spring. Nature. The best teacher. All that pressure under the earth building up until it exploded through the barriers. A magnificent release of water, soaring into the sky.

The meaning? Her analytical mind could come up with ideas. But the truth was in her soul. No use in forcing it. Perhaps if she relaxed and meditated, it would come to her. She stopped paddling and closed her eyes, unconsciously letting Annie do the work.

•

Annie's arms strained to paddle. She must be out of shape. However, the effort also felt good. The stress of the past few days trickled out of her body.

How to describe what had happened to her? Everyone wanted to know. She noticed the tree on the bank. A start. It mirrored how she felt inside. The tree's trunk was broken and twisted. However, it still had enough life force to create leaves on the remaining branches.

Behind the tree, she glimpsed an intriguing opening. Ancient trees and moss-covered boulders—fairyland. A tingling sensation in her heart. Her grandmother, Victoria. She had been extraordinary. A Christian sage, who weaved together the Bible, nature, and the metaphysical world. That summer. How she'd cried when her parents dropped her off to go on a missionary trip. Then the perfect cure: her grandmother and Annie's special mission. Explore the forest and find a magical place to create a fairy village. Together, they designed glens, stick houses, rock caves, and gardens. Afterwards, they prayed, inviting the fairies to come and live there. Annie also made a silent vow to protect the fairies and their stories. Every day, they'd check the village and find a new flower, a colorful mushroom, or a special rock. A sign from the fairies. It was magical.

Bedtime became special. The anticipation of having fairy dreams awaited her. Such an imagination—just like her grandmother's. Victoria might have lost her rational mind, but never her playful imagination. If given a choice, Annie would choose the latter. What had happened to that little girl? So carefree. Annie wanted her back.

•

Sondra paddled closer to Annie and Jo. It had been quiet long enough. Sondra looked at Annie's serious, sweaty face. Did Annie know that Jo had stopped paddling?

Time to lighten the mood. Make up a funny song, like they had as kids. "There's my Annie, she has quite the fanny. Hey ho, away we go. And there's my friend Jo, she's quite the ho! Hey ho, away we go."

Jo straightened up and dug her paddle into the river. "Come on, Annie, we need to get closer to her." Jo splashed Sondra. Missed. Of course, Sondra could expertly maneuver her canoe out of danger. Fine, if not water—then words. "There's my friend Sondra, she likes to bug ya."

Sondra stopped paddling, allowing Jo and Annie to get closer. Her turn. "Here's my friend Jo, she paddles really slow." Sondra dipped her paddle in the water and splashed Annie and Jo. Their faces! The shock of the cold water would wear off. Better get away before they retaliated.

Sure enough, Jo and Annie worked hard to reach her. But no problem. A piece of cake to keep enough distance. She relished the frustration on Jo's face.

"Come on, Annie, smack her with a song," Jo pleaded.

"There's Sondra and Jo, where did they go—when I needed them." Shit. Don't make them feel bad and bring down the mood. "Hey, I'm sorry. It's not your fault."

"True, but we should have been there for you, Annie. I'm sorry," Jo said.

Yes! A breakthrough. Sondra backpaddled to join them. "Annie, I'm sorry too. We're here now. We want to talk to you. But girls, I have an emergency. I really have to pee. My bladder is about to burst. Please help me find a spot. Pronto. I can hear the rapids coming up. All that jolting. It won't be water in the bottom of the canoe if I don't get relief."

"What was that phrase? TMI? And Hank was hip?" Jo asked.

"I did hear that Sondra fell into Hank's arms at the baseball field," Annie looked over at Sondra. Wow. Sondra was squirming like gnats were biting her. Maybe they should stop.

"Have some mercy!"

Jo observed the marshy banks. "You didn't pick the right time to have an emergency."

"Excuse me. Who knows when they're about to have an emergency?"

"She's got a point," Annie said. "I can relate."

"Just look for a shallow spot, anything. I can squat. I've got strong quads."

"There!" Jo pointed to a small mound of earth covered with long grass and broken branches. An oasis in the middle of the river.

Sondra clenched her core muscles and powered over to the island. She made it. Hallelujah! She scrambled out of the canoe and pulled down her pants.

"Sondra, stop! Look behind you," Annie shouted.

Sondra turned. No way. Her heart thudded. She wanted to shout, but her tongue wouldn't move. A huge beaver with enormous teeth and angry eyes. Swimming right at her, full tilt, leaving a motor-sized wake behind. Why? She looked to her side. The pile of branches mixed with mud. His den.

"Oh shit!" Why weren't her arms and legs cooperating? *Move!* She'd never felt so uncoordinated. She stumbled around, pulling up her pants before tumbling backward into the water. She struggled to get up while her pants slid back down. Jo and Annie's howls of laughter thundered in her ears.

The beaver was getting closer, its menacing teeth bared to attack. No time to waste. Sondra pulled the canoe off the island. Her paddle flipped out and floated away. No! She lumbered after it, her wet pants hugging her knees, hindering her progress. She finally grabbed it. A loud crunch behind her. The beaver? Her body froze. A jab of pain. The canoe rammed into the back of her knees, tossing her into a deep hole of water.

Sondra felt strange, a lightness under her feet. She'd been spared from crashing on the rocks. But how? The beaver? She scanned the water. Nothing. Gratitude filled her body and acted as a life jacket as she bobbed around.

The underlying current dragged her back onto a shallow, sandy bed. *Stand up and act cool.* Right—as if that was possible. She wavered between being pissed off and enjoying the hilarity of what had just happened. There really wasn't a choice. It had been an incredible comedy act—one that couldn't be reproduced. Jo and Annie caught up to her, tears of laughter streaming down their faces.

"Stop! I still have to pee."

"Hey, Annie, do you know any good jokes?" Jo asked.

"My last knock-knock joke wasn't very funny," Annie admitted.

"Actually—my muscles are clenched from being terrified. It's going to take the rapids to loosen me up."

"There's a spot right after the rapids where we can stop," Jo said. "Annie, what do you think?"

"I think watching her run from the beaver, pants halfway down, was the funniest thing I've ever seen. Sondra, if you could have seen your face!"

"I've seen enough scary pictures of my face lately. I don't have to imagine."

"Impossible—unless someone played a trick on you."

Why had she let that slip? Sondra knew better than to give them any clues. Their minds were sharp. Getting bitten by that beaver would be more pleasant than admitting what happened—and the blackmail. *Quick—make up something and hit the rapids.*

Sondra climbed into the canoe. "I'm finding more wrinkles every day. Let's enjoy those rapids before my bladder changes its mind."

Around the bend, the rapids greeted Sondra with a magnificent roar. It was up to her to lead the way. This was what she loved. Total focus. Get in the zone and flow.

What route to take? The river dropped a few feet, with a chute running through the middle. A good place to start. After that, her instincts would guide her. Sondra took off. A warrior charging into battle. No fear. No turning back.

The current sucked Sondra down the chute. The canoe flew up in the water, then smashed down with an emphatic jolt. A boulder right in front of her. She paddled hard to the left. Good decision. Left—right—right—left. The spray of the turbulent water battered her face. Exhilaration coursed through her body as she neared the end. *Damn it! No!* Images burst into her mind. Adam, lying on top of her naked body. Emily, snickering as she tossed the photos at Sondra. She couldn't escape. She sideswiped a boulder and had to straighten herself out.

Annie and Jo passed her by. They grinned at her, lifting their paddles into the air like champions showing off their trophies.

The show wasn't over yet.

Sondra engaged her core, used long paddle strokes, trying to catch the fast current. It worked. She knelt on her seat and lifted her arms in a 'V' for victory as she passed them.

"And you wonder why we pick on you!" Annie shouted.

Sondra could barely hear her. Her victory movement had activated her bladder. She had to find land—fast!

Jo shook her head, faking annoyance. "We have to find something to keep her ego in check." But Sondra—you had to love her. They were back. The three of them on this great adventure. How fun was that? And their banter was part of it.

Oops. Too late. Jo spotted the rock in front of them. No way to avoid it. "Annie, hold on!" Their canoe slammed into the rock. The current caught the back, then spun them around, sending them backward into calmer water.

"Wait—no wisecracks from Sondra?" Annie asked.

"Maybe she's doing a victory dance." Jo spotted Sondra's canoe on the nearby grassy bank. Sondra was running toward a cluster of bushes.

"Oh no, I think that's where—Sondra, stop! Get out of there!" Jo yelled.

Annie and Jo landed on the bank as Sondra pulled down her pants.

Sondra squatted behind a bush. "Thank heavens!"

"You aren't in heaven. Get out of there!"

"Now what? A snake? Don't go pulling one of your jokes on me, Jo."

"Don't you remember what three-leaf waxy plants are?"

"No, I don't remember and don't care."

"That's where Louie and I first did it. The most amazing night of my life became the week from hell. Going to the hospital the next day with poison ivy all over my body. The whole town found out about it. All those jokes I had to endure."

"Shit." Sondra looked down at the poison ivy plants brushing against her bare skin. "I can't stop now! Maybe my pee will kill it?"

"I'll get some soap," Jo offered.

"Wonderful. I get to wash my tush with you laughing at me. The universe is enjoying punishing me," Sondra muttered.

"Hey, I tried to stop you."

Annie spotted a narrow path that looked like a deer trail. "I'm going to walk into the woods. I like my privacy. See you in a bit."

•

Annie followed the path. The packed dirt transitioned into trampled grass, then disappeared. A memory rolled through her mind. She was sixteen, in a hiking phase where she created her own paths. The delight of the adventure, not knowing what the destination was going to look like. Never afraid to go alone. In fact, she liked it that way. She could toss aside her teenage persona and become childlike. She created markers made up of sticks, rocks, and hair ribbons to find her way back, and for the animals and fairies.

How life had changed. A small nudge of sadness. *Stop. Don't go there.*

*Stay here. Look around.* A small clearing. A majestic sycamore tree in front of her. The bark was smooth and cool under her hand.

Annie leaned her cheek against the trunk. Comforting. Why not ground herself, like Sondra had taught her the last time they were together? *Focus on the energy at the bottom of your spine. Now send that energy down your legs, out your feet, merging with this tree's roots. Visualize the roots going to the center of the earth. Then absorb the energy and let it flow upward.*

Annie held onto the tree as a powerful throbbing sensation rocked her entire body. Incredible. She wasn't sure if she was holding onto the tree anymore or if it was holding her. Her mind became quiet. There—her soul. The hint of light. The contrast. The place she'd been in lately had been dark.

Annie took a slow, deep breath. A loud crunch. A branch snapped. What was it? She opened her eyes and peered around the tree. Spectacular. A deer held her in his gaze from behind the neighboring tree. Their eyes connected. The deer tilted its head, scrutinizing whether Annie was a friend or predator. *Don't breathe. Stay still.* The deer came out, stepping forward, eyes still connected. It was mesmerizing.

Laughter invaded the silence. Sondra and Jo. The deer turned and leaped over a fallen log and disappeared into the forest. Annie felt strangely powerful, as if she had received a gift. Her hand floated to her heart.

It didn't feel so empty anymore.

# CHAPTER THIRTY

ANNIE CUPPED HER HANDS AROUND her mouth and hollered. "Okay, Sondra, haul that poison-ivy-infected, almost-beaver-bitten butt over here and join me. You take the front, because I'm steering. After lunch we can switch around," Annie commanded from the back of the canoe.

"I came all the way from L.A. to get bossed around by Jo. Now, micromanaged by you?"

"How do you think I manage a husband, four boys, a church, school, and community activities? Need I go on?"

Sondra shoved the canoe off the shore and hopped in the front. "Nope. I'll take my place. That sounds exhausting to me."

*Exhausting.* Dr. Hensley had used the same word after listening to Annie's schedule. One thing to hear it—another to live it. The thought poked at Annie, like a nut waiting to be cracked open to discover the truth.

A slight bang. Annie's body jolted out of its reverie. Jo was right next to her, their canoes side by side. Jo's face looked intense.

Was the interrogation about to begin? Annie's stomach muscles clenched.

"I drove out and saw Thelma yesterday," Jo said.

"I love that woman. What words of wisdom did she share, or should I say stories?"

"There was a story for me. I'm still thinking about it. However, she had a message for you."

Annie was quiet and kept on paddling.

"Don't you want to know? She would never be hurtful."

"Thelma has a way of seeing inside a person's soul. It frightens me. I may not be ready to know."

"She didn't share anything that deep. It's quite practical and helpful."

"Okay then, hit me."

"She thinks you're splattering."

"Splattering, spattering, or scattering? I've done them all. The most painful was splattering on the bathroom floor." Annie bit the inside of her cheek. She had to stop doing this. Jo had a horrified look on her face. "Sorry, I know that's not funny. I keep trying these dark jokes, but nobody likes them. I'd rather hear what Thelma said."

"Have you heard of sweeping back your energy?"

"No. But, I've fantasized about a flying broom. I could sweep up my mess, then escape for a while. But bummer—they don't sell them online yet."

Jo playfully tossed a handful of trail mix at Annie. "Hey, I'm trying to be serious here."

Annie picked up the pieces that landed on her lap and popped them into her mouth. "Alright, you have my full attention. Splatter away. I actually like that word. But first, spatter me with more of that mix. You can even scatter it about."

Jo aimed—the perfect throw. All of it landed on Annie's lap. "There! Now pay attention. You splatter when you give your energy away to people or tasks where you don't receive the energy back. Eventually, your energy is depleted. You hit a wall, empty and lost."

"No denying it—I splattered. But you're a mom. You get it. Nonstop action."

"It doesn't have to be. We have choices. Kids need time-outs to slow down. Why not us? All you do is stop when you're feeling tired. Then take a few minutes and visualize all the things you did up until that moment. As you visualize those tasks—imagine drawing that energy back into your body. Sweep your arms out and wrap them around your body while you declare out loud: 'I'm taking my energy back.'" Jo demonstrated with a hug around her own body.

"It could take me hours to do that. Have you tried it?"

"Many times. It's actually mind-blowing to realize how much I do. It's a way to practice self-love. But I have a tendency to screw it up by criticizing myself for not practicing it more. I can be my worst enemy. Tell me, why can't we slow down for a few minutes? Why are we so hard on ourselves? It's crazy—right?"

Annie nodded. "We've been trained to be productive. To complete as many tasks as possible in a day. We take pride in it. I'm not sure if it's the Scandinavian, Lutheran way of life or just being a woman. I watched my grandmother, mother, and now me. It's ingrained in my subconscious, part of my value system. I actually feel guilty to sit down during the day unless I'm saying a prayer. Maybe that's why I got so exhausted. I needed a time-out for me. I'm going to practice it right now. Watch."

Annie stopped paddling, leaned back. Now, this should be fun. How long before Sondra caught on? They were in slow-moving water. It would be harder for Sondra to paddle. A breeze picked up, blowing against them. A tingling sensation as the wind blew the anxiety out of her body.

A soft laugh. Jo.

Sondra turned her head. "What's going on back there?"

Annie pointed toward a cluster of pine trees on the other side of the river. "We're arguing. Is that an eagle? There ahead on your right. Jo says it's a hawk."

Sondra's eyes scanned the trees. "I don't see anything."

"It's huge. Let's get closer and prove Jo's wrong." Annie enthusiastically dipped her paddle in the water and pulled hard. Sure enough. It worked. Perfect. Sondra followed her lead, putting her full body into her strokes.

Annie set her paddle across her lap and propped her feet on top of the canoe sides. Now this was the life. Sondra was actually making progress. Impressive. The wind picked up. A huffing sound—like someone breathing through labor pains. Was that Sondra panting? "You okay up there?"

"This wind is really tough."

Annie gave Jo a thumbs-up sign. "Jo isn't having a problem."

Jo caught on and pulled her canoe ahead of Sondra. That would spur Sondra on.

"First one to the eagle is a rotten egg!" Jo announced.

"A rotten egg? Are we twelve again? How about a bet?" Sondra offered.

"Whoever loses, has to clean up the dishes after dinner tonight," Annie suggested.

Annie's time-out was turning into a comedy. She had to keep it going. "Come on, Sondra. I'm sick of doing dishes!"

It was quite the show. Annie noticed how Jo barely dipped her paddle in the water, letting them catch up. Once they did, Jo took off. Sondra's competitive spirit kicked in, mimicking an Olympic rower, her muscles straining. Should she help out? No—she had to learn to relax. Enjoy the entertainment.

Jo turned around and gave Annie a wave. Oh—no. Sondra whipped around to check on Annie.

Annie grabbed her paddle as if she was in mid-stroke. But her legs weren't as quick and clumsily thudded to the floor. Sondra gave her a look of astonishment.

"You little poop!"

"I wanted to see how strong your muscles were. Especially since you're always at the gym and can't call me back. So—who's the poop now?" Annie whacked her paddle against the water, drenching Sondra.

Sondra gasped and splashed Annie back.

Laughter burst out of Annie, surprising herself. "Oh my God! Shit! That's refreshing. Like being baptized. I can start anew." Annie pointed toward Jo, paddling away at high speed. "What do you think?"

"Time for a water party!" Annie put her muscles into it and their canoe flew across the water. Now, that was strange. Jo had stopped and was clambering out of her canoe. The sandbar! Jo was stuck, not enough time to push off and escape. Jo stood up and faced them—looking like the lone warrior who knew the battle was lost.

Annie and Sondra came close and relentlessly splashed Jo.

Jo tried to use her paddle as a shield, but it was hopeless. "Stop!"

"What's the magic word?"

"Fine! Please!"

Annie clanked her paddle against Sondra's, celebrating their success.

Water dripped everywhere off of Jo. She looked like a monsoon survivor. "I'm so drenched. I can barely move. I've got to dry off."

"How about our favorite beach? It's right around the bend. We can all dry off," Annie suggested.

# CHAPTER THIRTY-ONE

THE BEACH. AN OASIS. Jo dangled her good leg over the side of the canoe. She felt stiff, like dried-out, warped cardboard. Now for her other leg. Her hamstrings ached from her crazy riding attempt with Zac.

Annie and Sondra were already out of their canoe, stretching. No need to draw their attention. *One deep breath. Grit your teeth and do it.* Jo used her arms to lift her body and swung her other leg around. Shit. The canoe tipped. She struggled to find her balance. Her shoe caught the rim of the canoe. Jo twirled in the air and plunged into the water, landing on her hands and knees.

Annie waded into the water and pulled Jo to her feet. "Are you alright?"

"I'm fine. Except I'm sopping wet again."

"That's the second time today that you've been on your hands and knees. Maybe the universe is trying to tell you something," Sondra chided.

"Should I bring up the beaver?" Jo retorted.

"At least your landing didn't leave you in the hospital," Annie said. "Keep up your antics and everyone will forget about my incident. But for now, why don't we take off our shirts and pants. Keep the rest on, shall we?"

They stripped down to their underwear and bras. A tree branch served as the perfect clothesline. They hung their shirts and pants to dry in the sun.

"This takes me back," Jo commented. "Remember our skinny-dipping days?"

"Hank and I were just talking about that. How the three of us would run, screaming, naked into the woods, worried the boys would see us."

"Hank? Isn't skinny-dipping a taboo topic to discuss with a pastor's wife?" Sondra asked.

"Like you said—Hank is hip. A lot has changed since you left."

"Like being afraid of the boys seeing my boobs. The sight of them sagging would scare them off," Jo joked.

"Did Louie say you had saggy boobs?" Sondra asked.

"No, but my mirror did."

Sondra stretched out and went into a sequence of yoga warrior and sun salutation poses. "Remind me later to share what my mirror told me."

"What are you doing?" Annie asked.

"Some power yoga positions. It centers and calms my mind. It also strengthens my muscles, so my boobs won't get saggy like Jo's. It's a type of physical prayer. Come on, try it."

"I can't reverse my saggy boobs from breastfeeding, but the rest sounds good."

Annie mimicked Sondra's moves, exaggerating them on purpose. "Come on, Jo. Join us. Tighten up those boobs you keep talking about."

"I'll stick to my gym workouts. But you're putting on quite the show. Too bad I left my cell phone at home, or I'd be recording this."

Sondra dropped her pose. "Don't even think about recording us."

Jo strode up to Sondra, hands on her hips, with her most fierce, no-nonsense look. "Sondra, what's going on? You usually love attention."

"Maybe in the past, but not anymore. I'm here for Annie—and for you, if you need me."

"Maybe you need us? You're dropping hints. We're not stupid. We're your two best friends. Talk."

"I'm great. Maybe you're trying to project your struggles on me. Don't you have a huge decision coming up about Louie?"

"You don't get to change the subject."

Sondra's stomach grumbled with hunger. Could she spill her guts right now? If she talked about it, she'd get sick and lose her appetite. Best to hold them off. "You're right. I have a few problems to solve. But I need food. I never got to eat breakfast—customers were lining up outside the door."

"Okay, later. A free pass for now."

Sondra opened the cooler. "What did Kate and the boys pack us for lunch? Let's see—my favorite! Peanut-butter-and-jelly sandwiches. I haven't had one of these in years."

"Come over any time. It's my standby for my four eating machines," Annie remarked. "My favorite sandwich was your mom's fancy cucumber-and-cream-cheese ones for our tea parties. Remember those awful cookies my grandmother made when she'd forget a main ingredient? Your mom was so sweet. I saw her secretly switch out the cookies. My grandmother never knew the difference."

"She really was kind, wasn't she?"

"Your mother was an inspiration. She lived her best each day," Annie said.

"I don't know how she was so strong. She was still making meals for people in need, mere weeks before her death. She even created a cookbook with all her favorite recipes to leave for me and my dad. I was never able to open it. I don't know why. It's still in the kitchen drawer. My dad tried to make a few things, but they never tasted the same."

"When we get back, take it out and cook something for us," Annie said.

"Maybe," Sondra looked over at Jo. "What? No witty or bossy comment from you?"

"Nope. I think you should do that. But I'm hungry, so get busy and pass out those sandwiches."

Sondra rolled her eyes and passed a sandwich to Jo and another to Annie.

Jo unwrapped hers. "Look, I have a message inside. It says, *These sandwiches are made with love, Mark.*"

Sondra examined hers. "I have one too. It says, *Peanut butter protein is good for your muscles. Love, Luke.*"

"That's my sports boy." Annie unwrapped her message. "*Tell Mom not to worry like she always does, but to have fun. Matthew.*"

Sondra laughed, "Sounds like a teenage boy."

Annie pressed the message against her heart. "Sounds like a start."

"Annie, I'm glad," Jo said. "Since Sondra isn't ready to tell us what's going on, how about you?"

"Right now, the sun is shining and I'm with my two best friends. I don't want to ruin this moment. I'm surprised John didn't write one."

Sondra dug around in the cooler. "Wait—a container of grapes with a picture taped to it." She handed it to Annie.

"It's us cooking hot dogs over a campfire with big smiles."

"Your boys are awesome. I lost out by not having kids. Probably better for them."

"Sondra, you'd be a great mom. It's not too late—if you really wanted to."

"But it'd be risky for the baby."

"You're not that old. Things have changed. But I'm happy to share my boys with you."

"You can be the fairy godmother to my girls," Jo offered.

"It's a deal. I now magically have six children and it didn't even hurt! If you don't mind, I'd like to meditate on that thought. It feels so good in this sun." Sondra closed her eyes.

Annie gathered up the notes and tucked them into her backpack. A nap sounded perfect.

•

Jo leaned her head against a tree trunk. The stress from the past few days hit her. This place made her think of Louie. They'd spent a lot of time on the river. She couldn't avoid facing the big question anymore. Why was she divorcing him? Was she making the biggest mistake of her life?

Louie. The summer they'd met had been a roller coaster. Sondra's mother dying. Sondra mad and frustrated. The three of them getting into trouble, with Sondra leading the way. Their parents doling out the punishment. Sondra had been sent to a fancy summer camp. Annie left for Bible camp. And Jo had gotten the worst of it—kitchen duty at the bar. A greasy, messy job.

Jo recalled the relief when her parents finally took pity on her. Jo had begged to go see Thelma. Her dad had been eager to drive her. Unusual, except there was a bar along the way. But no, the minute they hit the backroads, he stopped the truck, telling her to take the wheel. She'd been so excited. Then, learning to use the shift. Her dad bumping his head on the windshield, exaggerating the pain—making her laugh.

Jo had been eager to impress Thelma when they arrived, but nobody was around. Then the sound of Thelma's voice and wolves howling. Her fearless sprint into the woods—ready to save Thelma.

Instead, she met Louie, Thelma's grandson—and her world changed for the better.

There was Thelma, howling with a boy. Jo had tried to stop her momentum, but no luck. She smacked into Louie. She would have knocked over a lesser boy, but Louie's strong arms, even then, caught her from falling. She had looked up and tumbled into the depth of Louie's liquid brown eyes.

Jo hadn't thought a boy could be beautiful, but Louie was, inside and out, like his parents. His mom was beautiful, with dark hair and perfect skin. A chemistry professor and a healer like Thelma, her mother. His father the opposite, with blond hair and light skin. A special education teacher, patient and kind to everyone.

Louie's disappointment in leaving California to move to Minneapolis evaporated. He had begged to stay for the summer, and his parents agreed. Life became amazing, filled with days of climbing trees, fishing, and exploring the forest.

The following summers, Louie came back. Their fearsome threesome became a foursome. All those years, she never dated anyone else. Their first kiss at fifteen. Even at that age, Sondra had already gone through a number of boyfriends before Hank. Annie was secretly dating an older boy, who drove them to remote farmers' fields. They'd listened to music on the car's radio until each couple would drift away, finding a special spot to make out. The memories lulled Jo to sleep.

# CHAPTER THIRTY-TWO

ANNIE JERKED AWAKE, CONFUSED. REALITY rushed in. She looked over at Sondra and Jo, sleeping. They looked peaceful—different from when they were awake. Something was going on with both of them; they just weren't telling. Not so different from herself.

Jo. She couldn't divorce Louie. He was a good man—a rare soul. Jo and Louie had made each other better, until things got bad with Jo's drinking. Annie needed to convince Jo to stop and think.

Sondra was another story. Sondra had never really recovered from losing her mom. Even the highest-paid psychologist didn't help. The deep wound refused to heal. The funeral—her grandfather leading the service. His words—calm and comforting, versus the hell and brimstone he preached. When Annie sang the closing song, they had cried. A moment of bonding that had lasted their lifetime. Now Sondra was talking about her mom and dropping hints. Was it a cry for help? Why wouldn't she tell them anything?

How ironic. Annie had done the same with Dan. Her comments, hoping Dan would catch on. Angry when he didn't. She could have been straightforward. How much was his fault? With four boys, there was always something going on. Perhaps all that chaos prevented her from being heard. Maybe she needed to take charge and make decisions instead of reacting to everything around her. Yes, her soul embraced that idea. The revelation was almost too much to handle. What a blessing to have this time to think.

Annie watched a broken branch float by, twirling in the current, mirroring her own life spinning around. At least she was still floating! She checked their clothes—almost dry. Time to wade in the water and look for stones that spoke to her. There—a shiny one. It felt good in her hand. The message? Enjoy the moment, stop analyzing, and let the answers come. A good idea.

Another rock, but no pockets. She did have her bra. Perfect. There—a green and blue rock. It looked like a person, maybe a princess. She remembered amusing her parents by singing stories about rocks she'd found. Her imagination kicked in. She began to sing; the words unabashedly flowed.

·

Sondra woke up first. Annie's voice. It was dreamlike. She nudged Jo awake, putting a finger to her lips. The water rushing over the rocks and the birds singing along with Annie. It was a masterpiece.

Annie was examining a big rock when she noticed Jo and Sondra watching her.

"Please don't stop. I love it when you sing," Sondra pleaded.

"That's okay."

"It's not okay. Besides, what's up with you not being the choir director?" Jo asked.

"Somebody joined the church who has a degree in music education. She wanted to direct, so I stepped aside."

"What? And keep that voice to yourself? I believe that's a sin," Sondra said.

"I was being a pastor's wife."

Jo stood up. "Does *pastor* mean *martyr?*"

"Excuse me?"

"All we've heard from the moment we got home is, Annie does this and Annie does that. No wonder you needed drugs."

"I wasn't taking drugs. They were prescriptions."

"That's not the point. Some people get a sense of reward by sacrificing themselves for others. It's not a bad thing. I see it a lot in my AA meetings. But it's draining. They end up choosing the pity card to get the attention they need, or they can't take it anymore and blow up."

"Shit. I did blow up my life, actually my whole family's life. Are you saying it's my fault?"

"No! I'm trying to help you to help yourself."

Annie tossed the big rock into the water. "I'm getting a bit confused here. I'm either having a pity party or I'm blowing up."

"Hey, I'm sorry. I'm probably wrong. I was only sharing a thought," Jo apologized.

Sondra stood up and stretched. "Well, you could be more sensitive and not pick on Annie. However, Annie, you better still be singing at church. It was the only reason that I attended. But don't tell Dan that."

"The new director doesn't believe in solos. She also changed the practice time so it conflicts with the boys' schedules. It's really no big deal."

"Well, I say—that bitch!" Sondra spouted.

"That witchy bitch," Jo added.

"I've got a twitch for that bitchy witch," Sondra continued. "Your turn. Annie. Come on, stop sulking. It'll feel good."

"Fine. I've got a—" Annie stopped. The sound of loud voices drifted into their space.

"We better be quick before that twitchy bitch finds us!" Sondra shouted.

Sondra pulled on her shirt. The voices were louder now. Perfect time for some payback. She grabbed all their clothes and dashed up the bank. Jo was close behind. Sondra cut to the left, dodging Jo. Now! Sondra heaved the clothes down the bank away from Annie. *Yes!* A massive pine tree straight ahead—thick enough to hide behind.

Jo headed toward the clothes as four canoes filled with Boy Scouts rounded the bend. No time to retrieve them. Better to hide. Jo spun around and joined Sondra. "Do you really want to keep this battle going?"

"Shh—watch Annie. This is hilarious."

Annie took five steps toward the clothes, then five steps backward up the bank, performing a line dance with her indecision. The Scouts saw her and paddled faster.

Annie cupped her hands under her rock-filled bra and scrambled up the bank. Her bra heaved up and down, threatening to snap. She huddled behind Sondra. "You better watch out that I don't crush you with my bra."

She peeked out. "I can't understand what they're saying. They sound excited. They probably think we're naked up here. I can't believe you did that."

"You two are always picking on me. I'm not even close to being even." Sondra stepped out from behind the tree. "Do you have a first-aid kit?"

The Scouts were elbowing and shoving each other, trying to

get a look. One of the boys yelled, "Do you need help?"

Annie yanked Sondra back. "You don't have your shorts on. What are you thinking?"

"I have my underwear on. I'm sure the boys have seen a girl in a bikini by now." Sondra grinned as she shoved Jo out from behind the tree.

Jo ducked back and tried to wrestle Sondra out into the open. The two of them went back and forth until Jo stepped on a sharp stick. "Ouch!"

The tallest Boy Scout grabbed a first-aid kit. "We're coming up."

"Girls, stop it right now." Annie looked out. "I know those boys. You two stay put. I'll take care of this." She cleared her throat and then lowered her voice, so it was deep and booming. "Stop right there. We're okay. I know who you are and your parents' phone numbers. Put those clothes back where you found them or you'll be stripped of your badges."

The boys immediately dropped the clothes. "Yes, ma'am. Sorry, ma'am. We were only following the code to help those in need." The tall Scout motioned to the others. Within seconds, they piled into their canoes and took off.

"We've got another memory to cherish," Sondra grinned.

"At least we didn't demolish their dream of what a naked girl looks like," Jo laughed.

Annie strutted around with her bra stuffed with rocks. "Speak for yourself. I'm looking quite stacked right now."

## CHAPTER THIRTY-THREE

ANNIE PLUCKED THE COLLECTED ROCKS from her bra and set them into the canoe. That had been quite the show. She felt lighter already.

Jo came over and studied Annie's pile of rocks. "You're bringing all of them? That's a lot of extra weight. You're going to have to paddle by yourself."

"Fine with me." Annie pushed off. "They're my new friends."

"Hey, wait up!" Sondra mimicked Jo's pose: hands on hips, glaring. "Do I look familiar? Let's get going. It's time to get Annie to open up."

Jo shoved the canoe offshore and scrambled in with Sondra. "Do I really look that scary?"

"Remember that creepy glow-in-the-dark goblin Halloween mask?"

"Got it. I'll paddle extra hard."

"You better. I'm in the back, so don't forget I'm watching your every move."

They paddled together in perfect unison. It took only a minute to catch up to Annie.

"I forgot about your rocks," Sondra said. "Jo still gets crow feathers. Me—nothing. A big fat zero."

"Look in front of you. Someone is here to bring you good luck."

Sondra saw it on the bow: a magnificent red, green, and black dragonfly enjoying the ride. She leaned over and studied it. "He looks majestic, like a miniature dragon with wings. Actually, I think it's a female. She's smiling at me."

"Maybe she's your totem," Jo said.

"I understand the feathers, but what's with this totem thing? If it brings good luck, then I'd like one."

"It can be good luck, if you listen to their messages. For centuries, people from different cultures have believed that we can forge a bond with a specific animal, bird, reptile—even an insect. And whatever you bond with becomes your totem. By studying their characteristics, you can gain insight to make better decisions. It's like having a spiritual coach on your life journey. You can even meditate on them and ask for guidance."

"Do you know the meaning of a dragonfly?" Sondra asked.

"I do. It's fascinating." Jo kept paddling. This was turning out well. Barter with Sondra to open up about what was bothering her. It might help Annie to share.

"Please tell me something good," Sondra begged.

It worked. Sondra was on the hook. "Only if you tell me something first."

"What do you want?"

"Something is bugging you. What's going on?"

Sondra set her paddle down and tapped on her sternum. Time to release some of her guilt. "Okay, I slept with a client."

"Whoa—I didn't see that coming," Jo sputtered.

Annie pulled her canoe close to listen. "What about James?"

"He doesn't know. I'm still trying to figure out what to do. Maybe this dragonfly can help."

"That's it? No details?"

"First, the 4-1-1 on the dragonfly before she flies away. I don't want to miss her message."

Jo looked at Sondra's face. It was intense. *The 4-1-1.* That was Hank's expression. Jo's resolve to push Sondra dissolved. Let Sondra talk when she was ready—at least for now. "Okay—this is what I remember. People with the dragonfly totem can be highly emotional and passionate. This can work for them as they pursue their goals. However, it can also work against them if they deny their true emotions. They can miss the lessons to be learned. They need to develop ways to keep emotional balance and a clear mind. Often the message is that it's time to change and find a new way of thinking."

"Are you making this up?"

"No, I promise. I listened to Thelma and read her books."

Sondra placed her finger close to the dragonfly. It crawled onto her finger and onto the back of her hand. "Okay, I heard you. Time for a change."

"There's more. A dragonfly often carries a soul on its wings, someone who cares about you. Maybe that's your mother and she's here to help you."

"I wish she could." Sondra lifted her hand. The dragonfly hovered around her before flying away. "I messed up. I feel guilty. However, I'd rather share later, around a campfire."

"I agree with Sondra. We have tonight." Annie picked up one of her rocks. "But what about me? I like how my rock feels, but it doesn't send messages."

"Do you see an animal in your dreams? Or has an animal crossed your path recently?"

A mosquito landed on Annie's arm and bit her. She slapped at it but missed. "Damn thing. It doesn't get to be my totem. My dreams are like that mosquito. They keep me up at night, tormenting me along with Dan's snoring. But I did see a deer this morning. Plus, I love the movie *Bambi*. I've watched it a hundred times with my boys. We always cried when the mother died. I can't stand that part."

"I still cry every time I watch *Dumbo* with the girls," Jo shared.

"Why does the mom have to die in fairy tales like *Cinderella* and *Sleeping Beauty*?" Sondra asked. "It stinks."

"Think about it. Back then, when those stories were created, girls got thrown out on the street for the smallest mistake. Life could really suck for women," Annie said.

"Then the storytellers added the delusion that if the girls were sweet, kind, and pretty, a prince would come along and rescue them," Jo added. "What's with that?"

Sondra stood up in the canoe and shook her butt. "I believe it's the tale in the term, fairy tale. A guy always needs to have a little tail."

"Amen!" Annie laughed.

The canoe rocked side to side as Sondra scratched the upper part of her butt. "This feels good. Maybe that mosquito bit me too."

"Now you're acting like a guy," Jo scoffed. "Sit down before we capsize."

"Fine!" Sondra plopped down on her butt. Her hands ached to keep scratching. She squirmed around on her seat trying to relieve the itchiness. She caught Jo's glare and made a face back at her. *Okay, think. Don't scratch. What you focus on is where your energy flows.* Sondra dipped her hands into the water, drawing her attention to how the coolness felt on her skin. Better.

"Back to Annie," Jo stated. "The deer is a sign to be gentle and loving with yourself and others. You may need to ask if you're being too critical, because nobody is perfect. It's time to reflect if you're trying to force something to happen. A deer showing up signifies that a new energy is about to be born around an old or new dream."

"That's a lot to take in," Annie said. "Thank you, Jo. You're like an encyclopedia."

Sondra shook her head. "I'd say she's more like a psychic. She's kind of freaking me out. She said that Louie's totem is a wolf. Now, a wolf must be worthier than any prince."

"Stop pushing Louie on me."

"Am I doing that?" Sondra grinned.

"And stop working your toothpaste-commercial smile at me while you're at it."

"Come on, Jo. I'm with Sondra. Give us a little something."

"Alright! The wolf represents the wild spirit—part of what drew me to Louie. They're friendly, social, and highly intelligent and won't fight unnecessarily. There are ancient stories about wolves and crows developing playful friendships. The wolf communicates using body language, while the crow talks. Wolves have a strong sense of family, are loyal, faithful, and mate for life."

"That's why we love Louie. We've known him since we were kids. We can count on him to be there—no matter what." Sondra said.

"I do know about crows from the Bible. Elijah, the prophet, was fed by a crow when he was hiding in the desert. Egyptians and other cultures believed that a crow represented magic. When a crow showed up, it was time to recreate your life. The crow is intelligent and a symbol of spiritual strength. That's a compliment for you, Jo," Annie stated.

"Are you calling me a crow?" Jo asked as they paddled under branches of a tall, majestic pine tree.

Before Annie could respond, a group of crows flew out from the tree, cawing at them while flying away.

They all stopped paddling, speechless.

Jo felt her body tremble. A bolt of energy coursed through her. She lifted her hand at the crows high in the sky. "I got the message!"

•

Annie noticed how the river had taken over, moving them forward without any paddling. So many profound messages. They were being guided through an area where the mossy banks led into the forest. Magnificent pine trees flung their branches high into the sky. A miracle. Annie had witnessed many in her life, between her and Dan. God was still around. She felt a tug—like someone had cast a fishing line and snagged her. A connection. Was that hope? Happiness? Why label it?

"I love all of this!" Annie proclaimed, waving her paddle around, gesturing to the forest, the river, and sky. "Thanks for coming to save me. I love you both."

"I love you too," Jo replied.

"I love you more," Sondra said.

Jo rolled her eyes at Sondra. "Really?"

"It's just an expression. No need to get uptight about it."

"Stop quibbling! We've got fast water. Let's be rapids warriors!" Annie yelled. The turbulent water tossed the canoe around. Her rock pile toppled over and danced along the canoe bottom. Annie's spirit rose to the challenge, maneuvering her canoe around fallen trees and boulders.

Sondra and Jo came up to her side. Annie felt a yearning to be ahead, to lead this time. She paddled harder. The river was wide, but the water was converging to the center. Why? The answer: ten yards ahead—a small waterfall. A gradual, three-foot drop where the water shot through, leading into calmer waters. It was like being an arrow on the string of a bow, ready to be released. No time to think. Be fearless. Annie held her paddle over her head, a hand on each end, and let the canoe rocket down the falls.

She did it!

A release of pressure. Were those tears streaming down her cheeks? Annie brushed them aside as Sondra and Jo caught up to her. They all hoisted their paddles even higher. True elation.

"That was awesome!" Sondra shouted. "I wouldn't want sex if I could do that every day."

"It was great, but I'll keep my sex," Annie replied.

"I do miss that feeling," Jo admitted.

"I'm sure Louie still wants to make you feel that way," Sondra said.

"You're relentless."

Sondra flung her hair back. "That's what makes me—me." Sondra turned her head around and sniffed the air. "What's that smell?"

"It's not me. I've got my super deodorant on," Jo said.

"Lilacs. My mom." Sondra felt the familiar pain. It was like a volcano. Rumbling up from the depths of her stomach and into her heart. It happened like that. The pain buried deep in her gut either rose like steam or exploded. The memory erupted. The poor, rich girl, without a mother. The whispers that her mother was a closet smoker. People used to believe only smokers or coal workers got lung cancer. She knew better. The only thing her mother smelled of was sweet lilacs.

Annie looked around. "I don't see any bushes. Maybe it's a wood fairy?"

"Damn lung cancer," Sondra said.

"Damn liver disease," Jo added. "What's going to happen to us as we get older?"

Annie shivered. "Thanks for that wonderful thought. I was enjoying myself."

"Sorry, I have a way of making things negative."

"That's not true. You're funny, witty, and make people laugh."

"My AA group wouldn't agree with you. They think I'm an interrogation specialist."

"You are good at it," Sondra said. "But come on—you're not that bad."

"I can be a jerk sometimes—that terrible stubborn streak in me."

"Is that why you're not giving Louie another chance?" Sondra asked.

"You're the wolf and the crow. Both of you are supposed to mate for life," Annie added.

"Maybe not all the tales are true," Jo said.

"Stop squashing my dreams when they're just beginning!" Annie said.

"Right now, my dreams are of a nice dinner and a soft bed," Sondra muttered.

Annie could feel her exuberance transform into fatigue. The hours on the river had been a mixture of fun and intense thinking. That damn sadness was seeping into her body. She hated the feeling. She couldn't give into it. Stop it by using gratitude. Start with the obvious, simple things. She had the boys. Dan hadn't condemned her and actually seemed concerned. She was with Sondra and Annie. She was in a canoe. The sun was shining. She had tater-tot casserole last night with Jell-O. That thought made her laugh. It was working!

Annie glanced over at Sondra, who was grimacing. They better stop soon. "Why don't we soak in our victories for the day. Find our camping spot for the night?"

"Perfect," Sondra said. "Don't laugh, but my butt is getting worse. It really itches. I pray it's psychological and not poison ivy."

"I'm not checking that scene out," Jo said.

"I didn't ask you to. Please, Annie? Maybe later if it doesn't get better? I'll be forever grateful."

"I'll do this act of charity for you. But I'm only looking."

"Thank you! How about that spot ahead to the left?" Sondra pointed to a small clearing with signs of previous campers. A firepit existed and the underbrush had been cleared away. It was perfect.

# CHAPTER THIRTY-FOUR

SONDRA EXHALED A SIGH. OFF the water and onto flat ground in their camping site. She couldn't believe how sore her muscles were. Her daily energy routine should get her blood pumping and distract her need to scratch. Mix in some Qigong with yoga and breathwork. She circled her hips, arms, and legs, drawing figure-eights with her body, imaging it with her mind and breathing through the movements.

"You look like a contortionist," Annie teased. "Those moves could spice up my sex life. Seventeen years with the same man can get a bit stale."

"It's great for connecting to those deep muscles that are harder to reach. I'm happy to teach you, as long as you don't mock me this time."

"I'll be serious. I promise." Annie swung her arms around and then her whole body. Her muscles were loosening up. Nice.

"You're doing great. Next is a tree pose. Great for balancing and focusing your mind. Ground your feet. Lift one leg and place the bottom of your foot on your calf or above your knee. Like this." Sondra balanced perfectly and rested her foot high on the inside of her thigh. "Once here, you can grow your branches and blossom." Sondra stretched her arms out to the side and drew them up into the air.

Annie rocked her feet back and forth. Balanced. She slowly drew her foot up to her calf. Still stable. Now grow her branches and blossom. *Concentrate.* Her standing leg wobbled, then trembled with the effort. Nope, she was going down. She toppled onto her butt. "It must have been the wind."

Jo picked a leaf and tossed it into the air. It floated straight down. "I don't see any sign of a wind."

"At least I tried. What's your excuse?"

"I pulled my hamstring about a week ago. My new move while trying to have sex."

"I knew you were holding back. Why didn't you tell us that you and Louie connected? How was it? Tell us everything," Annie demanded.

"First of all, the key word is 'trying,' and it wasn't Louie."

"We drove all the way from the airport together and you didn't tell me anything?" Sondra grumbled.

"What do you mean, it wasn't Louie?" Annie felt a rush of disappointment. Damn it. How could her emotions be such a roller coaster? She had never felt so unstable. Was this how it felt to fight depression? Her role was to be strong, to handle anything. She was the pastor's wife.

"Don't worry, in the end nothing really happened. A number of spirits made sure of that."

"Maybe it was the holy spirit." The words popped out of Annie's mouth. They startled her. Did she believe them? Or was she trained in her rhetoric?

Sondra interjected, wiggling her butt around. "I can't take it anymore! I have to scratch, but it hurts when I do. Both of you—we have to talk. Mandatory confessions around the campfire tonight. Nobody can escape. But Jo, can you find that lotion your mother-in-law made? I need help. This is torture!"

"Pronto." Jo dug into her backpack and handed the lotion to Annie. "Charity time. This might work. It has ingredients for mosquito bites and diaper rash."

Sondra started pulling down her pants.

"Wait one second. I'm out of here. I'll unpack the canoes. Annie can practice her sainthood."

Annie gestured Sondra to follow her into the woods. "Let's get out of sight in case more Boy Scouts come by. Bad enough you tortured them, showing off in your underwear. They don't need to see the real thing."

•

Jo hauled their gear from the canoes. Three trips, but she didn't mind. Sondra's butt must be a mess. They still hadn't come out of the woods. On a positive note, she could hear them laughing.

Jo opened up the tent bag and dumped the contents on the ground. Why so many pieces? Weren't the manufacturers supposed to make things easier versus harder? She spread the tent canvas on the ground. She could discern the shape of a tent. A good sign.

Now for the poles. She gathered them up. What were all these sizes? In the past, there had been only one size. What kind of tent was this? Directions? She turned the bag over and shook it. Screws, bolts, and hooks tumbled out. It looked like a graduate exam for a mechanical engineer. It reminded her of putting together Jessica's crib. Louie's endless calls to customer service, doing his best not to swear. Afterwards—their celebration. A picnic dinner on the living room floor. The dessert that set them up for fun, messy, playful sex.

Jo's body heated up at the memory. It had been incredible. How many good memories had she chosen to ignore? Was there enough to build a future on? Maybe they didn't need to build on the past. Start fresh. No expectations. The only constant would be the love they still had for each other.

The sounds of chatter broke through her thoughts. Annie and Sondra were back.

"Thank you, Annie, for being my butt friend. Oops, I mean best friend," Sondra laughed.

"I won't say 'any time.' Although if yoga keeps your butt that toned—it's my new hobby. James is a fool to pass on that!"

Her best friends. A wave of gratitude almost knocked Jo over. "Annie, you amaze me with your humor. What's the verdict? Poison ivy?"

"Not sure, too early to tell if the red is from scratching."

"Well, I'm done scratching my head trying to put this tent together. It had to be created by some overzealous man. Look!" Jo pointed to the mess. "And no directions to be found."

Annie searched through their gear. "Did you check this?" She held up an envelope from Sondra's backpack.

Sondra snatched the envelope. "There it is. I was afraid I'd lost it. An important real estate deal."

"You brought it on this trip?"

"I meant to leave it at home." Sondra shoved it into her back pocket. "Let me take a look. My dad might have thrown them away. He unwrapped it for us, so we didn't have to deal with the packaging."

"I appreciate his good heart. However, the tent was your responsibility. Therefore, you get the pleasure of putting it together.

I'm sure Annie can help you. I'll go get firewood," Jo said.

"Hold on! I just completed my last act of charity! You told me to stop being a martyr. Why don't you help, Sondra?"

"You and Dan camp a lot. You'll do a better job than me. But if you prefer, I can build a fort with branches, like when we were kids. Remember?"

"I still have nightmares about our sleepover in your fort. Those ravenous mosquitoes swarming over us, delighted to discover their dinner."

"And don't forget all the screaming and running to reach Thelma's house before a bear caught us. I'm making an executive decision. No tent created by Jo. Annie, if you can deal with my butt—a tent should be a piece of cake. Right?"

"Absolutely. We'll make it gorgeous. Jo, go have fun gathering firewood."

"I'm happy to do that. But I did love my forts." Jo huffed loudly as she hiked off into the woods, acting offended.

# CHAPTER THIRTY-FIVE

JO FELT HER BODY CALMING down. Interesting. She hadn't realized she'd been holding onto tension. She needed to be alone to process her feelings. But first, the firewood. Look for wood that would burn cleanly. Great for cooking and conversation. Perfect. A fallen tree. The large branches were easy to snap off. It didn't take long before her arms were full and aching from the weight. Time to head back.

Wait—the light changed between a clump of birch trees, indicating an opening. She walked closer. There it was—a perfect dream spot. Soft, wild grass had sprouted up. A fallen tree trunk covered with moss waited for her. Louie was the only person she had ever shared her special spots with. They would lie down together and meditate, trying out-of-body techniques to let their spirits soar above the trees.

Annie and Sondra were right: Louie was a good man. He loved Annie and Sondra too and had been a big part of their lives. That question again. Why the divorce? Could her stubborn inability to overcome her shame be the answer? The thought stung—the venom stronger than a rattlesnake bite.

This was a sacred place. Jo needed to honor its energy. She leaned her back against the fallen tree and visualized walking through the veil. The mist between this world and the one that couldn't be seen with human eyes. A pulsing sensation, stronger than her heartbeat, pumped through her veins. Louie must be thinking of her.

A breeze gathered strength and transformed into Louie's arms circling around her, loving her. The wind became his hands stroking her skin, his lips caressing hers. She loved the way he loved her. He could be gentle and soft or strong and wild. Without effort, the barriers around her love for Louie began evaporating. She sank into the feeling and consciously willed the universe to send her love to Louie.

A shout broke Jo's trance. Now a lot of cursing. Annie and Sondra. It sounded like trouble. Jo silently thanked the universe and Mother Earth for their help. She gathered up the firewood and hustled back to the campsite.

Annie and Sondra were pounding the last corner stake into the ground. They were grinning, covered in sweat and dirt, full of pride.

"We did it!" Sondra proclaimed.

Jo stared at the misshapen tent. Branches helped to support the poles holding up the sides. Annie's rocks were piled on the corners to anchor the tent down. One strong wind and they'd be clinging to the tent like a parachute.

Jo dumped the wood next to the fire pit. "I'm speechless. What is it?"

"Our home for the night. At least it will keep the mosquitoes out," Sondra said.

Annie stepped backward. She tipped her head side to side, admiring it. "I think it's very artistic."

"More like yin and yang," Jo said, tilting her own head.

"I love it, very Zen." Sondra high-fived Annie. "To my Zen buddy."

"Okay, Zen and butt buddies, how about dinner?" Jo said. "My stomach is grumbling. What's on the menu?"

Annie opened up the small cooler. "Looks like hot dogs, sweet potatoes, and an assortment of exotic beverages."

"Gross. A hot dog? I'm afraid to ask what an exotic beverage is," Sondra said.

Jo peered into the cooler. "Juice boxes! We also have water, tea, and coffee. Where are the matches?"

"I didn't pack any. I thought you were going to. We better find them. There's no way I'm eating a cold hot dog," Sondra said.

"Maybe you stuck them in that envelope you're hiding," Annie suggested. "I can check."

"I'll look." Sondra looked inside. Those awful photos. Why did she bring them? Did she unconsciously want to torture herself? It was obvious that Annie was suspicious. "No matches—but they were on our checklist."

"In that case, I've done my butt and tent duty. You two can figure it out," Annie said. "I'm heading down to the river to clean up. Be back in a bit."

Jo and Sondra watched Annie disappear down the path.

"I can't believe we forgot the matches. It won't be pleasant in the woods tonight without a fire. Plus, we packed s'mores. It's not the same without a melted marshmallow," Jo grumbled.

"At least I was smart and remembered my phone. We can search how to start a fire without matches."

"I didn't bring mine because there isn't any reception out here."

"What if something happened to the kids? How would they contact you?"

"Thelma would find a way or send Louie."

"Well, I do have a Blackberry and it should work anywhere." Sondra pulled her phone out of a watertight container. She tried to connect to the Internet—nothing. "Okay, you're right about one thing. But I have the flashlight app. We'll be able to see in the dark."

"So now you're okay with cold hot dogs?"

"Let's use Annie's rocks. Rub them together like in the movies."

"I think you've lived in Hollywood too long."

"Do you have a better idea, Miss Smarty Pants?"

Jo carefully picked up two rocks from a corner. "Whoever gets the fire going first gets to sleep in the middle."

"Why the middle?"

"Those poles don't look very sturdy. A bear could grab anyone from the side."

A bear? Another thing to be afraid of. Damn it. Sondra gathered up dry grass, small twigs, and two rocks from Annie's collection.

"I know you're making up the story about the bear. I'm not that naïve. But remember our plan. Annie relaxing by the campfire while we coax her to share her story?" Sondra hit the rocks against each other. "So, stop watching me and start trying."

"All right." Jo gathered grass and twigs and joined Sondra.

•

Annie could hear the sound of rocks smacking against each other. What were they doing? She snuck up behind them. Really? They were hitting rocks together? Their arms must be getting sore. Time to show them a thing or two.

She grabbed two rocks and knelt beside them, then struck

her rocks together with a soft, sliding motion. A spark flew onto the twigs, blossoming into a flame. Annie fed it more twigs, then added larger sticks.

"Showoff," Jo muttered.

"I told you they were my friends."

"I'm impressed," Sondra said.

"Den mother for the Boy Scouts. I learned a few things, including how to survive a bunch of overexcited boys constantly trying to outdo each other."

"I appreciate it. By the way, I call dibs on the right side of the tent," Sondra announced.

"Why would you do that?" Annie asked.

"There's less space for a bear to fit there by that tree."

"I don't even need to ask."

# CHAPTER THIRTY-SIX

SONDRA DEVOURED HER SWEET POTATO. Why couldn't it satisfy her hunger? She was still ravenous, her stomach begging for more. Could she actually eat a hot dog on a carb-loaded white bun? The boys had packed extra hot dogs instead of vegetables. Jo and Annie looked delighted as they roasted their second one. Sondra sucked on the straw of her juice box. Actually, it was pretty good, but couldn't compare to the cheap wine they used to pass around the campfire.

There was that small bottle of scotch her dad had bequeathed her, in case of an emergency. Her dad, Jack—what an incredible surprise. The awkward dad suddenly super-cool. Was this an emergency? Probably not. She reminded herself of her new, unbreakable rule: no more drinking on an empty stomach.

A perfectly charred hot dog on a stick appeared in front of Sondra. Annie. In her other hand was a bun. "It's 100 percent beef."

"I haven't eaten meat in years that wasn't free-range, organic, and prepared by a top chef. And carbs? Totally taboo in L.A."

"Skip the bun and eat it off the stick. Pretend it's James, for God's sake. You know what to do."

"I can't believe you said that!"

"Just because I'm the pastor's wife doesn't mean that I don't like sex."

"Quite obvious—four boys."

"I can't believe that, after all the guys you've been with, you're terrified to put a hot dog in your mouth."

"Hey, you're my Zen butt buddy, remember? You promised not to pick on me anymore."

"I'll take the Zen part. You keep your butt. Now eat. I know you're hungry. I hear your stomach growling all the way across the campfire."

Damn. The hot dog smelled good. Sondra grabbed the bun and shoved the hot dog into it. She could do this. *Eat quickly. Don't think about it.*

Jo sauntered over and squirted mustard on Sondra's hot dog. "Here, this will make it easier. Think of it as a lubricant."

"You two are furiously persistent. I'm not sure if you're funny or mean!"

"Persistent and definitely funny. Now gobble that hot dog up. It's your time to confess. You promised. Remember?"

"Can I do a dare instead?"

"We're too old for that. We all have to confess. No judgment, only support," Annie said.

Shit. Jo and Annie both looked serious, with arms crossed over their chests. Might as well slam the hot dog down. Start the horror show. Sondra closed her eyes and took a few bites. Doable. The mustard helped. Focus on that. Three more bites. No more. She tossed the remains in the fire. Her stomach lurched. It wasn't the hot dog—it was the confession.

Sondra put her head into her hands. What words to speak? So far, they had only been in her head. Nothing spoken out loud to make it real. Words that she might have to repeat to James, her father, and others. How could she trust those obscene pictures would disappear, even if she paid the blackmail money? But she could trust her two best friends. If she couldn't tell them, then she was truly lost.

"The client that I slept with, I actually began having feelings for. That's what makes it harder. I've avoided temptation from some of the hottest guys in Hollywood. I'm mad at myself that after years of therapy, I still ended up cheating on James."

"Wasn't James enough for you?" Annie asked.

"Enough? There was the companionship, a great social life, house, money. But the sex, along with the physical intimacy, disappeared. Lots of promises with no follow-through. Maybe three times in the past two years. I missed being touched, held, and reassured that I wasn't alone in this world. It was hard. Wait—it wasn't hard!" Sondra looked up. "That was a joke."

Annie touched Sondra's hand in support. "Kind of a sad one. Being alone is difficult."

"Being alone is okay. Feeling alone sucks. My thoughts haunt me. My mind digs up every regret. I was frustrated and confused. I wanted to have sex, to feel that high, to feel beautiful and sexy. But it wasn't happening with my husband. I was contemplating a sexless marriage. Then this guy came along and took advantage of me."

"Took advantage? How is that possible? You're too savvy for that. Perhaps deep down, you wanted a reason to leave James," Jo pressed.

"Not at this expensive cost." Shoot. Another slip. How to cover it up? Sondra licked a drop of mustard off her fingers, stalling for a moment. She'd have to open herself up more. Be vulnerable. That would distract them. "Maybe you're right. Deep down, I was imagining a different life. One with this guy. But it was all a game. He knew I was lonely and became exactly what I needed. My karma came back to me. I've used guys for sex in the past. That's what he did to me. He was already in a relationship. Things are really screwed up. I'm not sure what to do next."

"God forgives you, no matter what. I'm sure James loves you. If you're afraid he's going to find out, then tell him first. Open up the conversation that you need about the future," Annie said.

"I do believe James loves me, but is it the right kind of love? Even though this guy was a fake, it showed me what I was missing. You're right. I need to tell my husband. Otherwise, I'll be controlled the rest of my life." Darn. Another clue. No more mustard to lick off her hands.

"I didn't know James was a control freak. You're too smart to live with that. Maybe you should be thinking about a divorce," Jo said.

"Divorce is a huge decision. Not something to rush into. And Jo, I don't think you're doing it for the right reasons," Annie said.

"Don't be shy in telling me how you feel, Annie," Jo retorted.

"We said complete honesty. And Sondra, I'm sure if you're really honest, James will forgive you."

"But how do I forgive myself? Just ask God? Is that what you're going to do? Do you really believe that or is that Dan talking? Because if you believe it, then God forgives you too."

"In some religions they don't forgive suicides, even if they're accidental," Annie said.

"Screw that!" Jo proclaimed. "God did not create religion, man did. God created the Earth, the sky, human beings to love and care about each other. And don't doubt for a moment that God forgives you too, Annie. He doesn't need to forgive you, he understands. And one last thing—I didn't hear Sondra say, even once, that she was happy with James. Only that the trimmings were enough."

Annie felt a jolt of recognition and exploded into laughter.

"Excuse me. What's so funny about that?"

"You sound like a pastor! However, that means God understands you, too." Annie gasped between bouts of laughter.

"So now you have to have the last word, like Sondra?" Jo exclaimed, hands on hips.

Annie pulled herself together. She knew Jo's posture. "It was a really good sermon."

Jo dropped her pose. "Thanks. It was pretty good. Your turn, Annie."

"Hold on. Sondra has a little more to tell before I confess."

Sondra sucked up the last of her juice box. Maybe if she had mixed some scotch in it, she would feel more courageous. But then liquid courage always evaporated the following day. "What's up with you two? Did you both develop psychic powers?"

"I spent a lot of time with my grandmother and Thelma. You can imagine what I learned, hanging out with a pastor's wife and a healer."

Feeling trapped, Sondra rubbed her eyes, wishing the action could erase her memory. Should she tell them about the blackmail? They were intuitive and hard to fool, but this trip was about Annie. Once it was out, they'd spend the rest of the night trying to solve her problem. Better to sacrifice her pride. Provide one more distraction. "Okay, you caught on that I don't feel good about myself right now. Something happened."

"You hooked us. Keep going," Jo said.

"First of all, I'm sorry that I'm terrible about keeping in touch.

My excuses sound shallow, false. In L.A, things are different. The pace is crazy and everyone, including myself, becomes self-centered. Therefore, in order to earn your forgiveness, I'm willing to share my humiliation."

"Bring it on. We're waiting," Annie responded.

"It'd been months since James and I had sex. My vibrator became my best friend. He even has a name—Tony. After another disappointing night, I took out my vibrator. But I made a huge mistake." Sondra stood up for dramatic effect. "I glanced in the mirror right when I had an orgasm. I looked like this!" She scrunched up her facial muscles and made a grotesque face.

Sure enough, Annie and Jo looked horrified, then hung onto each other, howling with laughter.

Jo crossed her legs and stumbled around. "Stop! I'm going to pee my pants."

Annie doubled over, laughing, and sank to her knees, holding her stomach. "I'm going to get a cramp."

"That's enough!" Sondra clapped her hands to get their attention. "I bet you don't look great having an orgasm either."

"After seeing your face, I'm never going to look in the mirror!" Jo stood still, took a deep breath, and slowly uncrossed her legs.

"Me neither." Annie brushed tears from her face.

Sondra pulled Annie to her feet. She'd said enough. For now. "Okay, Annie. I've humiliated myself. It's time for you to spill your guts. Bring it on. My turn to laugh."

"Don't count on that. It's depressing. We need a cup of tea. Let's see if Thelma packed anything for that." Annie pulled out tea bags and sniffed them. "Peppermint. That should lift us up." She pulled the metal teapot off the fire.

Annie twirled her tea bag in her cup. Where to start? Her explanation didn't have to be perfect. Actually, how could it be?

*Start somewhere, even if it's a confusing stream of consciousness. Get the words out. Loosen the power they hold over your dark emotions.* It could feel like sunshine brightening a dark room. She tossed her tea bag into the fire and took a sip. *Fortification. Be brave.*

"These past few months, I kept falling into this well of sorrow. I had no intention or desire to go there. I lost myself, my soul. Who I really was. It happened slowly over the years. I gave pieces of myself away to help others, leaving no time for playing the piano, writing songs—the list goes on. I wasn't angry. Everyone was grateful and it felt good. But then it changed. This sadness crept in. It was persistent. I expected Dan to see my misery and rescue me. Why couldn't he see how much I gave up for him and the church? Didn't he miss the old me? I became so angry with him."

The words sank into Annie's soul. *The truth. Don't stop and analyze them. Let them pour out.* "I'm sure your question is like everyone else's. Did I attempt suicide? Maybe I did. Maybe I didn't. Whatever it was, it wasn't deliberate or conscious. I was sliding down a dark path. I did pray to God, but no answer. He didn't seem to be anywhere, at least for me. I wanted to blame someone, anyone, including me."

Annie looked into the flames dancing in the fire. The words were finally out. A pressure pulsated in her chest. Fear. Annie finished her tea and set it aside. She could do this. Three deep breaths.

"What really freaks me out is that I could have died. If I had—would my kids think it happened on purpose? That they weren't enough for me? I keep thinking these awful thoughts. How in one split second, a person can accidentally take one extra pill, or take a gun and not mean to pull the trigger. And it could be too late. If Dan hadn't found me, half-naked and unconscious on the floor—would I be here tonight?"

Annie looked at their faces, brimming with compassion. Her shoulders hunched over, protecting her heart from the emotional pain. She wrapped her arms around herself. "I never knew how serious depression could become. I'm grateful that I got the chance to live. But I'm scared. How am I going to deal with everything and everyone? I don't want to go back to that dark place. Alone, and incredibly sad."

"Annie, I'm so sorry that I didn't come and see you sooner. I wasn't a good friend," Sondra whispered.

"I'm sorry, too." Jo reached out and touched Annie's shoulder.

"It's nobody's fault, maybe not even my own. The doctor called it a situational crisis and thought the pills would help. They dampened the sharp edges of my emotions. But they didn't solve my problems. I'm realizing how much I needed to talk. Somehow the sadness morphed into depression. If you can top my shame, you're welcome to it. I'll gladly take second place."

"There's no shame in that. Not like my cheating," Sondra said.

"Or my getting drunk while taking care of the girls and putting my family in danger," Jo added. "You're here now. Alive. With us."

"I'm so grateful. One lesson learned is that hints don't work. I haven't been clear about what I needed. But then again, I'm still not completely sure what I need. Shit, I'm getting depressed hearing myself talk. Quick, somebody cheer me up!"

Sondra and Jo were quiet.

"This is a first. Nobody is going to compete? Find out who is funnier?"

Jo and Sondra shook their heads.

"Then I'll tell you about my hilarious disguise. When I started taking more pills, I didn't want to go back to my regular doctor. Instead, I went to neighboring pharmacies and even a free clinic. I had this funky outfit with huge sunglasses, a long black wig from Halloween, topped with a big, floppy gardening hat from a Goodwill store."

"You sound like a movie star trying not to be recognized," Sondra said. "I've got to see it when we get home."

"Too late. The outfit is in the trash. I'm embarrassed thinking about it. But I'll admit, it made me feel kind of sexy. Like I was a mysterious person, wearing a disguise, and nobody recognized me. It was a treat after having to behave like the perfect pastor's wife every place I go."

"I can share a little bit about disguises," Jo said.

"Perfect. I've shared enough for one night! I sound pathetic."

"You sound like a loving, caring person," Sondra said.

"Thanks."

"Get over here. I promise not to squeeze too hard." Jo gave Annie a gentle hug. "What's your plan if you start feeling depressed again?"

"I'll be working with a therapist, but I'm open to your advice."

Jo resonated with the topic. "Take it one day, one hour, or on a bad day—one minute at a time. The famous AA motto. It's powerful. I remind myself the feeling will pass. In treatment, we created a list of things to do to shift our attention. Some of my favorites are dancing with the kids, going for a walk, going to the gym, putting on upbeat music and singing along. It's different for everyone. Personally, I have to get out of my head and into my body to overcome the cravings. I even took up kickboxing. Check out these moves."

Jo bounced around the firepit, boxing with the shadows of the flames. She kicked her leg to the side. A painful twinge from the damn hamstring. Not good. She'd better sit.

"That's quite impressive, but I'll pass on that. There's enough fighting between the boys. Sondra, any words of wisdom?"

"Even with my expensive years of therapy, my brain can act like a hamster, running around and around on the same thought. I learned the 'STOP' method, where I put my hand up in the air and actually say, 'Stop!' Then I ask if my thought serves me. The answer is always no. Then I praise myself for stopping and choose how I want to feel. I pick an emotion, like, 'I choose confidence.' Then of course, there's my yoga. It integrates my body, mind, and spirit. If all that fails, then I try to change my environment." Sondra looked around at the forest surrounding them. "We achieved that tonight."

Annie stood up. "Those are great. I can sing and dance. And now I even have yoga. Check me out." Annie went into a warrior pose, with her arms pointing straight at Jo. "You, it's time to confess about your disguise and cheating on Louie."

"I don't consider it cheating. Our divorce will be final in a few months."

"Is that what you really want?" Sondra asked.

"Do I get to tell my story or not?" Jo regretted bringing up the disguise. It wasn't funny anymore. But they had agreed to confess, which meant complete honesty. She could at least try to make it sound like fun.

Sondra nodded her head. "Sorry, go ahead. But interrogation is part of the process."

"I'll keep that in mind. So—there was this guy at an AA meeting. I know it was wrong, so no lectures! He was a hat man, with a good imagination for playing games. I wore a cowboy hat, if that gives you an idea."

"Okay, stop with the sex story. Don't make me jealous. That's just a game. What's your true confession?" Sondra asked.

"When I got the call about Annie, everything changed. My world slammed to a stop. I had been in high gear, staying busy, not wanting to think about the divorce. I'd convinced myself that it would be easier to walk away. Have a clean start. But it's amazing. These past few days, being back home—it's offered a different perspective. Life is messy and some of the best parts are in the mess. They become the cherished stories."

Jo looked inside her cup of tea. The scent of peppermint encouraged her, giving her a message. She closed her eyes and took a sip, letting it slide down her throat, clearing her voice. *Keep talking.* A revelation was going to occur through her words. Her body shivered in response.

"I've made my amends to a lot of people, but not to Louie. I didn't know why. After I saw Thelma, I went to the cemetery and talked to my dad. I know it sounds weird, but you know me. The anger I'd buried with him—for letting alcohol take his life from us—erupted. But once I released it, there was this surreal moment of forgiveness. It opened me up. The distortions are disappearing. Running away from my marriage was easier than facing all my mistakes. There wasn't any alcohol to numb the pain." The truth felt like fireworks exploding within her body.

Jo looked down at her trembling hands. She rubbed them together, then shook them. Thelma's technique to shake off old energy. She stood up, shook her arms and legs, then stomped her feet on the ground.

"Are you okay?" Sondra asked.

"I had to ground myself there. You do yoga—you get it." Jo found a large stick, then grabbed a marshmallow out of the bag, the one next to the graham crackers and chocolate bars close to Annie. She shoved the marshmallow on the end of the stick and began to roast it. "I need some sugar to continue. Here, indulge with me." Jo passed the bag to Annie. "We can prep for our s'mores."

"Happy to join you. Keep sharing." Annie said.

"That isn't enough?"

Sondra shook her head. "Not even close."

"Fine." Jo sat and looked into the flames again. "It's been hard to forgive myself for my drinking and destruction. The burden is heavy, even though I've worked the steps. People have forgiven me. But I still struggle to forgive myself. The guilt comes up out of nowhere. Sometimes it feels like yesterday, when I hit rock bottom."

Jo's hand trembled again. What was going on? What was in that tea? Her lips trembled as she vomited up her words. "Somewhere inside of my soul, I want to continue to beat myself up. I don't deserve to be happy. I'm not sure that I love myself. I reject things that make me happy, except for my daughters."

"What?" Annie stood up, unable to stop her growing frustration. "First of all, I think that's your ego talking and not your soul. And secondly, are you really going to take out that shovel and dig up that old shit? It's already become fertilizer. You are amazing, loving, and stronger than ever! You accused me of being a martyr. You're doing the same number on yourself."

Jo's jaw dropped. "There's my Annie, with one of her famous 'Annie-isms.' It's about time she showed up!"

"Yes, I'm here. Ladies, after hearing all of our sad stories—I believe it's time we reinvent ourselves!" Annie pulled her shoulders back and stuck out her chin. She felt powerful. Time to show them—she still had it. Wait—her marshmallow was burning. She grabbed her stick and blew out the flames.

Annie strutted around the campfire, striking a few sexy poses. What song fit the mood? She'd always loved listening to Dionne Warwick singing, 'I'll Never Fall in Love Again.' Perfect. Make up her own words, like she did with her dad. Bring on the show.

A few more struts and go!

"Guess what I got when I fell in love? A household of boys who never help me, and a husband who forgot the real me. But I'm still in love with him. Yes, I still love all of them."

Annie swung around. She felt wild! Her marshmallow flew off her stick, barely missing Jo. She grabbed another marshmallow and reloaded her stick.

Annie's joy was contagious. Not wanting to miss out on the fun, Jo grabbed her marshmallow stick. The perfect microphone. "Guess what I got when I fell in love? Flabby boobs but two great kids. Maybe it's time that I forgive, so I'll probably love again. Yes! I'm still in love with him."

Jo bumped her hip into Annie's, sharing their secret stare. The one they used whenever Sondra wanted to sing. Annie shook her head.

Jo glanced at Sondra. Oops. Sondra had caught their exchange and looked crestfallen. Oh, what the heck. Her eardrums would heal. Jo handed the stick to Sondra.

Sondra knew she was the butt of their singing jokes. So what? She didn't care. She loved to sing, even if she was out of tune. Annie was right. It was time to reinvent themselves. Step into that abundant field of confidence! She shoved two marshmallows on her stick then climbed on top of a sawed-off tree trunk. Belt it out. Torture them if necessary. "Guess what I got when I fell in love?"

Jo and Annie covered their ears and grimaced.

"Knock it off! You have to listen. This is the best one. Now I have to start over." Sondra took off her marshmallows and whipped them at Annie and Jo. "Guess what I got when I fell in love? An older man who doesn't want me, and a vibrator who still loves me. But I hope that James can really love me again. But I know that I'll love my vibrator again."

Annie had a flash of intuition. What was inside that envelope Sondra was hiding? If Sondra was in trouble, would she tell them? Probably not. Sondra would be too afraid of upsetting her. Annie needed a plan. Sondra still had to be hungry. Annie made a few s'mores, put them on a plate, and walked over to Sondra.

Annie picked up a s'more and took a huge bite. The gooey marshmallow spilled out the sides. "I forgot how good these tasted. I always thought they should be considered a sin." Annie moaned and groaned with pleasure. Another bite. Drip a little marshmallow onto Sondra's hair. "Oops. Sorry. I didn't mean to spill on you. Oh, did you want one?"

"You just got marshmallow in my hair! You better share one after doing that!" Sondra tried to pull the marshmallow out.

"After you finish telling us what else is going on. Otherwise, no s'more for you." Annie held the plate over her head and turned to Jo. "Jo, would you like one?"

Jo hustled over and grabbed one. She took a bite, slowly licking the chocolate off her lips. "You're right, Annie. This is better than sex. The richness of the marshmallow and chocolate melted together. It swirls around your mouth and ends with a satisfying crunch."

"Come on. I confessed everything." Sondra stood up. She tried to grab a s'more, but Annie spun around and avoided her reach.

"No, you didn't. You forget that I'm a mom. I'm highly trained to sniff out half-truths and lies."

"You two probably didn't confess everything either. Everyone here is a little confused. So, give!" Sondra reached for the plate as Annie handed it off to Jo.

"See! You admitted that you didn't tell the whole truth. Isn't that right, Jo?"

"Absolutely."

Sondra lunged for the plate, but Jo deftly passed it back to Annie.

"There isn't much more to tell. I need nourishment to think clearly. Now give me one!"

Sondra leaped to the side, attempting to intercept the plate as Annie passed it back to Jo. Sondra was faster this time and caught the edge. She almost had it. No! The plate soared into the air. The s'mores separated and performed acrobatic twists before landing. Pieces scattered on top of Annie's head...then Jo's...then her own.

Sondra scraped a chunk of the mixture from her forehead and shoved it into her mouth. "Delicious, but I'll still need my friend, Tony."

Annie reached up. Pieces were smeared all over her head. "This feels worse than having gum stuck in your hair."

Jo removed a few pieces sliding down the side of her face. "It still tastes good, maybe a new conditioner for the ladies in L.A.? What do you think, Sondra?"

"Hmm...let me see." Sondra scraped off another chunk and tasted it. "It tastes good, smells good, but it's stickier than the worst lie we've ever told."

"Ladies—you know what this means?" Annie said. "Skinny-dipping!"

"But I don't want to get wet again," Sondra complained. Now, this was an emergency. She pulled the scotch out of her gear bag. "It's going to feel cold. Do you mind if I indulge in a little liquid courage?"

Jo picked chocolate out of Annie's hair. "Go for it. I've got my nightcap here."

Annie snatched the flask out of Sondra's hands and took a big gulp.

"Wow, that's wicked. Where'd you get that?"

"Dad gave it to me. It's top-shelf."

Annie took another sip.

Jo grabbed the flask away from her. "Hey, you shouldn't be doing that!"

"Lighten up. It was pills, not liquor, and it was an accident." Annie grabbed it, took another swig, then handed it back to Sondra. "The communion wine is better." She winked at Sondra, then took off running. "Last one to the river has to clean up the mess."

# CHAPTER THIRTY-SEVEN

ANNIE MADE IT TO THE river first. Sondra and Jo scrambled down the bank, pushing and shoving each other. They were a riot to watch.

"I won!" Jo exclaimed.

"No way. I had you by a good foot."

"I declare a tie," Annie announced. "But does it matter? Look."

The moonlight shimmered on the water. It looked magical.

"It's beautiful, but it was cold earlier." Sondra drank some of the scotch, then set the flask on the riverbank. "Whoa, that is strong stuff. Okay, no peeking. I'm very sensitive about how my butt looks right now. I can't handle you making fun of me."

"Don't worry about that. I have a saggy belly after all the boys. No amount of Pilates or crunches made it go away."

"Let's turn around. I'll count to ten while we strip." Jo started counting.

They stripped down and raced into the river, shrieking as the frigid water hit their bare skin.

Sondra gasped. "It's freezing!"

"My boobs perked up for the first time in years," Jo said.

"It's cold because we've been sitting around a warm fire built by incredible me. And yes, you're welcome. Don't forget all the heat we got by spending a little time in hell, sharing our stories."

"We're in heaven now. Paddle around. You'll warm up," Jo said.

"Except that I have to get this marshmallow out of my hair. Thanks to Annie, who started it all," Sondra muttered.

"Stop being a baby." Annie ducked under the water and came up with sand in her hand. "Here, I'll help you scrub it out." Annie swam over and rubbed the sand into Sondra's hair. "Time to rinse." She reached out and dunked Sondra under the water.

Sondra came up sputtering, "Who are you? I thought you were depressed? Now all you do is joke and pick on me!"

"I'm sorry. I feel high on being naked and liberated in this water. This is happiness. I want to hold onto this feeling forever!" Annie disappeared under the water, doing somersaults. She surfaced, exhilarated. "I can still do five in a row!"

"I want to try!" Sondra thrashed beneath the surface, then popped up, coughing water. "I did two until something slimy scraped against my leg."

"Probably a carp. A bunch were swimming in this hole when we pulled the canoes up," Jo said.

"How big were those carp?" Sondra asked.

"They were small. You weren't afraid of them as a kid. Why start now?"

"You're right. Let's be fearless and float on our backs like we used to." Sondra flipped over on her back and looked up into the star-studded sky. "Annie, you're right, this is happiness."

Annie pointed at the sky. "I think that was a shooting star."

Jo joined them. "I missed it. Where?"

"Which one? There are millions of them tonight," Sondra said. It felt incredible. The peacefulness and sensation of the water and the sky blended together.

"Please tell me a happy story. I'm starting to feel sad," Annie requested, breaking the silence.

"Why would you feel sad?" Sondra asked.

"You're both leaving in a few days."

"Did I ever tell you my dirty dancing story?" Jo asked.

"First, it's a cowboy hat, now dirty dancing?" Sondra exclaimed.

"Get your mind out of the sex shop. This is a nice story. Louie and I had watched the movie *Dirty Dancing* together. We loved it and went to the movie three times. Well, at least I loved it and he pretended to. I wanted to try that lift, so we canoed to where we had lunch today. It was a full moon. The forest was illuminated with all the moonlight. There was so much energy in the air, even the daytime animals were up, moving around."

"Weren't you afraid of skunks, wolves, or even bears?" Sondra asked.

"Not at all. I swear the animals loved the music and were dancing with us. We had brought one of those huge boom boxes to play the song track. We practiced that lift in the water over and over. Louie would lift me over his head like a professional dancer and spin me around. I remember looking at the sky and seeing all the stars—just like tonight."

"That's the most romantic thing you've given Louie credit for," Sondra said.

"What are you—" Jo was interrupted by a snap coming from the forest on the opposite bank. A loud crash. "Insinuating—" A louder snap, as if a large branch was breaking.

Sondra pointed toward a shadow, growing bigger. Creating crashing sounds as it approached.

"A bear?" Sondra ran out of the water, screaming. She grabbed her clothes and lurched toward the campsite.

"Wait for me. Jo can be the bait!" Annie shouted, running out of the water.

Jo could hear their screams ripping through the air. That noise would scare off any bear. She squinted her eyes and tried to make out the shadow. Another snap. Now heavy breathing. Shit—maybe it was a bear. She let out an involuntary scream as she raced out of the water.

# CHAPTER THIRTY-EIGHT

Annie added wood to the fire, transforming it from a gentle blaze to roaring flames. One more piece. Perfect. Enough light was cast about the site. That should offer reassurance that nothing would approach them. Well—at least they would see it coming. Annie turned her naked backside to the fire. She closed her eyes and enjoyed the heat stroking her body. It was enrapturing.

"I can see you're not modest now," Jo commented, gingerly putting on her jeans. That hamstring was twitching. She hadn't been able to rest it. Why hadn't she brought old sweatpants?

"I'm completely liberated. With four boys in the house, the only time I get to be naked is in the shower or having sex with Dan. But damn it, I really have to pee."

Sondra tied the laces of her running shoes. "You're going to be a party for the mosquitoes unless you get dressed. At least I'm prepared if something chases us."

"Shoot. I left my shoes by the river. I better not leave them overnight. I'm sure whatever animal that was, it's gone by now. Be right back." Jo zipped up her pants. *Just walk slow. Don't limp or they'll notice and baby you.* Right now—she felt a need to be alone again. Something was pulling at her.

Annie reluctantly put on her clothes. "Wish me luck, since nobody packed any repellent."

"That was on Jo's list. You're not going to leave me alone, are you?" Sondra asked.

"You're a big girl. I'd suggest cleaning up the s'more mess—even though you tied with Jo. Better to suck it up than have the sugar attracting unwanted friends. If you hear noises, do your warrior yoga moves. You'll scare that bear off—if that's what it was."

Sondra watched Annie disappear into the woods. Really? She surveyed the s'more mess. She'd seen worse. She could deal with it. But what was that rattling noise? She went into a warrior pose and was rewarded by a breeze caressing her face. It was just the wind. But another log on the fire wouldn't hurt.

·

Jo looked up at the moon. It had risen higher. The frogs were in full voice, croaking loudly to attract a mate. Was that an owl in that tree? It would be fun to share this with Louie, Jessica, and Hunter. She hadn't even thought about things like that. She'd been focusing so much on the negative and what could go wrong. When was she going to change?

Jo took a deep breath and relaxed her shoulders. She hadn't even realized how tight she was. Her shoes? She spied them—there by Sondra's flask. Jo opened it and smelled it. Scotch. It used to take the edge off. It had even tricked her into believing she was more creative with it.

What a shitload of lies. She wasn't that person anymore. That edge. It could be painful and uncomfortable, but it was part of being fully present and alive. Jo took one last sniff. She felt powerful with her choice, whipping it across the river. Yes.

Jo looked up at the stars and shouted, "Yes, I still love Louie." What? Tears again? What the hell. Her spirit guides weren't going to let her out of this one. Time to release all the toxins building up inside of her. This time the tears were frustration for the pain she had caused Louie. But like Annie said—acknowledge her strength in fighting her way back to sobriety. She was here and had a chance at this crossroads right now.

A hand on her shoulder. Jo looked up. Annie.

"Rub those tears in. They're good for you."

"You and Sondra are right. Louie is a good guy. I pushed him away because I didn't feel worthy of him. He was stronger than me. He could stop drinking and I couldn't. I'm sorry. I sound like such a whiner."

Annie sat beside her. "No, you don't. I'm sad that you carried that weight all by yourself. I could have been there for you."

"There you go again, ready to sacrifice yourself. You need to be there for you. All the choices I made and will make are mine. I know it and own it. I should have been there for you, instead of wallowing in this poor-me stuff."

"You were busy fighting a disease, raising two little girls, and holding down a job. I wouldn't call that wallowing. Plus, guilt is exhausting. Forgiveness is a gift you can give to yourself, whether you believe in God or not. Think of the positives, like, at the top of the list, what a good mother you are. I'm going to have to live those words myself."

"It isn't easy, Annie. Alcoholism is like having a friend who's actually an evil wizard in disguise. He makes you laugh, play, and dance. Then, when you least expect it, he stabs you in the back. It hurts a little, but you forget because he's fun to be with. The trap is set. Slowly, you begin to feel powerless to fight back. You ignore that you're hurting people you care about. Yet—eventually, you have to choose to give up or fight and stab him back."

"Well, I'm glad you decided to stab that wizard."

"Annie, you're the best. Thanks for not dying."

"We're both lucky. A few inches to the right—I could have sliced my head open."

"I believe it's time we leave our fuckups behind. Don't give them any more power."

"Is that an AA saying? I like it."

"I heard something similar in a movie and instinctively related to it."

"I relate, too. Let's help each other." Annie leaned her shoulder against Jo's. She felt blessed by the depth of their friendship. Maybe God had been listening to her, after all.

Their peace was interrupted by Sondra's scream. Jo jumped up and looked around for a big stick.

"Relax. She probably found the frog I put in her sleeping bag."

"That's why I love you, Annie."

"Love you too, Jo."

# CHAPTER THIRTY-NINE

ANNIE CRAWLED OUT OF HER sleeping bag. Her dream had manifested itself. The first one up, with no plans but to enjoy the day. She stirred the remains of last night's fire. Awesome, there were still embers. A good sign. Breakfast time. She heated up water for tea and coffee and found a muffin. Blueberry lemon? She took a bite. It melted in her mouth. Delicious. A rustling from the tent. Jo emerged. A happy sight. "Good morning. How are you doing?"

"Emotionally, great. Physically, another story." Jo stretched her arms and legs. "The last time I slept on the ground was when I passed out and woke up with a major hangover. I'm glad those days are over."

Jo looked over at the tent. The poles were jerking around, and the sides were shaking. Was it going to collapse? "Sondra tossed and turned all night. I hope her poison ivy didn't spread."

"I applied more lotion to her poor butt before bed. My punishment for the frog. I have plenty of ointment back home. Hopefully, seven more hours won't hurt." Annie handed Jo a muffin. "Now for the coffee." She found the packet, poured it into the cup, and mixed in the hot water. She handed it to Jo.

"You don't have to make coffee for me. Get out of your martyr role."

"Okay." Annie grabbed the cup out of Jo's hands and took a sip. "Incredible. Better than tea this morning. Find your own packet. And if you don't want that scrumptious muffin, I'll eat it. Kate still has the magic touch."

"You too? That muffin has my magic in it. I'll keep my muffin and make my own coffee." Jo dug in their food pack and held up a packet. "Score. The last one. Hope Sondra doesn't want it. But like they say—the early bird gets the worm."

"What about worms?" Sondra crawled out of bed. "No, don't tell me." Her stomach spasmed. Another wave of nausea. Sondra ran her hands through her hair. She hoped she didn't look as rough as she felt.

"Not as cushy as your bed in L.A.?" Jo asked.

"Not even close. Those hot dogs made me sick. Does anyone else have a stomachache?" Sondra bent over and groaned.

"I'm fine," Annie said.

Jo stirred her coffee into the hot water. "Maybe it was the scotch?"

"Three sips of scotch wouldn't do this."

"Maybe a blueberry muffin will calm your stomach." Annie suggested.

"Or you can have my coffee," Jo offered.

Sondra waved the coffee away. "Do we have any bottled water? The river water had a funny taste."

"You drank the water?" Annie asked.

"When we were skinny-dipping. I had to get the taste of scotch out of my mouth. Who knows how much I drank, trying to do those somersaults? Plus, if I recall—somebody dunked me."

"Sorry about the dunking. Shit. I wasn't thinking. The water isn't clean like it was years ago. You can pick up parasites."

"I saw a warning sign about giardia at the landing," Jo said.

"Giardia? What's that? It sounds like a sexual disease." Sondra felt clammy as uneasiness bore into her mind.

"I'm not sure, but they wouldn't let us in the water if it was fatal." Jo saw the fear on Sondra's face. Damn. Why hadn't she kept her mouth closed? Better to act normal, not let Sondra dwell on it. "You'll be okay. You're tough. It's probably all the gourmet food your body is missing."

"Thanks for your support, Jo. I'll go find a quiet spot in the woods now."

"Watch out for poison ivy," Annie said.

"Too late." Sondra scratched her butt as she stalked off.

## CHAPTER FORTY

JO SCANNED THE FOREST. THE tent had been struck and the canoes packed. Water had doused the fire. All set to go. Where was Sondra? Jo felt a prickly feeling run up her arms—guilt. She could have been more sensitive. It was so easy to fall back into their old relationship of exchanging barbs. Yet, Sondra was vulnerable underneath it all. Those childhood nights, sneaking out after midnight to hang out in Sondra's bedroom. The times when Sondra couldn't sleep or stop crying. Eventually, the tears dried up, Hank appeared, and Sondra developed a pretense that nothing bothered her.

Finally! Sondra, lumbering out of the forest, clutching a water bottle. She looked better.

Sondra saw Jo and Annie waiting for her. Damn. She couldn't get sick. Another spasm. No—not again. She rubbed her stomach using a circular motion. Better. Reassure her body that everything was going to be okay. Climb into the canoe and act nonchalant. Everyone gets diarrhea now and then. Right?

"Sorry I took so long. Go ahead and push off. I'll be fine."

"Do you want one of us to paddle with you?" Annie asked.

"No, that's okay. It's best if I solo it. I'm not going to provide any gassy topics for Jo to tease me about."

"Then we'll stay in front and avoid being downwind. After sleeping in the tent with no ventilation, the fresh air sure smells good," Jo said.

"See, I told you."

"As payback for that remark, we'll switch at the next stop. You can have the front and Jo gets the back," Annie promised.

Jo looked up at the sky. Still a lot of sun, but large gray clouds were gathering in the distance. "We better get going. This weather could change on us."

Annie pushed off and they started downriver. Happiness soaked into Annie's body. This was how she wanted to feel. In sync with Jo, their paddles barely causing a ripple in the water. It was so peaceful. Turtles perched on a fallen log. A family of ducks swimming in front of them. A cry of a hawk. Annie looked up, admiring as it circled above them.

"Jo, that hawk reminds me of the old Sondra. Full of spirit, soaring above her obstacles. I was never a fan of James. I wonder if Sondra thought conforming and settling down would save her. I actually think it dampened her spark," Annie said.

"Have you told her that?" Jo asked.

"Of course not. How could I assume that I was right? It annoys me when someone tells me how I feel. How can we really understand the situation until we experience it ourselves? Life doesn't end just because you make a mistake. Wait. Did I just say that?" Annie asked.

"You did. It was quite prophetic. I always hoped Sondra would find her way back to Hank."

Jo looked over her shoulder to check on Sondra. "Are you pouting back there?"

"No. I'm enjoying the beauty. Nobody is picking on me."

"We're trying to toughen you up. That way, when you face James, it won't be so hard," Jo said.

Sondra didn't reply.

"What? No joke about James not being hard? Time to take a break. The current is picking up. We're coming close to our next rapids," Annie said.

"No, it's better to keep going. I'm curious—did you pack Pepto Bismol?" Sondra asked.

Annie gestured to Jo. "Let's pull over, we need to talk." They turned the canoe sideways to block Sondra, forcing her to paddle to the riverbank with them.

Annie hopped out of the canoe and landed in the shallow water. She grabbed the bow of Sondra's canoe and pulled it onshore.

"Really, I'm fine," Sondra protested.

"Well, if I had a poison ivy butt and diarrhea, I wouldn't be fine!" Annie exclaimed.

Jo handed Sondra a bottle of water. "We didn't bring anything for diarrhea. So, you need to drink plenty of water. I added some electrolyte powder to it."

"Thanks, Jo. You must think I'm sick to be nice to me."

"I'm always nice to you! I thought you liked my joking around."

"I do. But my brain isn't working fast enough to outdo you like I usually do." Sondra forced a smile.

Annie felt Sondra's forehead. "You're running a slight fever. Jo, anything in your famous backpack for that?"

"I'm not dying," Sondra said.

"We know, but let us mother you for a moment." Jo held up a medicine bottle. "I love how this backpack has secret pouches to store things, kind of like us."

Sondra brushed away tears sliding down her face. "Dumb tears. This is your fault for making me feel sentimental."

"I'll take the blame and offer a suggestion. Why don't we agree to ban any tough acts today?"

"Is that even possible for you?" Sondra asked.

"Of course."

"Deal," Annie said. "Let's start by switching canoes. Jo, you take Sondra, who can lead us through the rapids."

"Okay, but first I need the bathroom." Sondra raced into the woods.

# CHAPTER FORTY-ONE

ANNIE'S EARS REVERBERATED WITH THE rumble of the fast-approaching rapids. A loud boom. What was that? Another boom. Thunder. Raindrops splattered down. Too late to get off the river. Annie took a deep breath and shouted, "Pull over to the right bank once we get through."

Sondra raised her paddle, indicating she'd received the message. The rain pounded down now, making it hard to see. Sondra's adrenaline kicked in. *Rise to the occasion. Ignore your stomach.* The fast current propelled them into the middle of the rapids. She'd have to yell for Jo to hear her. Damn. A rock. Too late. They swept sideways. Sondra paddled hard to straighten them out. Another rock. "Right! Left! Left! Right. Oh shit!"

A huge boulder. They slammed into it. The canoe threatened to tip. Sondra strained hard, pushing to dislodge them. One more push and they were free. A large branch smacked against the side of the canoe and spun it around. No way. She wasn't going to finish these rapids going backward. Sondra dug her paddle into the bottom of the river, forcing the canoe to turn and straighten out. A rush of salt in her mouth. Sweat. She could feel a hot stream of it running down her face.

But they were through the rapids.

Where was Annie? Sondra's heart pounded. She squinted through the rain. Thank heavens, Annie was safe, on the bank, waving them over.

Jo steadied the canoe so Sondra could get out, then clambered over the side, plunging into the water. Oh well. She was so wet, it didn't matter. She half-ran, half-hobbled up the bank, forcing her ailing hamstring into action. She made it. Panting with relief, she huddled with Annie and Sondra under an enormous pine tree. The perfect umbrella.

Annie wiped her face and grinned. "That was awesome. I loved how we held onto our strength and power!"

"I was feeling relieved, but powerful describes it better." Jo leaned her face against the tree trunk and inhaled. "Smell that pine bark and needles. I want to be strong like this tree."

"I wish we could bottle that energy for when we needed it." Sondra leaned her back against the tree and scratched it like a bear. "Now this feels good."

"You're shivering," Annie said.

"I've been wet most of this trip. Besides, I didn't sleep well, trying to release the Adam asshole stress stored up in my body."

"So, this asshole has a name? Adam?" Jo asked.

Sondra noticed their smirks. "Don't even go there. Adam and Eve and temptation."

"I'm not saying a word," Annie replied. "Looks like the rain stopped. We have five hours of paddling before we reach our meeting point. Let's get you out of those wet clothes. You can wrap up in a sleeping bag to warm up."

"Good idea. Let's go." Sondra led the way. The bank was slick from the rain. Sondra slid down sideways like a snowboarder, gracefully keeping her balance.

Where was the second canoe? Sondra scanned the river. "We have a problem. The canoe with the cooler is gone."

Jo's good mood plummeted. "Along with the tent, my life jacket, two sleeping bags and the fancy gear bag. It's my fault. I'm so sorry. I should have tied it up."

"No reason to panic." Annie breathed in for four counts, held it, then slowly let it out. She had wilderness survival skills. Jo knew the woods. Annie checked the remaining canoe. "We have Jo's backpack. Should be a few granola bars and some water." She rummaged inside the bag. Only two bars left. Three bottles of water. How had that happened? No reason to let them worry. She was being a friend, not a martyr. It was different. "Who wants a granola bar? I'm still stuffed from breakfast."

"I'm not hungry. But I'll take a bottle of water," Sondra said. "Jo, you should eat a bar. You worked hard."

"I lost my appetite along with the canoe."

"Stop it. Don't feel bad. It doesn't serve you. We'll find the canoe downriver. Besides, we have a job to do." Annie nodded to Jo. "Ready?"

Annie and Jo started tugging Sondra's shirt off.

Sondra stepped backward, swatting at their hands. "Stop it! I can do this. You two are worse than a teenage boy hoping for sex."

Sondra peeled off her wet clothes. Her skin stung, like peeling off a Band-Aid that had been on too long. Oh no. Poison ivy all over her legs and stomach. Her back throbbed. It must be there as well.

Annie reached out and held Sondra's hand. "You poor thing. Jo, let's try a different lotion."

Jo searched the backpack. Wait—only two granola bars and two bottles of water? Annie, the martyr. But she understood. Probably good to protect Sondra. Keep looking. What could be in that bright pink bottle? Jo checked the ingredients. "This is crazy! It's like Pepto Bismol for the skin. I'll apply it this time. I forgot to share that I'm immune to poison ivy after my incident with Louie."

Jo enjoyed Annie's look of disbelief. Better to keep the mood light. Jump into her bossy demeanor. "Annie, get the sleeping bag out. The inside should be dry."

"I'm ready." Sondra squeezed her eyes shut. The lotion felt cool and calmed the painful tingling.

Annie wrapped the sleeping bag around Sondra. "There, all better."

"So, this is how I get sympathy?"

"Who said anything about sympathy?" Jo smiled. "This is all about the love. Now climb in the middle of the canoe and rest. Annie and I will paddle."

Annie took the back while Jo took the front. Sondra leaned her head against the backpack and closed her eyes. Gratitude. Universe—thank you.

The sun burst out from behind the clouds in full force, as if apologizing for deserting them.

# CHAPTER FORTY-TWO

Jo FELT A HEADACHE COMING on, a dull throbbing from her temples. Probably eye strain from her hypervigilance in looking for the canoe. How could she have been so careless? Enough! Annie was right. Beating herself up was only hurting her. What would she be saying if Annie or Sondra had lost it? She wouldn't be chewing them out. Why not treat herself with kindness too? Jo felt a wisp of pride. She was getting better at recognizing her unproductive thoughts and turning them around.

Jo noticed a huge oak tree fifty feet ahead that was split down the middle. It must have suffered a lightning strike. Half of it had fallen into the river, spreading its branches, leaving only a narrow passageway that hugged the opposite bank. What was the shiny thing hidden in the tangle of branches, jammed against the split tree trunk? Was that the canoe? Yes!

"I see it!" Jo pointed to the canoe. Oh, happy day! Lunch was in the cooler.

"Let's paddle over to the bank and make a plan," Annie replied.

"We don't want to get caught in that mess." Annie gently patted Sondra's shoulders to wake her up.

"Are we there yet?" Sondra sleepily asked.

"Afraid not, but we found the canoe."

Jo remembered this part of the river. They never stopped here since the banks were steep, rocky, and lined with scraggly bushes. It wasn't easy to find a spot to tie up. Jo finally flung a rope over a bent tree that looked as if it was praying. Close enough. She'd have to climb over the side into the waist-high water. Jo's hamstring quivered at the thought. But she was the one who lost the canoe. She couldn't ask Annie to get it.

"You two stay here. It shouldn't be hard to dislodge." Jo clenched her teeth and got into the water. Focus on the canoe. It was only twenty feet away. The rocks below her feet were jagged and slippery. Maybe swimming would be easier? She tried, but her hamstring ached at the action. She was almost there.

The branches acted like an army, blocking her way. She tried to break them, but they were alive and resisted. She'd have to fight her way through. Look for a path with the least resistance. There. A small opening with smaller branches. She bent the branches back and was able to move forward. When she released a branch, it slapped her in the face. *Shit, that hurt. Stay positive.*

Jo was a few feet from the canoe now. There! She grabbed the edge of the canoe and pulled it toward her. The current grabbed it back, slamming it against the tree trunk. Her frustration flared. Screw this. She'd win this game of tug-of-war. One—two—three—four—five tries. A scream gurgled, wanting to escape from the bottom of her throat. No, she'd scare Annie and Sondra. *Okay, Spirit Guides. How about a little help here?*

Jo closed her eyes. Words drifted into her consciousness. *Slow down. Clear your head.* Jo listened to the sounds of the forest, calming her nerves and sending her a message. *Look around you.* The paddle on the back seat. She could climb into the canoe and use the paddle to push it out. Go with the flow of the current instead of against it. Brilliant. But she still needed to get closer. How? A crow cawed as it flew above her. *Of course. Thank you. Go above this tapestry of branches.* It could hold her.

Jo took a deep breath, then exhaled it like a karate chop. She hoisted herself onto the intertwined branches. It worked! She dragged her body carefully across the branches and slid into the canoe. Should be easy now. She grabbed the paddle, leaned forward, and dug into the mixture of branches, pulling hard. The canoe screeched across the branches as it propelled forward. Success!

Oh no. This couldn't be happening. One of the branches jutted upwards against the side of the canoe, causing it to tip to the right. Water trickled in over the side, then became a steady stream. Jo shifted her weight to rock the canoe in the opposite direction. It didn't budge. The momentum of the water pouring over the side was too forceful. The canoe sank lower. She spotted the cooler jammed under the crossbars. Quick. Kick it out. It might stay afloat. But it was too late. She felt like a bystander. This couldn't be real. In a slow surreal motion, the canoe flipped over, taking her with it.

Jo was trapped. Sandwiched between the canoe and the riverbed. Her face smashed against the riverbed. Sand gritted between her teeth. Her eyelids pressed against rocks. *Keep your eyes shut. Don't let the rocks scrape them.* She couldn't move. The canoe must be jammed under the tree trunk. She had to get out. She tried to kick her legs, but they only smashed up against the canoe. Her arms? She stretched them out in front of her. The movement caused the canoe to shift a few inches upwards before it smashed back down against her. Pain roared through her body. Was she going to die?

Water infiltrated her nostrils, streaming down her throat and into her lungs. How much longer could she hold her breath?

For the first time, it hit her. She wasn't invincible. Even when she screwed up, she'd never thought it could end in death. What about Jessica and Hunter? At least they had a great dad. *Louie.* He'd never know she still loved him. They wouldn't have a chance to be a family again.

No. Not yet. She couldn't give up. Jo swept her arms out, blindly searching for branches to pull herself out. She grasped a few, but they slipped out of her hand. There was nothing else to hang onto. Just be grateful for the life she had. The people she loved.

Jo let go of struggling. Her body completely relaxed. Her mind floated into a dream state. She felt warm, almost hot. Was that her spirit leaving her body? Then a presence beside her. Without effort, her body flattened to align itself along the riverbed. Now her body was moving forward. Was she going to heaven or to hell? Please let it be heaven. A whooshing sound echoed in her ears. A slight bump against her head. Her eyelids fluttered open. She was inches above the riverbed. The rocky bottom transitioned to sand as the current propelled her downriver.

She was alive!

The pressure in Jo's lungs built, ready to explode. She felt dizzy and disoriented. She had to breathe. Now! She used her arms to break the surface. Air! She gulped it in. The overturned canoe swept by her. She had to get it. Their gear was in there. It was too deep to walk. She'd have to swim. She kicked her legs and her hamstring screamed in pain. *Forget it. Let it go.* She watched the canoe bottom bob up and down before it disappeared out of sight. Something bumped against her back. Their tent! She captured it and held it close like a coveted trophy.

Jo made it to the shore and collapsed, looking up at the sky. The blue was magnificent. She felt exalted! Yes—that was the word. Jo stood up and experienced a rush of rapturous joy. She had a second chance. She was alive. Jo raised her arms upward and shouted, "Thank you!"

Jo turned around. Sondra and Annie were still in their canoe. Their faces expressed horror and fear. Jo waved at them. Even her hamstring felt better. Jo noticed that Sondra was dressed. That was good. Jo gestured to them to stay far to the right. They got the message as they paddled over to the opposite bank and avoided the treacherous branches. It took only minutes for them to reach her.

"Did you see my miracle?" Jo danced around, unable to contain her exuberance.

"We witnessed it. You scared the shit out of me. Which, by the way—thank you. But damn it, Jo. Don't ever take a risk like that again. I need my friends," Sondra exclaimed.

Jo felt her arms and legs. "I'm really here! I can't explain it. I was a goner. Trapped. But the moment that I let go—it changed. The current took me out. I can't wait to share this with Louie."

"That was horrifying. I didn't think you could hold your breath that long." Annie started to cry and wrapped her arms around Jo. "But it's also beautiful. Your belief. You have one hell of a guardian angel watching over you."

"For a pastor's wife, you sure do swear a lot," Jo said.

Annie stopped crying and released Jo. "I usually say only hell and damnation. They're not swear words, since they're in the Bible."

"We've heard a lot of *shits* and even a few f-bombs. I thought Sondra was the queen of swearing. But you've surpassed her."

Annie grinned. "Maybe it's not cool, being the pastor's wife and a mother. But what the hell. I'll take that crown and wear it with pride."

Sondra reached over and tapped Jo's cheek. "What's your secret? Your face glows. It's radiating light. Like you had a diamond facial."

"As you know, I'm a trendsetter. Just scrape your face against a riverbed for an intense exfoliation. By the end of this trip, we'll have created an entire product line."

"Let's skip adding more product lines through pain. We have four hours left. It should be a piece of cake after all we've been through," Annie said.

"Except Jo is sopping wet." Sondra handed her the sleeping bag. "Here, take this."

"No, thank you. Just because I'm immune to poison ivy doesn't mean I want to cover my body with material that's soaked with it."

"We'll reverse the sides. The sun will dry up any seepage," Annie said.

"Let's share one of these granola bars to celebrate Jo's victory." Sondra dug into the backpack. What? Only two bars left? What about the water? She held up the two bottles. "Why didn't you tell me we were almost out of water? I'm sorry that I drank so many."

"Don't worry." Jo reached into the backpack. "I packed a few energy gels I eat after a big workout. That should get us by. See." Jo opened the packets and passed them around.

Sondra's stomach cramped. *Settle down. You don't need water right now. Be happy.* She chewed on the gel. "Not bad. They remind me of the Jell-O molds my mom made for the church's potluck dinners."

"Not even close. Your mom was an artist with Jell-O. I loved how she used fresh berries to create a design, then swirled fresh whipped cream on top," Jo mumbled, gel stuck on her teeth.

"If you need to see a regular Jell-O mold, come over and check out my refrigerator. Our stoic Scandinavian community shows their feelings by making Jell-O molds—and casseroles. At least, the boys had something to eat while I was recovering," Annie commented. "In reflection, according to my fridge, I must have scared the hell out of them."

# CHAPTER FORTY-THREE

Annie climbed into the back of the canoe. She was going to keep an eye on Jo and Sondra.

Jo wrapped herself in the sleeping bag. Time to get going. She'd have to hop with her good leg. She gave it a try. It reminded her of pillow sack races with the kids. A nice memory. She made it to the canoe without falling on the uneven riverbank. Now—how to get in? Maybe lean sideways and roll into the seat? It worked.

Sondra pushed the canoe off the shore and deftly climbed into the front. "Is that a new canoe dance or are you saddle sore from riding a cowboy?"

"Just tired. I had to listen to you snore. You scared away any bears or beavers for miles."

"Then you better start snoring," Sondra ordered.

"Not a problem." Jo rearranged the sleeping bag and propped her leg on the tent. Elevation would help. Ignore the throbbing. Too bad she'd given Sondra her Advil stash. But that poison ivy—it deserved a painkiller. She snuggled deeper into the sleeping bag. So cozy. Let the river rock her to sleep. Within seconds, she was out.

"Annie, you must be tired. You've had to do the heavy lifting today," Sondra said.

"This has been an incredible day! Jo's miracle when we thought she would surely drown under that canoe. I feel great. No fights to break up, no meetings to attend, or groceries to buy. Shit. Oops— sorry, Lord. I meant damn. I don't want to think about what I have to go back to."

"Could you assign your worst church duties to someone you secretly dislike, or the biggest sinner? You could pull it off. You're good at that mother-guilt-trip thing."

Annie clanked her paddle against Sondra's. "Excellent idea. I have a few people that pop to mind!"

"I don't mean to be obtrusive, but can I hire a house cleaner for you? I owe you ten years of birthday gifts. You never missed mine. I've been such a schmuck."

"Thanks, Sondra. It's a good idea. We could swing that financially. I'd rather have you buy me a day at a spa—or make that a week. I do hope you realize how sweet and loving you are."

"What are you talking about? I'm a tough, no-nonsense businesswoman!"

"Yeah, right. One that supports a shelter."

The shelter. The girls. Sondra was supposed to be the role model. She really was in a corner. Pay the blackmail money and hope for the best? Her hands trembled with anger. Her spirit didn't seem to be in agreement.

"I know you're married, so I've never asked you this. But since it's just you and me. Did you ever regret not giving Hank a chance?"

"I need to think about that." Hank? A gentle, warm feeling

pushed away her anger. Sondra had loved seeing Hank again. But, long ago, she'd torched that bridge with him standing on it. She must have left some painful scars.

What was that noise? Was some huge, monstrous bug ready to attack her? She looked around. Jo, as ordered, was snoring.

Sondra pointed to Jo. "Was I that loud?"

"Louder. At least I can hear the falls coming up."

"They're not that big. We used to go over them as kids."

"True. But that was years ago. They began releasing water from the dam up north. Add a few rainy summers and erosion. It changed. The water is high. The falls, unforgiving. Last year, a teenager, only sixteen, went through it in early spring and—"

"What happened?" Beads of sweat broke out on Sondra's forehead. Her whole body felt on fire as fear flooded her system.

"Sondra, we shouldn't talk about this. You look really upset."

"Just tell me!"

"Fine! The water was icy cold. He got caught in the whirlpool under the falls. He didn't have a life jacket on and drowned. I'm surprised your dad didn't tell you. The entire town was devastated."

"I sucked at returning his calls. I have to give him credit. He called me faithfully once a week. I rarely picked up. But he never shared news like that. I'm still his little girl to protect." Sondra shook her head. "That's awful. We better portage around the falls."

"Absolutely." Annie took a closer look at Sondra. "Your face is dripping with sweat."

"Guess my fever came back. Must be the water. The poison ivy in my private parts is punishment for the other sin I committed."

"You still have your sense of humor."

Sondra did. Amazing. That survival tool was embedded in her DNA. It might be the only thing she'd have left. Those pictures— the orgasm one. Perfect fodder for all the late-night talk shows.

And James—the humiliation for both of them. She wasn't brave enough. Fuck. She had to pay them off. Use all her savings—her trust fund. Make up an excuse to borrow the rest from her dad. She wouldn't go to James. Never.

Sondra could hear the thundering of the falls. As teenagers, going over the falls had been a thrill, better than a carnival ride. Something innocent was now dangerous. Similar to her desire for intimacy. Sondra couldn't avoid it—she was afraid. Her ability to be confident or fake it had evaporated. All she wanted was to run away. She had to get her emotions under control. Slow down the cortisol rush. Use her Qigong practice. Sondra set down her paddle. She vigorously rubbed her entire scalp, not caring about her hair, then gently pushed on her third eye. Was Annie shouting at her?

Sondra looked over her shoulder. "I'm sorry. What did you say?"

Annie pointed over to the right. "Over there. Looks like the portage trail. Let's try it."

Wow. Sondra looked frazzled, her hair bunched up and tangled. Annie never should have mentioned the boy who drowned. Time to get the fun back. Everything had become too serious.

"I'll wake up Jo." Annie had this. A silly song to the tune of *You Are My Sunshine.* Annie gave Jo a little nudge, then belted out, "Jo is our sunshine, she likes to look fine. Jo likes to act tough every day, but we know her, and we do love her, so we just laugh when Jo pushes us away."

Sure enough, Jo lifted her head. "Very clever, Annie. What's going on?"

"We're getting close to the waterfall."

"Fun! It'll be a blast to go over it."

Sondra swiveled around, her eyebrows furrowed. "Not this

time. We're portaging around it. We're not going to die like that teenage boy."

Jo shot up straight and looked around. She began getting dressed.

"You got her attention," Annie said.

# CHAPTER FORTY-FOUR

Sondra clambered out of the canoe and onto the shore. Everything was spinning. Acid raced up her throat. She fell to her knees and clutched the earth. Her stomach wrenched; her organs clenched together. Then relief. She rested her forehead on the earth. Cool and supportive. Shit. The concern on Jo and Annie's faces.

"Don't look at me like that. Just a little puke. With all your kids, you've seen it before."

"No more tough acts, remember?" Annie sputtered in frustration.

"Fine. I feel awful, but admitting it isn't going to help us get home." Sondra managed to rock back on her heels.

Jo reached into the backpack and pulled out the last water bottle. She squatted beside Sondra. "Here, sip on this. Obviously, the gels were too much for your stomach."

"What about you two? You must be thirsty."

"I'm seriously digging those gel chews. Jo, can you give me one?" Annie asked.

Jo dug into the backpack. Four pieces left. The meeting point was a few hours away. Jo handed one to Annie, then popped one into her mouth. She shoved the rest into the backpack before Annie could see the dwindling supply.

"I feel a surge of energy already." Jo stood up, flexing her biceps. "Come on, Annie. Let's carry the canoe. We can wrap the sleeping bag around the crossbars. I'll wear the backpack. Sondra, can you manage the tent? Glad your dad spoiled us with the lightweight one."

"What's with the two of you? Is it that hard to shed the tough act? Jo, I know your leg is hurting. Can't we drag the canoe?" Annie asked.

"Yeah, it hurts, but it's a muscle. It'll heal. We can't sit here. Considering the heavy underbrush, carrying it will be easier. I showed you my super biceps. We can go slowly."

Sondra gave them a weak smile. "I've got the tent. And I'll wear the life jacket. My new fashion statement."

"We were always a great team." Annie gave them each a high five. She was impressed with her own stamina. Being a pastor's wife and a mother of four was paying off. Her boys. She missed sitting around the campfire, laughing, singing, and playing silly word games with them. Baseball and soccer—always causing interference. But no more. She was going to pick a camping date, and nothing would get in the way.

If Annie and Jo could stay positive, Sondra could too. All these years, Sondra had searched for something or someone to lean on. What did she really believe? Was heaven up there? Was God real? Sondra closed her eyes and visualized her soul, her entelechy inside, wanting to connect. The energetic feeling was real. She'd given up church, yet she'd seen enough to believe in a higher power—full of love. The name didn't matter. Her favorite saying, "The one who is known by a thousand names in ten thousand languages." "I am," would do for now. Why not say a prayer? Shock Annie and Jo.

"Okay. Listen up. I'm going to say a prayer for us." Sondra stood and raised her arms to the sky. "Dear I am, please give us the strength to get the canoe around the waterfall. Thank you. Namaste." Sondra grinned, ignoring their surprised expressions.

"Alright, let's get this party started." Sondra took off down the path. *Positive thoughts attract positive things. Look how I'm beating down this underbrush and creating this beautiful path. I'm even avoiding the rocks so everyone can walk easily.* An image of her dad popped into her mind. Give him a bear hug. That'd surprise him. And Hank—she was still married, but maybe they could be friends again? He was authentic. She admired his ease at interacting with her dad and all the kids. Oops, what about James? No good feeling there. What did that mean? She tripped over a rock. Warning that she'd better pay attention.

"Quick time-out." Jo set down the canoe. She sat on a rock and rubbed her leg. "At least it's not poison ivy."

Jo surveyed the overgrown path. Hardly any trampled-down grass now. "Not many people canoeing these days. I was hoping those Boy Scouts would have cleared a trail. How much farther until we get to the top?"

"Maybe forty yards," Annie guessed.

Sondra wiped the sweat from her face, unable to hide her trembling hands. "Jo, do you want some water? I'm pretty sure I'm not contagious." She pushed the water bottle toward her friend.

Jo waved the bottle away. "I'll pass. Nothing personal. I never finish my girls' food. It grosses me out. Louie used to chase me around the house, threatening to feed me leftover baby food." Louie's arms—how she'd love to crawl into them right now.

Sondra looked like a wreck. Annie actually looked refreshed. She was tired. How could she keep going? The sun shared its warmth on her face, giving her an idea. One of her favorite rituals.

"Sondra, I promise that I'm not competing for the best prayer. But we could all use a boost. Let's honor the four directions." Jo stood and faced the east. "To the east, to the sun that rises and the air that we breathe." Jo turned ninety degrees. "To the south, for the fire that transforms us." Jo turned to the west. "To water, the substance of life." Last turn to the north. "To the earth and our ancestors. We honor you. We give thanks and ask for your blessings. As it is above, so it is below." Jo bowed in gratitude. A surge of energy. Much better.

## CHAPTER FORTY-FIVE

JO GRABBED THE BOW OF the canoe. "Ready?"

Sondra nodded. Time to lead the way. The underbrush wasn't the problem. It was the young saplings, their branches crisscrossing the path. They resisted her efforts to move them, causing her to stumble around. Her patience vanished. Anger took over, fueled by thoughts of Adam and Emily. Sondra let out a primal yell, grabbed a big stick, and wielded it like a machete. She whacked the branches, breaking them, charging down the path like an enraged warrior. It felt exhilarating! All the regrets and guilt she'd accumulated over the past week streamed out of her body. No more.

Sondra charged into the clearing by the waterfall, waving her stick around, ready to attack any predator. She skidded to a stop. Where was she? A magical, lost kingdom? Was she dehydrated and hallucinating a mirage? Or maybe she had time-traveled? Hell, anything was possible. Right? She dropped her stick. The waterfall's roar stunned her. It called to her.

Sondra's legs trembled. She sank to the ground and crawled

over to the edge. She could hear Annie and Jo join her. Good, they'd made it. She hung her feet over the edge, mesmerized by the water gushing down the twelve-foot drop. It demanded silent reverence. There was the whirlpool. If death had happened here, surely rebirth could as well.

·

Annie's eyes were drawn toward the opposite bank. The sight was enchanting, as if an artist had painted a masterpiece and hung it across the river. There was an air of mystery. Lush ferns and oddly-shaped trees appeared to be guarding a hidden treasure.

A movement. Annie squinted her eyes. There, stepping out of the shadows, a deer. Goosebumps. The deer eased into the opening and locked eyes with Annie. Annie pressed her hands against her heart. Could it be the one she saw before? Was it following her to share a message?

The deer took a drink, then turned and vanished into the woods.

"Definitely your totem," Jo whispered. "An affirmation of what a great mom you are."

"That was so mystical. I can't even be jealous," Sondra said.

"You had a friend riding on the top of your head for an hour," Annie shared.

Sondra ran her hand over her head. "What are you talking about? Was something in my hair besides s'mores from last night?"

"Don't freak out. Just a lovely dragonfly. Your mother coming to check on you."

"All these incredible things happening. Everyone has a totem. Our trip will surely go smoothly now," Jo declared.

Sondra felt a strong chill run through her body. Her teeth chattered. Moments before, she'd been feverish. How strange.

"I'm surprised you're cold with that life jacket on," Jo said.

Sondra hugged the life jacket. "It's my security blanket."

"We can untie the sleeping bag and wrap you in that," Annie offered.

"Maybe once we get into the canoe."

"Jo, you ready? We can drag the canoe across the clearing. Going downhill should be easy."

Jo massaged her hamstring. "My leg needs a pep talk."

"What about using my bra like an ace bandage?" Sondra suggested.

"Actually, I have a wind jacket in my backpack." Jo pulled it out. This could work. She wrapped it around her hamstring. The sleeves hung out the side, but the supportive pressure felt great. "Brilliant idea, Sondra."

Sondra gave her a weak smile. "See, I care about you too."

"I'll take the back and push. Jo, take the front and pull. Sondra, follow behind us," Annie instructed. "If the bank is slippery, we don't want to hit you with the canoe."

"I appreciate that." Although being knocked unconscious might be an improvement over how she was feeling. But after Annie hitting her head, Sondra couldn't joke about it.

"Ready!" Annie bent over and pushed hard, using her core muscles to take the strain off Jo. They made it across the clearing. Great. Now downhill. Shit. They'd have to carry it. They lifted the canoe. Why did it feel heavier? Her arms ached. The terrain didn't help, with its sharp rocks and thorny bushes.

Could Annie just pull it herself? Worth a try. Tell Jo to stop. Why was Jo jerking around? The canoe swung radically side to side. The jacket! The sleeves were tangled in a thorn bush. Jo dropped the canoe and tumbled into a cluster of thorn bushes. A sick feeling of dread wrapped around Annie's chest, like a boa constrictor squeezing out her life force. She couldn't let the canoe hit Jo. It was slipping out of her hands. One choice. Heave her end toward the river, away from Jo. Her left arm screamed in pain at the effort.

Annie watched the canoe slide over the bushes toward the steep bank. Sondra ran past her toward Jo, who was swearing like a madwoman. *Snap out of it! Go help Jo.* The thorn bushes showed no mercy as they pricked Annie's fingers, drawing blood. Finally, Jo was free.

Sondra pointed toward the bank. "The canoe!" The canoe gained momentum as it slid downhill.

They stood together in shock, watching the canoe rocket over the edge of the bank, landing upright in the river. The current appeared to welcome it as it merrily floated away.

"Damn and hell!" Annie shouted. No way was that canoe getting away. She ran down the bank and plunged into the river. The cold temperature shocked her. Maybe there was a cold spring underneath her. Better keep moving her muscles so they didn't tighten up. Swim toward the canoe! Her arms were moving, and her legs were kicking, but no progress. What was going on? Then the whirlpool caught her. It maliciously tugged her underwater, spinning her around. *Don't panic. Fight! Think of the boys, Dan, Sondra, Jo—yourself!*

Annie was spinning faster now. The whirlpool was like a demon, tenaciously gripping her ankles, pulling her down into its dark vortex. Her lungs throbbed, begging to breathe. Her back slammed against the rocky ledge under the waterfall. The jutting rocks clawed at her back, slowing down her momentum. Her chance. Where did the whirlpool connect with the downstream current? The only way out.

There! Rays of sunlight hit the river's surface, displaying rivulets of water flowing off to the side. She was not going to be a victim. She deserved the chance to reinvent herself. She was worth it.

The whirlpool mocked her as it yanked her back into its swirling pit. No! She was invincible. She was Annie. *Swim to your new life.* She swam like an Olympian, propelling herself forward. Almost to the surface.

Annie's head exploded out of the water. She gulped in the fresh air, choking with relief. She'd done it! She felt lighter—stronger. She was alive. Maybe that damn whirlpool had sucked out the heaviness of her guilt and the need for forgiveness. Her feet touched the ground. The canoe rocked in the current, thirty feet away, temporarily caught on a boulder, hesitating—teasing her.

Run!

Had an angel put wings on her feet? Annie flew across the rocks until a gust of wind almost knocked her over. No! The canoe shifted off the rock and continued downstream. She could still grab it. Only ten feet away. Another gust of wind. Annie fell backward on her butt. The canoe jauntily picked up speed. She watched in desperation as it rounded the bend.

Game over.

Annie let the cold water soothe her aching body. Her whole body ached. *Toughen up.* It wasn't going to help sitting here, acting betrayed. Annie turned to check on Jo and Sondra. Unbelievable! They were waving their arms, giving her victory signals. "Yes, God. Those are my best friends, thank you."

Annie stumbled toward the riverbank. The river bottom went from rocks to a thick mud. Wasn't the whirlpool enough? Why was the river turning from a friend into an enemy? Was God mad at her for doubting him? Annie felt her energy dissipate. She needed a break, but there wasn't a place to sit. It was only marsh running alongside the riverbank. Why didn't she walk over to the other side? It looked nice over there. She dropped her head in despair. Then two sets of arms wrapped around her.

"You were like a goddess out there, fearless! I've never seen you like that before!" Sondra exclaimed.

"I lost the canoe."

Jo hugged even harder. "Who cares? That was spectacular! You were a superhero, fighting the forces of nature."

A warm feeling of pride replaced Annie's despair. "Thanks! I actually amazed myself. Superhero Annie. I like the sound of that. So, here we are. The big question is—now what?"

"When the canoe makes it to the meeting place, the guys will know something is wrong. They'll look for us," Sondra said.

"If it doesn't get hung up, tip, and sink. It could take hours before they start searching. My boys are going to freak out. We need a plan."

"First, we need to get out of this muck." Jo could feel herself sinking, mud slithering up her shins. She could barely lift her leg.

"Do you hear buzzing, like a chainsaw?" Sondra asked.

Jo looked around. A gray shadow was speeding toward them. "Mosquitoes!" They swarmed all over Jo, delighting in her inability to move, devouring her.

"We have to cross the river!" Annie shouted.

"I can't move." Jo gagged as mosquitoes torpedoed down her throat.

Annie and Sondra grabbed Jo by her armpits and pulled.

Jo could feel the mud reluctantly releasing her. Wait. Her right shoe. The mud victoriously captured it. Let it go. There must be a thousand mosquitoes. They were taking chunks out of her body. Pure misery. She could barely see Annie and Sondra.

Sondra slid off her life jacket. "Jo, wear this. Give me your backpack. You can barely walk. If you fall, you'll float. Annie, follow behind Jo."

"You're sick. I can lead the way." Annie swatted the mosquitoes attacking her face.

"Don't argue with me. Do you want to be their last supper?"

Annie shook her head.

"Then let's go." Sondra led the way, waving the backpack in front of her, as if she was Moses parting the Red Sea.

The mosquitoes chased them halfway across the river before giving up their delicious treat.

# CHAPTER FORTY-SIX

SONDRA MADE IT TO THE bank first, grabbed a tree branch, and pulled herself up. No mosquitoes. She could breathe. She tossed the backpack and tent to the side. Now for Jo. Sondra spun around and saw fear wash across Jo's face.

Jo maneuvered her way through the rocky bed. Agony. The rocks jabbed at her shoeless foot. Careful. Watch where she was stepping. Why hadn't she grabbed her shoe from the muck? She scratched at the multitude of bites on her arms. Her answer. Sondra had made it to the bank. Her turn now. She took another step forward, but her foot slid and turned at an odd angle between two large rocks hiding under the water. Excruciating pain shot through her leg. She tried to move, but her foot was jammed. Jo grabbed her calf and pulled. Her leg muscles shook uncontrollably and gave out. *Don't fall!* Jo flailed her arms, trying to keep her balance. No hope. She needed to protect herself. Tuck her chin in and pray the life jacket would cushion her fall.

Annie watched Jo's arms windmill. Was she goofing off, or

did the mosquitoes return? Jo was wobbling now—falling backward. Annie hurtled over the remaining rocks and stretched out her arms. She grabbed the life jacket's collar, protecting Jo's head from smashing against the rocks. "Help!"

Sondra hurled herself into the river. A rush of adrenaline shot through her body. She effortlessly shoved aside the rocks trapping Jo's feet. "We need to carry her to shore."

Sondra picked up Jo's legs while Annie hung onto the life jacket. They gently laid Jo down, then collapsed on either side of her.

Sondra's heart pounded. She'd almost lost both of her friends today. Her best friends. Maybe it was time to reprioritize her life. Her stupid blackmail was nothing. It wouldn't take her life. Sondra looked at the sky through the branches of a large oak tree. What would make her happy—at her soul level? She felt an inner intensity, as if the answer was right here. She looked at the clouds through the trees. The sight calmed her. Now the wind was rustling the leaves. Did someone whisper, "Everything will be okay?"

Annie sighed, "I'd love a cup of tea right now."

"Tea..." Sondra propped herself up on her elbows and looked around. "I know where we are. Our final tea party with my mom. I didn't know at the time that a few weeks later, she'd die."

Annie sat up. "I remember. Thelma and my grandmother insisted that we come and skip the county fair."

"I wonder if they knew?" Jo struggled to sit up. Every movement jarred her ankle.

"I think my mom did." Sondra wrapped her arms around herself, remembering the sweetness of her mother's hugs. "After our tea, my mom took me to the waterfall. She was so happy. We kicked off our shoes and dangled our feet into the rushing water, laughing at how it tickled. Then she got serious and held me tight."

Sondra got goosebumps. "She whispered to me that I could always meet her in my dreams, if I needed her. I'd forgotten that memory. What a gift to recall it."

Sondra reached out for Annie's and Jo's hands. They huddled close together, warming each other.

The cry of a crow broke their contemplative silence.

Annie spring-boarded to her feet. "Our plan! We're close to the old cabin. It's gone, but the driveway is still there. I can find it, walk out, and get help."

"Annie, it's been years. The woods have changed, just like the waterfall. You could get lost. We should stay together." Sondra's stomach cramped. She bent over, but thankfully nothing came out. "Just the dry heaves," she announced.

Annie felt Sondra's forehead. "You have a high temperature."

"I agree with Sondra. We still have the tent, the backpack, and each other." Jo unsnapped the life jacket and shrugged it off. The movement jerked her ankle. Jo gasped with pain. Her secret was out.

"Time to check your ankle." Annie unraveled the jacket and hung it on a tree to dry. "Damn jacket, causing so much trouble." This was going to hurt. She gingerly rolled down Jo's sock, biting the inside of her cheek to hold back her words. The ankle was furious, black and purple, hanging at an odd angle. Worse than when Mark had broken his. Jo wasn't even shedding a tear. Unbelievable. It had to be incredibly painful.

"What's the verdict?"

"You won't be doing aerobics at the gym for a while. I don't want to move it. But we can't let you sit there, wet and cold. I'm going to get a fire going and set up camp."

Annie spread the tent out to dry. No time to waste. Jo could go into shock. What if Sondra's fever got worse? Hurry up. Get a mixture of firewood. Pieces that would burn brightly and others that created smoke—in case the mosquitoes returned.

Jo grimaced each time she glanced at her ankle. It was a wreck. Her hamstring joined the chorus, her whole body singing in pain. "I hate feeling helpless like this."

"I agree. Hey, how about my cell phone? We should get reception here." Sondra opened up the backpack and took out the waterproof container. She checked out the cell phone. "Dry—but the battery is dead."

"How could it be dead when you didn't use it?"

"Last night. I used the flashlight app for numerous trips into the woods. I was trying to be brave and not wake you up. It must have drained the battery." Sondra looked inside the container and took out a pack of tissues. "These could have been useful earlier. What else? Hallelujah! Look!" Sondra held up a box of matches. "My dad must have packed them."

"Annie, you've got to see this. Fast!" Jo shouted.

Annie's heart thudded. Now what? Did Sondra pass out? Annie raced into the clearing and jolted to a stop. There stood Jo and Sondra, grinning, holding up a box of matches like a trophy. Thank you, Jesus!

"Where did you find them?" Annie asked.

"In the backpack, inside my waterproof cell-phone container," Sondra said.

Annie set down the firewood. "What else can we find in there? Let's empty it." Annie grabbed the backpack and turned it upside down. Three granola bars tumbled out. "Score!"

Annie shook the backpack. A t-shirt rolled out. Annie picked it up and smelled it. "Smells like a men's locker room." Annie tossed it to Jo. "It must be yours. We can use it to wrap up your ankle."

Jo smelled it. "Phew. This reminds me of when we snuck into the men's locker room while the guys were showering. All those wet penises. Such a turn-off."

"Then freaking out when the coach caught us. Good thing Sondra used her smile and made up some excuse," Annie said.

The blackmail photos. No smile or excuses could explain those. Sondra reached for the backpack. "No need to make a mess. I'll go through it."

Annie held it out of Sondra's reach. "No. It's time to really empty it out. Just in case something is stuck in one of those secret pockets." She shook it harder. The teapot tumbled out, tea bags, then the envelope with Jo's chew gels smeared over it. Annie pulled the gooey mess off, causing the photos to slide out of the envelope.

Annie picked them up and looked. "What the hell?"

Sondra's face turned white. "I didn't want you to worry."

"What's going on?" Jo asked.

Time to stop this nonsense and protect her friend. Annie tucked the photos under her armpit and snatched the matches from Sondra's hands. Time to light the fire. She stacked twigs then struck the match. Such a satisfying sound. It ignited perfectly. Incredible satisfaction to throw the photos on top of the blossoming blaze—into oblivion. Annie added more firewood just to make sure. The heat made her take a step back.

Now, how to help Sondra? Her grandfather and his sermons. Annie took a dramatic stance and raised her arms to the sky. "Dear God, rain down fire and brimstone onto these sinners. May they experience your wrath at their atrocious behavior. May your will be done."

Annie looked at Sondra's petrified face. Shit, she'd gone too far. Annie sat down beside Sondra and hugged her. "Not you! I was trying to be funny. That was from my grandfather, directed at the assholes who did that to you. You were innocent. Now tell us what happened. We're on your side."

"It sounds like a Hollywood movie, but unfortunately it's true. Adam..."

"The asshole?" Jo asked.

"Yes, that asshole. While we were having sex, his secretary—actually his boss and lover—secretly took pictures. Now they're blackmailing me for a lot of money in exchange for not telling James and spreading the photos all over the media."

"You know what I say to that?" Annie asked, not waiting for an answer. "Fuck them!"

"Oh great," Jo said. "Dan is never going to forgive us with your new attitude."

They all burst out laughing.

"The best part is that he will. He'll love me even more," Annie stated with total conviction. "Sondra, I don't believe you would have cheated on James if you hadn't been so unhappy. I don't have anything against divorce. Maybe it all happened for a reason. You don't have to be miserable the rest of your life. You deserve to be happy. But you're the only one who can figure that out."

"Wait. I don't get to see the pictures?" Jo asked.

"You really want to see Sondra naked?" Annie asked.

"No. I wanted more material to tease her with. I'm running out."

"Well, that's a relief," Sondra muttered.

"If I keep praising you, you won't know how to respond," Jo quipped.

"I'll think of something, if that day ever comes."

"You two can praise me while I put the tent up," Annie said. "Mosquito protection. Just in case it takes me awhile. I gathered two types of wood." She pointed to the stack closer to them. "This will create smoke to keep annoying flying creatures away. The other stack is dry and should burn brightly if you need light to see."

Sondra swallowed a few times. Annie was really going to try and walk out of the forest. *Keep the panic down.* Fear was making her hand shake. *Get busy.* That always helped. "I'll fetch some water and boil it. That's supposed to kill the bacteria. Right?"

Annie nodded.

"Good. Then I'll make you some tea. We can even dunk our granola bars in it. A tea ceremony to send you off on your mission." Sondra grabbed the teapot and headed toward the river.

•

Jo watched Annie expertly put the tent together within minutes. "I don't get it. Last night the tent looked like a shack ready to collapse."

"I was having fun with Sondra. It didn't matter what it looked like."

"Wise words from a wise woman."

Annie picked up the t-shirt and knelt by Jo. "I do have my moments. Now it's time to wrap that ankle."

Sondra joined them. "I'm ready to be the next tea brew master." She placed a rock on the fire and set the teapot on top. She peered over Annie's shoulders, "How's Jo's ankle?" Her hands instantly flew to her sternum and began tapping. "Oh my God. How can I help? Wait!" She ran over to the wood pile, pulled out a stick, and brought it over.

"Do you want to bite on this? I've seen women in movies do it during childbirth."

"No, thanks. Just give me your hand." Jo squeezed it hard. Shit. It did feel as bad as labor. Annie was being gentle, but it didn't matter.

Jo was crushing Sondra's hand. A rapid yoga breath would ease the pain. "Come on, Jo. Breathe with me. Annie's almost done."

The teapot whistled.

"There. All better." Annie kept her hands on Jo's ankle for a moment, sending it healing energy.

"Thanks, you two," Jo mumbled. "How about that cup of tea?"

"Not a problem." Annie passed around cups of steaming tea, then unwrapped the granola bars.

Sondra dunked her bar into her mug and took a bite. "This is good. Cheers to us, and our mothers, grandmothers, and all our ancestors. We did them proud today."

They clanked their mugs together.

"I better get going before dark. I hope it's safe to leave you two alone," Annie joked. "I don't want to come back here and find you wrestling like two bear cubs."

Sondra winced. "You had to mention bears again? I'm trying not to think about them."

"Sorry. I'm trying not to think about those mosquitoes. I feel like a teenager with a pimple outbreak. Which gives me an idea." Annie poured her leftover tea on the dirt beside her, making mud. She scooped it up and rubbed it on her face and arms.

"Ingenious. That will keep the mosquitoes off your face," Jo promised.

"Remember to wipe it off once you reach the main road, or nobody will stop for you. They might think you're a swamp monster," Sondra said.

"Take the windbreaker in case the mud wears off," Jo said. "And please be safe. We need you."

"I'll be safe. We aren't saying our last goodbyes. I'll be back in less than two hours. And I need you too."

Jo held onto Annie's hand for a moment. "Here's my wisdom. I know you believe in God and that he sends angels in many forms. So, if an animal or a bird approaches you, don't be afraid. They want to help you."

"So, if Annie sees a bear, is she supposed to walk up and shake his paw?" Sondra joked.

"I'm serious here."

"I know. Sorry. Here's my advice. If you feel threatened, visualize white energy surrounding you, protecting you. You can even add angels with swords or a purple flame. I swear it works. In fact, I should have been doing this instead of letting my fear take over."

"Sondra and Jo, you've both been nothing but brave and loving. Stay put and take care of each other. Love you both." A surge of love swirled around Annie's heart, causing her to blink back tears. *Stop it. No tears.* Better to leave them with lightheartedness. "And Jo, your boobs aren't flabby at all. Not that I was looking or anything!"

Annie gave them a big grin and disappeared into the forest.

# CHAPTER FORTY-SEVEN

Annie jerked to a halt. Which way to go? She deserved kudos for her confidence performance. Not bad at pretending she could find the old driveway. Fifteen years—probably best to follow the riverbank. At least, the cabin's cement foundation should still exist.

How far was it? A mile? Annie racked her mind. Damn. Another patch of intertwined bushes, the reason why her grandfather had built that path. The path! A surge of joy made her hop up and down—like John would. Annie relished the smile that spread across her face. There still was a kid inside of her.

That grueling week. Conspiring with her grandfather to create a path to the waterfalls. At the memory, Annie's hands rubbed her lower back. The pain of cutting down brush, pulling up weeds, moving rocks—and the bugs. Maybe that's where she'd learned to swear. Her grandfather had boomed out quite a few *hells* and *damns*.

Her grandmother's dementia. A torturous disease of the mind.

It'd been hard for everyone. But the path had given her grand-mother the freedom to walk through the forest and not get lost.

Annie could find it.

That huge pine tree looked familiar. Annie stepped closer. A track next to it looked like a path. A bit overgrown and narrow. Should she take it? It would lead her away from the riverbank but save precious time.

Go for it.

Annie bit her lip. She had to be smart. Don't get lost. Leave markers if she needed to backtrack. Her t-shirt would work. The windbreaker jacket would keep the bugs away. The t-shirt resist-ed tearing. She gritted her teeth with frustration. Did everything have to fight her? *No, don't go there. Stay positive.* She stepped on a sharp rock and picked it up. Perfect.

Sure enough, the rock ripped through the material. Awesome. Annie tied the first piece at eye level. Okay. How many steps could she take without losing sight of the marker? She carefully stepped backward. Twenty. Tie another piece. Her chin lifted as confidence flowed through her. She turned around and repeated the process, over and over again.

A grinding roar—like an old jalopy—reverberated through the forest. Yes! The road! Where were those sounds coming from? The sound vanished.

Silence except for the noises of the forest.

Annie looked at the sky. Where was the sun? Too many clouds to tell. Why couldn't she hear more cars? Where was the road, driveway, or the cabin's foundation? She was almost out of markers and the light was fading. The path was almost unrecog-nizable now.

Deer and other animals created paths too.

Three markers left.

Annie leaned against a tree. Every muscle ached. She shivered, feeling the temperature drop. *Come on, Annie, stay strong. Don't fall asleep and die like they do in the movies.* Fear slithered through her body, cold and slimy. In the whirlpool, there had been no time to think. Now it was decision time. Turn around or keep going?

She could pray.

Contrition lashed at Annie's mind for her immaturity at being angry and blaming God. God hadn't given her depression. Maybe what had happened was a gift. The famous saying, God works in mysterious ways. She'd seen it many times. Today—he had sent angels.

"I believe in you," Annie whispered.

Annie knelt.

No words. God knew what she needed. Sometimes it was best to be silent to make the connection. Dan had taught her that. Whenever they prayed together, magic happened.

Ouch! Damn it. The mosquitoes had discovered her uncovered head. Not even a minute of silence to hear an answer. Her stomach churned with indecision and worry. If she wasted any more time, what would happen to Sondra and Jo? She'd never forgive herself if she didn't try.

Trust.

No time to waste.

Another engine roaring. A pick-up truck? She had to be close to the road.

Run!

Annie embraced the surge of determination, racing along the path. Her foot hit a root extending upwards, and she catapulted through the air, then skidded to the edge of a steep gully. Her momentum carried her over; she rolled down the side. A tree straight ahead. Please God—not her head! Annie held out her arm to soften the blow. She crashed into the tree, her arm snapping. Pain hotter than a branding iron ripped through her body.

Everything went dark.

Annie's eyes fluttered open. Where was she? Annie could see a woman sitting next to a man by the waterfalls. Wait—that was her! The man's visage was Semitic, familiar in an uncanny way. Was it that emergency room doctor again? She stepped closer. No, this man was radiating with light. Her heart pounded. Jesus.

Jesus turned and gestured for her to join him. Annie watched herself stepping inside of her own body. How was this happening? It didn't matter. Jesus took her hand in his. Energy so full of love poured inside her. Jesus looked at her, his eyes streaming messages into her soul. All her worries, fears, and anxiety evaporated. A deep sense of peace expanded throughout her body, mixed with a sense of ecstasy.

Piano music filled the air. Annie could feel her lips moving and heard words pour out of her mouth. She was singing a song to Jesus, one that she'd never sung before. When she finished, Jesus slowly disappeared.

Annie's eyes snapped open. No more Jesus. She was back in the forest, halfway down a steep gully. Was someone holding a jackhammer to her head? No, the pain was coming from her arm. She tried to hold it up, but couldn't. Her forearm was broken, flopping to one side.

Something black flew by, skimming her hair. A bat! A scream screeched out of her mouth. Annie grabbed a patch of moss and plopped it on top of her head. The moss should ward off any flying creatures.

She circled her throbbing foot, testing her ankle. Only a minor sprain. She could still walk. What was that mass of dirt moving in front of her? She leaned over to examine it. Beetles! They were angry, rampaging up her legs toward her face. *Get going!* Annie crawled over the beetles' nest, grabbed onto a tree branch, and pulled herself up.

A tickle. She gagged as a beetle tried to pry her lips open. She swiped it away and shuddered at the thought of eating the damn thing.

Annie took a few steps, but the steep terrain brought her back to her knees. The moss slid off her head. How to keep it in place? She clutched her broken arm to her chest. Her bra! Use those yoga moves that Sondra had taught her to take it off, without exposing her bare chest to the mosquitoes.

Annie contorted her body, unhooked her bra, and shrugged it off. Dizziness from the pain assaulted her brain. *Ignore the pain. Remember, you're a warrior who birthed four boys.*

*Fortitude.*

Now for her arm. Not much to do but stabilize it. Annie found a stick the right size, placed it against her forearm, and wrapped the remaining markers around it. Time to get out of here. She crawled up the alley and made it to the top. Maybe a minute of light left. Where were the path and the markers? She could barely see anything. The night air was so cold, like stepping into a freezer. She couldn't stop shivering. Maybe she could sit, curl up in a ball, and rest? Someone would find her.

Stop it. Dangerous thoughts.

Which way to go? The melody of a song filled Annie's head. Jesus. She wasn't alone. Walk straight ahead. Annie shuffled forward, holding her broken arm against her chest, protecting it. What were the words she had sung to this melody?

A loud crash! Annie froze. Large branches breaking. The thud of large feet smacking the ground. A grassy, earthy scent tunneled into her nostrils. Annie squeezed her eyes shut.

*Don't move.*

A loud huff of breath stroked Annie's face. It was right in front of her. It wasn't attacking her—yet. What was it?

Annie slowly opened her eyes as a dim ray of light broke through the clouds.

A deer.

Annie stared at the deer. Was it real or an illusion? Did she have a concussion? It'd be her second one within days. Not a good thing. The deer cocked its head, studying her.

Annie felt a rush of warm air wrap around her body like a heated blanket. She stopped shivering. The words to the melody drifted out of her mouth in a soft whisper, "So don't give up on your life…"

The deer snorted and stomped its front hooves on the ground, demanding her attention.

Was this really happening? She believed in God. Why not believe that He sent this deer? The deer stepped closer, making eye contact with her. She could reach out and touch its head—if she wanted to. Jo's words. This was her special animal totem. Her remaining fear evaporated.

The deer turned and stepped away. It paused briefly and looked back at her.

"I'm coming," Annie whispered.

# CHAPTER FORTY-EIGHT

SONDRA HUDDLED BY JO, STARING into the fire. The flames leapt around, like mystical creatures dancing, sharing their wisdom. Captivating. Calming. Drawing her back to her predicament. The blackmail.

*I'll be alright. No more internal debate.* She welcomed the sweet taste of having some peace of mind.

Sondra took a sip of tea, the liquid bouncing in the mug. "I reek of wood smoke." Her hands trembled.

"Better than my body odor." Jo reached out to steady Sondra's hands—they were cold. Not a good sign.

Sondra pulled her hands away. "It's nothing. I'm just worried about Annie walking by herself in the dark. Help me change my thoughts. So why the divorce? You haven't said one negative word about Louie."

"I know." Jo squirmed around, trying to get comfortable, and bumped her ankle. "Shit, that hurts!"

"That's nothing compared to the pain of divorce. It'll be hard to fix once it's final."

"You're right."

"What?"

"You're right, but don't get too smug."

Sondra gently nudged Jo's shoulder. "Can't I be a little smug? It's so rare."

Jo nudged her back. "Sure. Why not. I'll even give you a bonus. Consider it my early birthday gift. Ready?"

Sondra grinned. "I'm ready to say I told you so."

Jo leaned back against the backpack and sighed. "I'm not going to bite on that. Here's my gift, wrapped in honesty without any shiny paper. Being with you and Annie made me feel worthy of being forgiven. It reminded me of who I really am. I think we've all been martyrs—just in different ways. Now your turn. What are you going to do about the blackmail?"

"I made a decision. I'm going to tell James. My dad, too. Talk about humiliation." Sondra rubbed her face. That damn orgasm photo. Why couldn't she get it out of her head?

"You're not alone. I know the feeling. However—I've got an idea about those assholes."

"Please share! I'll even give you credit."

"Tell your own story first. Take the power away from those jerks. Twist it your way. Expose them for the bad guys they are. Say that he did something painful. Maybe he pinched your nipple so hard that it caused you to make that face."

Sondra clapped. "Brilliant! Let's think up some more. Maybe he passed smelly gas when he came."

"Good one!" Jo high-fived Sondra. She loved their natural camaraderie. It comforted her. "Okay, I have another one—"

A loud howl interrupted them.

"What was that?" Sondra grabbed Jo's arm.

"Quick. Throw a bunch of wood on the fire."

Sondra tossed half the pile in, transforming it into a bonfire. "Now what?"

"Get our butts into the tent." Jo inched her way backward, trying not to aggravate her ankle.

"Hold on tight to your ankle. I'll help." Sondra grabbed Jo's armpits and dragged her into the tent. She scooted in behind Jo.

"Let's take a look." Jo cautiously opened the tent door flap and peeked outside. Numerous eyes glowed from the edges of their campsite. A flash of pain. Sondra's fingernails were digging a hole into her skin. Jo sucked in her breath. *Stay calm.*

The alpha wolf, their leader, stepped out from behind a tree and howled.

More wolves crept out of the forest, joining him.

"We need to treat them as friends, relate to them," Jo whispered to Sondra.

"Maybe you can bark at them?"

"Bark?"

"They look like big dogs. Turn around and wag your tail at them," Sondra whispered.

"Funny, but you gave me an idea. Watch." Jo made direct eye contact with the leader and kept it, not blinking until everything blurred. There. She felt a tingling. Their energies were merging as they made contact on a higher level, just like Thelma had taught her. Jo consciously focused on sending the leader gratitude for his friendship.

The leader howled.

Jo howled back.

The leader took a few steps closer, his nose sniffing, checking them out.

"I don't think he wants to be friends. He's probably hungry

and wants to eat us," Sondra frantically whispered.

Jo turned to Sondra. "He won't hurt us. Louie's animal totem is the wolf. Do you believe in shapeshifting?"

"Okay, Jo. I'm afraid the pain from your leg has gone to your head. Oh God, I think I'm going to be sick." Sondra pushed Jo aside, stuck her head out of the tent, and threw up.

The wolves crept backward.

"Okay, I know. I'm sick. Now go find something tastier than us!" Sondra shouted. "You may not scare Jo, but you scare the shit out of me."

The leader howled then took off through the woods. His pack followed.

"Okay, this must be a dream. I yelled at a pack of wolves, and they obeyed me."

"Try howling, it feels even better." Jo grinned.

"I can't howl."

"Oh—come on. Don't be such a stick in the mud. Nobody can see us. Be silly with me. It'll feel good. Reduce the stress in your body."

"Fine. But minimal wisecracks." Sondra let out a little yip.

"Nowhere close. Let it out. Like this." Jo bellowed out a howl.

Sondra looked up into the night sky. She cleared her throat and yelped a few times.

"What was that? You sounded half-donkey, half-wolf!"

"Give me a break. I need to practice." Sondra shook out her shoulders and lifted her chin. She had this. *Be the wolf.* She scrunched up her face, took a deep breath, and let loose a long, haunting howl. "That felt great!"

"I bet I can howl louder than you," Jo challenged.

"With my high stress level, I can surely out-howl you."

"Prove it."

Sondra howled.

Jo howled back—even louder.

Sondra pursed her lips. She gathered up all the stress in her body. *Now.* She ripped out a roaring howl.

Jo fell over to her side, laughing uncontrollably. "Bravo! You just turned a wolf into a lion!"

Sondra burst into laughter, clutching her stomach. "Oh my God, we just invented howling therapy. That was the best. We could travel the world teaching women how to howl."

"And Annie was worried about us fighting like bear cubs. If she could see us now."

Sondra shook her head. "We're quite the pair. We raced home to save Annie. Now she's out there trying to rescue us."

"You know what's crazy? If Annie hadn't taken all those pills, I probably wouldn't have come to the reunion. All these incredible moments and insights wouldn't have happened. Annie will be okay. Scoot over and warm me up. Even with our bonfire, I'm cold."

Sondra maneuvered to Jo's side. "Happy to share my body heat with you. We can spoon. Turn over, I'll wrap my arms around you."

Jo willingly complied. "Holy shit, Sondra, you're burning up. How much of that water did you really drink?"

"I took a few gulps, maybe more. It felt cleansing. Am I going to die?"

"You're not going to die. Annie is there. I can feel it. Our rescue team is coming."

"Sounds good," Sondra mumbled. Her tongue felt thick and awkward. Exhaustion ricocheted inside her body.

"It is good."

"I was right. You always have to have the last word."

"Yes, I do."

"That's why I love you."

Jo snuggled closer to Sondra. "Love you too. Now let's meditate and visualize Annie finding us help."

# CHAPTER FORTY-NINE

Aɴɴɪᴇ ʜᴜsᴛʟᴇᴅ ᴛᴏ ᴋᴇᴇᴘ ᴜᴘ with the deer. It leapt over another fallen log. If it was her friend, wouldn't it find an easier pathway? Damn. The deer had the audacity to break into a trot. It wove in and out of the trees, with a sense of urgency. Did it know something about Jo and Sondra? Were they okay? Annie grazed her broken arm against a branch. Shit, that hurt.

Focus. Keep up. Annie stumbled and saw the ground coming. Not again! This time she regained her balance, feeling the support of something soft and feather-like lifting her. She was not going crazy. *Keep your faith.*

Words to the melody in her head again. They must have a special meaning. Might as well sing them out loud. "It's hard when times get tough. You think—you've had enough. You feel like you're falling down. But don't give up on your life. Let it go."

It became completely dark now, as if someone had shut off the last nightlight. Annie couldn't see the deer anymore. Shit. *Stop walking.* Could she hear it? No branches snapping or leaves being trampled on. The acidic bite of despair assaulted her mouth.

Now what? Annie stilled her mind. Music—but not in her head. She peered through the trees. A faint light. She stepped toward it. The light became brighter. The music louder. The sound of a church choir. It had to be coming from her grandfather's old country church. She recognized the song. 'Shall We Gather at the River.'

That song? God did have a sense of humor. Another sign that He had been listening all along.

Annie picked up her pace. There was the road! Almost there. The music stopped. *Please don't finish practice and shut off the lights.* Doors banged open and shut as people left the church.

*Hurry!*

*Run!*

Annie's broken arm slapped against her body. Bile rose from her stomach into her mouth. Annie choked on it, losing her breath. Her legs crumpled in exhaustion. She collapsed onto her stomach, smashing her broken arm against the ground.

Annie's body convulsed with pain. Her mind was slipping into unconsciousness. She moved her lips, tasting the earth beneath her. *Don't give up. Fight.* A car door slammed. Familiar voices. Her family was shouting. "Has anyone seen Annie? We've been driving up and down the road looking for her."

Excited voices. Annie couldn't understand what they were saying. She rolled over onto her back. *Let them know you're here.* Annie tried to yell, but she couldn't get the words out.

Why couldn't she talk?

The melody again. Try to sing. New words spilled out of her mouth without trying. "Sometimes you have to fight, to survive the endless night."

Annie stopped. Had anyone heard her? Dan! His voice,

shouting, "Annie, where are you? Keep singing. We're here."

A surge of adrenaline. *Use it.* Annie closed her eyes, took a deep breath, and belted out, "It takes time to make things right. But don't give up on your life. Let it go."

Annie embraced the comfort of arms wrapping around her, hugging her.

"Mom!" Matthew's voice. His tears dripped onto her face. "Mom, are you okay? I'm sorry. I love you. Don't die."

Annie couldn't open her eyes. Was someone sitting on her face? Suffocating her? She gasped for air. Matthew sounded scared. She needed to reassure him. It wasn't his fault. She managed to whisper, "Matthew, I love you too."

Annie could hear Dan yelling, "Call 9-1-1." Was she dying?

So many voices.

"Dad, what's wrong with Mom?" John, his voice trembling. "There's moss on her head."

"That's how heroes look, battled and bruised," Dan answered.

"We can't let her go into shock. We learned about that in health class. She needs to sit up." Mark. His voice was strong with conviction. Would he grow up to be a doctor?

Then arms were everywhere, carefully supporting Annie into a sitting position.

"Look at Mom's arm. It must be broken. It looks worse than mine was." Luke. Mr. Sports. Would she live to see him play basketball again?

Yes. She was their mother. She was strong.

"Annie—stay awake! Where are Jo and Sondra?" Dan asked. "Nobody can find them."

Jo and Sondra were still by the waterfall! The thought acted like a crowbar, snapping her eyes open. Annie looked into the terrified faces of her sons. "Down by the river."

"No. That was the song the choir was singing," Dan said.

"I know, but Sondra and Annie are by the river, next to the waterfalls. Sondra's sick. Jo shattered her ankle. You know where it is. Hurry. Get help. I promised them."

Annie saw the faces of the choir, huddled behind her family. There was a long moment of reverence. Holiness. The choir bowed their heads and silently prayed. All that love and encouragement enveloped her in its grace.

The sirens of an ambulance, fire trucks, and police cars broke the moment. All this for her?

Dan wrapped his jacket around her shoulders. "I know exactly where the driveway and the waterfall are. Don't worry. We'll find them. The boys will stay with you."

Annie watched Dan get into a police car. Her husband. What an incredible man. His goodness far outweighed her complaints. And her boys, all huddled around her, trying to make her comfortable. This was her life and damn it—she was going to live it to the fullest. Teach the boys how to be true to themselves by starting with herself. Her authentic self.

Her resolution brought her a surge of love strong enough to blow out a fuse box. *Thank you, God, for my life.*

The medics approached with a stretcher. A needle poked Annie's arm. Blessed relief as the pain subsided. The melody of the song played in her mind. She really loved that song.

## PART FOUR

# Moving On

# CHAPTER FIFTY

SONDRA HUGGED THE SHEETS AND snuggled in. The smell of starch infiltrated her nostrils. It smelled so clean. A happy memory surfaced. Sunday afternoons with her dad. After church, picking up the famous local rotisserie chicken, then eating by the fireplace together. Her dad giving her the cartoons from the Sunday newspaper. How she loved sprawling on the floor, dozing on and off. Interesting how that memory had gotten buried under her childish anger. How many other good memories could she excavate?

Sondra rubbed her eyes. Where was she? The hospital. Right. Their rescue last night. Scenes trickled through her mind like a movie trailer. Hank's hand touching her face. Her dad telling her how much he loved her. The EMT putting her on a stretcher.

Something was pinching her arm. The IV line. The last time she'd seen one was when she visited her mom in the hospital. She braced her heart for the usual pain at the memory, but nothing. Instead, a sense of peace. How had that happened? *Don't question it. Embrace it.* Sondra checked the clock. How could it be 4:00 p.m.?

A swoosh of antiseptic air as the door opened. James stepped through, carrying flowers. Her body stiffened with fear. *Shit. Time to confess. Don't be a wimp.*

James casually handed her the flowers, but his eyes betrayed him. No hiding his raw pain. He knew.

James put his arms around her and held her close. What was happening? No words. No recriminations. Sondra bit the inside of her cheek. *Don't cry.*

Sondra's practiced words tumbled out. "I'm sorry. I really messed up. I understand if you can't forgive me. But I hope you will."

Cold air rushed in as James pulled away from her. "Emily came to see me. I was furious. Then your dad called, and it didn't matter. I hadn't felt fear for a long time. I had to see you. I'm happy that you're okay."

"Did she—?"

"Yes. All of them. I have the originals, never to be seen again."

"You paid them off?"

"Nobody blackmails me. A bad decision on their part. I slowed them down. I've got guys working on the rest. But with the Internet—who knows. Let's not worry about that now. What I really need to know…to understand…is why?"

Sondra took his hand that had always looked so strong. The one that kept her feet on the ground. Had her feet gotten so buried that her spirit couldn't fly?

"James, we've been doing this fake dance that our life is great. But no more hiding. It's time we confront our issues."

Sure enough, James's chin went up in the air. His sign of defiance and denial. "What are you talking about?"

306

"I'll say it. We don't have a sex life anymore. It's not just the sex, but the intimacy. I told you what I needed over and over again. You made promises but always broke them. It hurt. I never cheated on you before. I was vulnerable prey. Adam played me well. I was going to tell you but then—Annie. You know the rest." There. She'd done it. Nothing left to hide. It was up to James now.

James paced around the room. He looked like a prosecutor ready to nail the witness in front of a hungry jury. "I was worried when I married a younger woman. Yet you were so strong that my misgivings seemed silly. I tried to give you everything you needed."

"I needed you! How you used to love me. The way you'd reach out and hold me, skin to skin. It disappeared. It was hard to beg you to touch me, hold me, have sex with me."

"You know I'm bullheaded. It makes me successful. Having to take that pill made me feel like an old man. You're so beautiful. I hated looking at my aging body lying next to you. It was easier to avoid sex than to disappoint you."

"Why didn't you tell me that? It would have helped. Instead, I felt unworthy, undesirable—that I wasn't enough for you. It haunted me."

"Come home. We can figure it out."

"Why not start here? Stay for a few days. I need to make sure Annie is okay. Plus, you can get to know my dad."

"I can't. I've got that new building going on. The funky skyscraper that you love. I'll send my private jet when you're ready."

"But we just started being honest for the first time! You're not the carpenter carrying a hammer. They can get by for a few days." Sondra tapped her chest, trying to keep her frustration from exploding.

"Sondra, don't be offended, but I'm not comfortable here. I'm a city guy. Why don't I take your dad out for dinner? Just a couple of hours. Talk about you staying here with him for a while. My pilot doesn't mind flying at night. I'll hire a private nurse for you. Until then, we can talk every day." James took out his cell phone. "Let's schedule a daily call at 5:00 p.m."

"Sure, that sounds great." What a lie. Damn it. She was worthy. She was enough. He should be fighting for her. This wasn't all her fault. *Be Sondra.* But who was Sondra? *Shit.* Time to find out.

"By the way, the doctor identified a questionable drug in your bloodwork. Did Adam give you something? Did anything strange happen?"

"The doctor didn't tell me that. Why didn't you say something right away?"

"I wanted to hear what you had to say."

The champagne. Her awful headache. If Adam had slipped her something, it didn't matter. She'd been cognizant. "No. It was my decision. I'll talk to the doctor about it."

James's face froze into an expressionless steel shield. Sondra could feel the vibration of his emotional door slamming shut.

The sadness of the whole situation smacked in her gut. She didn't need anyone to tell her what the outcome was going to be. She could see it herself. But then a crack of lightness in her heart. Why was she trying so hard to make things work with James? Was it out of obligation? What about her? She deserved to be happy. Definitely a time to examine her own self-love.

James bent over and kissed her on the cheek. "Get some rest. I'll get hold of your dad."

The unexpected tenderness confused her. Sondra reached for James's hand, to pull him back, but he turned too quickly. Her hand flopped back onto the sheets.

The door shut. Good. Sondra felt an overwhelming need to be alone. What did she want? Could she ever be her true, authentic self with James? The truth hit her hard. She didn't know. A reason to stay here longer, maybe even a month. Her muscles relaxed with her resolution.

A knock on the door. A private nurse already? James probably had one on standby.

"Come in."

Hank.

He raised his hand in a tentative greeting. What was that emotion spreading through her body? It must be happiness from seeing a true friend.

Hank covered the room in five large strides. An old leather book was in his hands. "I saw James leaving. For a long trip, he got here pretty fast."

"It helps to have a private jet."

"I didn't know you were living in that world."

"Depends on how you define living."

"That life doesn't sound bad. It has to be more interesting than here."

"Don't sell this place short. I just had the adventure of a lifetime." Sondra pointed to the book. "What do you have there?"

Hank gave her the book, his hand brushing against her arm. "It fell off the bookshelf and hit my foot."

Shivers rippled through Sondra's body at the physical contact. What was wrong with her? James had just left! *Slow down.* Maybe there was an important message for her in the book. *Tune into your inner spiritual guidance.* Sondra rubbed her hands over the book, then randomly opened it. Really? A poem about a bear? Could the one animal she feared be her animal totem? Jo would love this.

Sondra silently read the poem. So unexpected. Haunting, beautiful words of having courage amidst one's fear. Such deep truth. She looked up at Hank. "Poetry?"

"I was in the drama section, trying to locate a copy of our high school play you starred in."

"The one where you were the talking tree?"

"You got it."

"I thought you despised that play?"

"Sometimes things you disliked have an odd way of becoming precious."

Sondra studied Hank. Was he trying to tell her something? *No. Don't read into his words.* "I'll cherish the book. Thank you." Then the question burst forth, "Why weren't you angry with me when we broke up? I didn't handle things very gracefully."

"We were kids. You needed to leave to live. I got that. I'm happy that you're happy now."

"Who said I was happy?" Oops. Too much disclosure. She could see the confusion on Hank's face. *Don't do this to him.* "What I mean is that life feels confusing right now. This trip changed me. I never realized how much I've missed Annie, Jo, my dad—even this town."

"This town?"

"I know. Don't laugh."

"Well, this town will always welcome you back." Hank walked to the door and tilted his baseball hat to her. "I'll always be here for you as a friend."

Sondra slid her hands under the sheet and squeezed her hands together. *Don't say anything. Do not get up and throw yourself into his arms to feel his lips on yours. You're married. What you had together is a memory. It's not real anymore.* Still—Sondra prayed his words were true.

# CHAPTER FIFTY-ONE

Jo EXAMINED HER CAST. HER ankle was a shattered mess. Anxiety crept in like a hungry lion, ready to pounce on her thoughts. How was she going to cope? What about her job? She had to calm down. Remember the serenity prayer. No changing what happened—so accept it. The courage to change the things she could? After their adventure, Jo could face Louie and make amends. But after Louie had seen her with Zac—would he still want to try? And what about the wisdom to know the difference? Face it, that was a lifelong lesson.

Jo poured another cup of tea from the thermos on the hospital tray. Whatever her mom had concocted was working miracles at reducing her ankle pain. Even the doctor had been amazed that she'd refused the pain medication. But she'd never again open the door to getting addicted to an artificial high. The only high Jo craved was what came naturally. These herbal teas—it'd be fun to learn how to concoct them. Her mother would love passing on her secrets.

Louie. Jo was obsessing over him. Could she will him to come and see her? Use their spiritual connection? Her eagerness to share these new insights was driving her crazier than the itch forming under the cast. Louie would understand her mystical, spiritual encounter.

Jo refilled her cup. When had her mother brought this thermos? Why wasn't her mother here now? It didn't make sense. Hmm—there was that dream last night. It had felt so real. But she'd always been a vivid dreamer. Still—maybe it had really happened? Jo's body tingled as she visualized how Louie had sat by her, stroking her hair. The best part—when he'd said that he loved her. But he wasn't here, either. Why wasn't anyone around? Jo hadn't even seen a nurse for a while.

Fear caused a rancid taste in Jo's mouth. Were Annie and Sondra okay? Maybe something terrible had happened and nobody wanted to tell her. She couldn't lose either one of them. They were more than her best friends. They had become her soulmates, bonded by confessing around the campfire. The trip had thrown incredible obstacles at them. Tempting them to give up. But instead, they had faced their demons and had come out stronger, determined to make changes. And the best part was all the laughter and love. Jo could feel her spine and shoulders straighten with pride for the courage they'd shown.

Was that a soft knock? Jo watched the door inch open. Someone was being cautious not to wake her up. It obviously wasn't a nurse. It must be her mom.

"Come out, come out, whoever you are."

Louie. He was here. Jo instinctively reached out her hand.

Louie didn't hesitate. He came and took it, connecting them.

"So last night was real?"

Louie looked Jo straight in the eye, exposing his love for her.

"As real as this is. It looks like you had an epic journey."

"We did." Jo gasped for breath as the memory sucked air out of her lungs. "I almost died."

Louie tightened his hand around Jo's. "What happened?"

"We lost the canoe. It got jammed under a tree limb. When I climbed in, it tipped. The water rushed in, flipping the canoe. I was trapped. I couldn't get out. Nothing worked. Then everything got quiet. I swear there was a loving presence beside me. I stopped fighting and relaxed my whole body. Somehow, the current pushed me out. The message was clear. Let go of the things that are keeping me stuck. Find a new path in my life."

Jo looked at Louie's face. His eyes were like a marquee, sending different flashing messages at her. Was that confusion, anger, or sadness that she was seeing? Then he shut his eyes as if he was closing his soul to her. When he opened them—his pain was clear.

Louie slowly withdrew his hand from hers. "Jo, if that's what you want, a new journey, I won't hold you back. I want you to be happy. I'll sign those divorce papers when we get back home."

"Wait, you have to hear the end of the story. I remember asking my mom about shapeshifting when I was little. When I went to see Thelma, a raven flew out of the woods. But as I got closer, it was Thelma. I was so confused. When I asked Thelma about it, she told me that if you paid complete attention, really focused— that you could see things change. It made me think. How do we really know what we are looking at in the first place?"

Louie brushed Jo's hair away from her eyes. "That's a great question. What do you think?"

Jo took Louie's hand back. Time to be brave. "In order for me to change, I had to forgive myself. Believe that I was worthy. I needed to love myself again. Let go of the shame. It took nearly dying and breaking my ankle to get there. But I'm here! And I believe if we look closely, we'll see that we've both changed. We can let go of the past that doesn't serve us. We can move on to create something really beautiful together. What do you think?"

Louie placed their joined hands on his heart. "Are you sure, Jo? My heart couldn't handle the anguish if you changed your mind."

"I'm perfectly sober, unless you put something in that tea you snuck in last night."

"My male nurse outfit didn't fool you?"

"Maybe for a moment, but please keep it. You looked awfully sexy in it."

"I like how that tea makes you think."

"It's also helping me to ask for forgiveness. I'm really sorry, Louie. Can you forgive me?"

Louie leaned over and pulled her close.

Jo breathed in his unique smell—of the sun rising, when everything was fresh with life. The sinewy muscles of his arms holding her felt exciting and intimidating at the same time.

"Sometimes it's better when the words are silent," Louie spoke softly. "I can share some of my wolf medicine with you, if you want me to."

Jo pulled Louie closer. "I'd like a little dose, please."

Jo felt Louie's lips on hers, kissing her gently at first, with a loving sweetness. Jo wanted more and pulled him halfway onto the bed with her. She kissed him back harder. Her hands slid under his shirt and up his back. She wanted to touch every part of him. It was as if someone had thrown a match on a dry stack of hay, igniting the fire they'd always had together.

It was perfect.

A burst of laughter and clapping.

Jo broke the embrace and craned her neck to see who was there.

Sure enough, Sondra leaned against the doorframe.

# CHAPTER FIFTY-TWO

ANNIE OPENED HER EYES. THERE was Dan. A déjà vu moment, back in the hospital, but much better than the last time. Dan was smiling at her with such love in his eyes.

"I'm so proud of you." Dan kissed her on the forehead.

"You're not mad that I took off without letting you know?"

"How could I be? You saved Sondra's and Jo's lives."

How could she explain what had happened? Time to try. No more holding back. "I wasn't alone. A deer disguised as an angel led the way. Okay, I know that sounds crazy."

"Not to me. What's crazy is that you walked through the dark with a broken arm and sprained ankle. That took incredible strength and willpower."

"An out-of-body experience and a song helped me through it, as well."

Dan touched Annie's cheek. "I want to hear it all, Annie. I've missed you. I'm sorry that I didn't understand how you lost yourself. How you felt that you had disappeared. But when I heard you sing—it all came back to me. My Annie. Your beautiful voice, bubbling laughter, and kind soul. I've been a selfish jerk."

The words she'd been waiting to hear. Dan's facial muscles were tight, intense with sincerity. She'd missed him, too. "I would never call you a jerk. You were consumed by the church and our family. It wasn't all your fault. It was mine too. I should have been more direct with what I needed, instead of playing the suffering martyr."

"In all honesty, I heard your words, but I didn't listen with my heart. Will you forgive me?"

"I already did. Being with Sondra and Jo, sharing like old times, was so healing. I knew that I needed to change. God had quite the lesson for me. Things escalated when I got sucked down into the whirlpool. It was truly like looking death in the face."

Dan reached out and held her good hand. "You're here now. But how did you end up in the whirlpool?"

"I didn't think. We were carrying the canoe over the portage trail and lost control. The canoe slid into the river. My adrenaline took over. I jumped in to save the canoe. Instead, the whirlpool captured me and dragged me under. There was the moment of stillness when I had no control. It was up to God. I banged against the rock wall. The message launched into my soul. You're never alone. There's always a way out. Just stop and look for it. Don't let a moment of panic determine your life." Annie shivered, realizing how profound and powerful her words were.

Dan bowed his head. "Thank you, God, for my beautiful, strong, amazing wife."

Annie felt Dan's tears dampen her hand. How could she have doubted their deep connection? She needed to rely on it now. "Dan, we both know this town loves to gossip. I want to be honest about everything. Tell the boys and our community that I was depressed and took medication to help. That I tried to hide it. I was afraid of the stigma—of being labeled. I don't believe our society knows how to address depression."

"Annie, I've got your back. I agree. People don't know what to say when someone admits they're depressed. I think you—wait—*we* can make a difference."

"I want to take it even further. I didn't try to commit suicide. But if I'd taken one more pill, or if I'd fallen the wrong way—you'd never know the truth. Those dark days. My sadness coming out of nowhere and haunting me. I can empathize how one can lose hope and make the wrong decision. I want to help. I want people to believe they are worthy, that they are enough."

"Annie, to me, to the boys, you are more than enough. But it's not what we believe, but what you believe. Be prepared, the boys are telling everyone that you're a hero. The fact that you're willing to share this message shows incredible bravery. Keep this up and they'll erect a statue at the park in your honor." Dan grinned.

"Please don't make me a saint! That got me into trouble the last time. I just want to be me. I had a vivid dream after I fell and broke my arm. I was with Jesus. He gave me words to a song about not giving up on life. To let go of the worries and have faith."

"Okay—no sainthood. But I hope you'll sing that song. And many others. The world needs your voice."

Annie's spirit leaped at the thought of singing again. Then reality hit. "I'll never have the time to do all this. I guess these are all long-term dreams."

"Help is on the way. The boys have a present for you."

"What in the world could that be?"

Dan reached inside his jacket pocket and pulled out an envelope. "For you."

"Money to take a long vacation?"

"Better than that."

Annie opened the envelope and pulled out slips of paper. "Hmm...this reminds me of fortune cookies. Let's see what's in my future."

Annie unfolded the first slip. *"Mom, I promise to make my own bed and put my dirty clothes in the hamper every single day, even on Saturdays! Love, John."*

"John was very proud to show me his bed this morning, even if it wasn't quite how you'd do it." Dan laughed.

"It will be perfect to me." Annie unfolded the next slip. *"Mom, I promise to do my homework right after I get home from sports. Love, Luke."* Annie rubbed her forehead. "Now that would be a relief. I hate bugging Luke every day. I hope he can keep his promise."

"Keep going. It gets even better."

"Okay, here goes!" Annie recognized the handwriting. Matthew. *"Mom, I promise to drive everyone to school in the van. I won't complain. But can I paint the van with sayings that will make people smile? Love, Matthew."*

Annie held the last slip to her heart. "I'm getting dizzy with joy."

"The last one is my favorite." Dan kissed her hand.

"Hey, I'm working here." Annie pulled her hand away. "Before I open it. What about you? Any slips of paper?"

"I hope my words will do. I hereby declare that I won't volunteer you for any work at the church. It's your decision going forward what you choose to do."

"That's going to be hard for you."

"Actually, it's the easiest thing I've ever done. You're an amazing wife, mother, and so much more. I want you to be happy again."

"Okay, now I'm almost speechless. Thank you."

Annie held the last slip in her hand. Her hand started to shake. This moment. Dan. She was so blessed. She handed Dan the slip. "Why don't you read it to me?"

"Sure." Dan unfolded it. *"Mom, I promise to babysit once a week so you and Dad can have a date night. Love, Mark."*

"I love date nights," Annie said.

"Me too. I think we should start right now." Dan raised her chin and kissed her passionately.

Annie kissed him back, feeling the energy soar between them. Love—the highest vibration of emotion.

The sound of cheering interrupted them.

Annie broke away to see Sondra pushing Jo toward them in a wheelchair. Their arms were up in a V, their infamous victory gesture.

"Dan just scored a home run!" Jo exclaimed.

"What's with all this kissing in the hospital!" Sondra pretended to wipe sweat off her forehead. "I had to interrupt a potential scandal between Jo and Louie. They were ready to break the rule of 'no sex in the hospital.'"

Dan stood up. "That's my exit cue. I don't want to think of your next adventure! If you got into that much trouble canoeing—what else could you three concoct together?"

"Hey, don't forget about all of our miracles. We gave you enough material for six to seven sermons," Sondra chided.

Dan gave Sondra a hug. "And I'm grateful. It's so good to see you, stranger. I hope you can stick around for a while."

"Count on it."

"Great, because there's a spot in the front pew saved just for you." Dan waved goodbye as he closed the door.

"Damn, Dan's good," Sondra muttered. "He got the last word, just like Jo."

# CHAPTER FIFTY-THREE

Annie's maternal instinct kicked in. She checked Jo and Sondra over. Not bad. Besides Jo's cast and dark circles around Sondra's eyes—they looked perfect. The sweet taste of joy, like their campfire s'mores, filled her senses. Her best friends had survived. "You two sure know how to pull a girl out of a depression."

Jo wheeled herself next to Annie's bed. "Of course, we do. It was all planned except for the beaver, poison ivy, fallen logs, a whirlpool, and monster mosquitoes."

"Well, it worked," Annie said. "I let go of my shame and my worries about the pill overdose. I even burned my superwoman cape. I'm ready to reinvent myself. What about you two?"

Sondra drew in a long, deep breath. She nonchalantly flipped her hair back, faking confidence. But why? This was Annie and Jo. If they could be vulnerable, she could too. The truth wasn't easy but critical to her happiness. "When James decided to fly back, the message was clear. He wants things on his terms. If I go back too soon, I may never learn how to love myself. It's time to stop relying on someone else to do it for me. So, Annie, I'm going to hang out for a while."

"Perfect! You can challenge Dan on his sermons, show Matthew how to throw a curveball, and teach me yoga. Those moves could come in handy for my date night."

"You and Dan and your sex. Just don't start making out in front of me. I plan to be celibate for a while."

Jo checked her watch. "Let's see—I'm going to bet you last one week."

"One week? James isn't here. I've had enough of men like Adam."

"Well, you did mention a vibrator named Tony. Sounds like a guy's name to me."

"Very funny."

"Well, if you get bored, my mom can use help. She had record sales with you waitressing. She was shocked at how many single men suddenly loved coffee. Although rumor has it, there is an exceptional bachelor." Jo scratched her head. "Annie, do you remember his name?"

This was what Annie loved. Their humor and ease with each other. "Wait—it's coming to me. Henry? No—got it! His name is Hank."

Sondra threw her arms in the air. "I just told you, I was going to be celibate. And I'm still married."

Jo groaned, rubbing her cast. "Sorry, I forgot. Must be the pain from my ankle."

"I don't buy that. You were laughing a minute ago."

"Oh my gosh. Are you two squabbling again?" Annie laughed. "How did you survive in that tent without me?"

Jo shrugged. "It was no big deal. Right, Sondra?"

Sondra grinned and nodded. "It was easy. We scared off

wolves, howled at the moon, spooned, and visualized you finding help."

"I'll add that to Dan's miracle sermon list. Jo, got any miracles to add? Is it true? You and Louie are back together?"

Jo's body pulsated with elation at the answer. Forgiveness—a divine gift. Liberating. Her words floated up and out from her soul. "I embraced my vulnerability and asked Louie for forgiveness. I was scared that he might say no, especially after seeing me with my failed one-nighter. But Louie was amazing. We're going to create a better version of ourselves—together. Jessica and Hunter are going to be so excited to be a family again."

"It's incredible. Our lives changed in less than a week. People call me a hero and say that I rescued you. But you actually saved me by coming here. Let's promise each other that we'll never give up. To remind each other that life can change for the better. Especially when times get tough. Actually, that's the message of this song that's been in my head ever since I fell in the forest. It's driving me a bit crazy."

"Then get those words out of there. We need to hear them," Jo said.

"I don't know—"

"Didn't we just talk about letting go? If you teach me the words, I'll sing it for you," Sondra threatened.

"Hurry, Annie, before she hurts my ears," Jo begged.

Annie laughed. "All right, here goes. I'm calling it, 'Don't give up on your life.'

"It's hard when times get tough
And you think you've had enough
And you feel like you're falling down
But don't give up on your life—let it go

"There are times when you have to cry
But it's not time to say goodbye
No matter what you're going through
So don't give up on your life—let it go

"There's magic in the air
And people who really care
You may not even know they're there
So don't give up on your life—let it go

"Sometimes you have to fight
To survive the endless night
It takes time to make things right
So don't give up on your life—let it go

"So don't give up on your life
Baby, don't give up on your life
Baby, don't give up on your life—let it go

"Sometimes you have to raise your chin
And dig your heels deeply in
And fight to begin again
But don't give up on your life—let it go

"When the storm is blowing strong
And your life is spinning around
And you can barely breathe
Don't give up on your life—let it go

"When you want to run and hide
Reach for your soul deep inside

And listen to what it says
So don't give up on your life—let it go

"There are the lives of those you've touched
You may not think it means very much
But it's a gift all of its own
So don't give up on your life—let it go

"So don't give up on your life
Baby, don't give up on your life
Baby, don't give up on your life—let it go."


THE END

## ACKNOWLEDGMENTS

This book took courage to write. I had to dig deep into my soul, relive certain life lessons, and combine them with the wisdom that I learned from others. When people say life is a journey—it certainly is! We get to evolve and hopefully become the best version of our authentic selves. I've had many teachers in my life, including my father and mother, who always provided unconditional love. I am lucky. I've been blessed to have so many wonderful people in my life and want to thank each and every one. However, I'm afraid that I'll miss a name, so please know that if you're reading this book—I want to thank you.

I do need to thank my husband, Herbert Rush, for being my soul mate and best friend. His patience was endless, listening to me for five years as I worked on hundreds of drafts!

I'm grateful to my big, fun, and loving family. Thanks to Kelly, David, and my grandchildren, Fiona, Josephine, Dean, and Joshua. Also, thanks to Jennifer, Christopher, and my grandchildren, Thomas, Joseph, and Jacob. They all love to read and bring such happiness to my life. My siblings, David, Doug, Renee, Lorene, and Roxanne are my lifeline and always lift me up.

I also want to thank my amazing girlfriends, who have been supportive of my journey and my book—too many names to list here! You know who you are and how much I love and appreciate you! You helped me create this story through our long talks and sharing the good and the hard times.

I want to thank those friends who read early drafts and gave me feedback, including Christine Griffin, Lisa Dolan, Sherry Stokes, Jill Denson, Paula IaCampo, Kathy Gram Katterfield, Mary Spear, Robin Moreland, Melissa Frisvold, Janet Cicon, Andrea Trank, and Barbara Francis.

I also want to thank Cathy Bagley and Alberta Stone Gouge for educating me on the proper terminology and sharing their knowledge of the Lac Courte Orielles Band of Lake Superior Chippewa, the Ojibwe tribe, so all could be honored.

I also need to thank my writing coach and editor, Carole Greene. She instructed me to take a moment before writing and center myself, to connect to my higher source and then let the words flow.

A final thank-you to Julie Schoerke Gallagher, whose childhood friendship with me was reignited after a long absence. Her support, along with our many laughs, gave me the last bit of confidence to step out fully into the world with the many messages in this book.

To me this book is about the power of friendship and the strength we give each other to never give up, to have the courage to be authentic and to give unconditional love, acceptance and support, to empower each other to let go of the past and embrace self-love and forgiveness.

With much love, Kristine Ochu

## ABOUT THE AUTHOR

Kristine Ochu is founder of "The Night of a Woman's Soul—Creating Your Amazing Life." She is a former Human Resource Executive with a MAIR from the University of Minnesota. Kristine has written screenplays and self-published a children's book. She is a member of the Global Women's Club, Women in Film and Video New England, the Harvard Square Script Writers, and various community groups. She lives in Amelia Island, Florida with her husband and their rescue golden retrievers.

You can learn more about her and find book discussion questions at www.KristineOchu.com.

1. Annie, Josephine, and Sondra were childhood friends, but their lives took them in different directions. After years apart, what allowed them to reconnect so quickly? Have you kept up with long-term friends?

2. Do you believe Annie, Josephine, and Sondra empowered each other, or that they empowered themselves? Have you had friends who empowered you in your life? If yes, what actions or words did they use to empower you?

3. Annie, Josephine, and Sondra all have their own stories. Which of these women did you find the most appealing, and why? Did you feel more compassion for one of the characters more than the others? Why or why not?

4. Josephine accuses Annie of being a martyr. Historically, a martyr was someone who suffered greatly for their cause. The definition evolved to include someone who has a "victim" mentality and may take on suffering in order to get praise or attention. Do you think Annie was playing the martyr role? Why or why not?

5. What strengths did Annie have that helped her during her journey by herself through the forest? Do you think her journey is a metaphor for some of the difficult journeys that women experience?

6. There is a theory that men and women communicate their needs differently. Do you believe this is true? If yes, how did these differences affect each of the characters with their husbands?

7. Annie, Josephine, and Sondra all needed to let go of their

mistakes to move forward. Why is letting go of the past or mistakes so difficult for people? What can help people through this process?

8. Josephine had a lot of guilt from her past alcoholic behavior. Why do you think it's so hard for people to forgive themselves?

9. At times, each of the characters struggled with self-love. What does self-love mean to you? Do you think women suffer from a lack of self-love? If yes, what are ways for people to practice this concept?

10. Various cultures around the world have spiritual beliefs about animals, birds, insects, and reptiles sending them messages. In the book, Josephine felt connected to the crow, Annie was drawn to the deer, and Sondra had a dragonfly land on her hand. Do you have any animals, birds, insects, or reptiles that you feel connected to? If yes, have there been times that you received a message that you needed to hear?

11. There are various energy, empowerment, and motivational tools used by the characters, including: meditation; visualization; "I am" statements; tapping, etc. Was there a tool that resonated with you? Have you used any of these tools during different times in your life? In what way did they help you?

12. Thelma was considered a healer in the community through her teas and her words. Have you had healers in your life? What forms did they take? Were they teachers, spiritual leaders, parents or friends?

13. Why do you think Sondra decided not to blame her behavior of sleeping with Adam on drugs or alcohol? Did you want her to give James another chance? Why or why not?

14. Sondra and Hank were reunited as friends. There is a debate

whether men and women who have been in a romantic relationship can "just" be friends. Do you think this is possible?

15. In the book the characters are able to confess their secrets with the pact of, "No judgment, only support." When you think of confessions, what are some of the things that come to mind?

16. Each of the characters practiced their spiritual beliefs in different ways. Annie through her prayers, Sondra through her yoga, and Josephine through her meditation. How do you define spirituality? Do you define it differently than religion?

17. Over the campfire, Sondra shares that, "Being alone is okay. Feeling alone sucks." Do you believe that loneliness is an epidemic in our society? If yes, what problems do you think it creates? What ways as an individual, or as a community, can we help address this issue?

18. Fire has often been associated with the concept of transformation and rebirth. As the characters confess their secrets around the campfire, how does it change them? Do you have memories around the campfire that are special to you? If yes, were any of them life-changing?